A Pinch

of

Promise

by Elizabeth Maddrey

Other Books by Elizabeth Maddrey

A is for Airstrip: A Missionary's Jungle Adventure

A Walk in the Valley: Christian Encouragement for Your Journey Through Infertility

'Taste of Romance' Series

A Splash of Substance

The 'Grant Us Grace' Series

Book One: Wisdom to Know

Book Two: Courage to Change

Book Three: Serenity to Accept

Novellas in the 'Grant Us Grace' world

Joint Venture

Novels in the 'Grant Us Grace' world

The 'Remnants' Series:

Book One: Faith Departed

Book Two: Hope Deferred

Book Three: Love Defined

Stand alone novellas

Kinsale Kisses: An Irish Romance

Scripture quoted by permission. Quotations designated (NIV) are from THE HOLY BIBLE: NEW INTERNATIONAL VERSION®. NIV®. Copyright © 1973, 1978, 1984 by Biblica. All rights reserved worldwide.

Cover design by HopeSprings Books.
Cover art photos ©iStockphoto.com/CGissemann used by permission.

Published in the United States of America by Elizabeth Maddrey
www.ElizabethMaddrey.com

Publisher's Note: This novel is a work of fiction. Names, characters, places, and incidents are either products of the author's imagination or used fictitiously. All characters are fictional, and any similarity to people living or dead is purely coincidental.

In memory of Kira
Though I didn't know you, your story touched my heart.

1

Rebecca Fischer pulled up her next appointment on her tablet. Her breath caught. Ben Taylor. The image of sandy brown hair and pale blue eyes flashed across her thoughts. Silly. There were probably hundreds—thousands, even—of people in the world with that name. Besides, Ben had never mentioned wanting to live in the D.C. area. And even over the course of one fleeting summer, it had been clear that Ben was going to get what he wanted.

Pushing away the ghosts of what might have been, Rebecca strolled through the sprawling therapy room, weaving between weight machines and treadmills. She crossed an expanse of floor mats where patients were stretching, some with the assistance of other physical therapists, resistance bands, and medicine balls. Conversations, grunts, groans, and the occasional whimper of pain ricocheted off the mirrored walls. She smiled as she stepped into the reception area.

"Mr. Taylor?" Rebecca's gaze drifted over the handful of people waiting. Her heart raced as a man about her age, complete with sandy brown hair, wobbled out of a chair.

"That's me." Ben adjusted the position of his crutches and inched his way across the room.

Rebecca pursed her lips, evaluating his progress. He hadn't been doing the range of motion exercises the surgeon had sent home with him. And he was babying his knee. "When was your surgery?"

"Friday."

Three days. She nodded. Not as bad as she'd thought. "All right. Been doing your exercises?"

Ben hunched his shoulders. "Trying to."

She held open the door into the main therapy room and gestured for him to go ahead of her. "I know it hurts. But if you want to get that full range of motion back, you'll need to do more than try. I'll help. I'm Rebecca, by the way. We'll start with a focus on getting your knee extension back. For now, if you're not here at therapy or doing your exercises, keep the immobilizer on and use your crutches. Either your surgeon or I will let you know when you can discontinue either one."

"Okay. And the swelling?"

"It'll go down, don't worry. I'll send you home with some instructions for that, as well." Rebecca stopped in front of a straight-backed chair positioned against the wall on the far side of the mats. Pale blue eyes met hers and the moisture in her mouth evaporated. "Have a seat."

When Ben was settled, she set his crutches out of reach and helped him remove the immobilizer. He shifted in the seat and flinched. "Now what?"

"Now we see how well you can extend your leg. I know you've been mostly straight in the brace, but you need to be able to get to what we call terminal knee extension, to regain your regular gait. If you want to grab the sides of the chair, that sometimes helps. Straighten your leg as far as you can."

Grimacing, Ben lifted his leg, straightening it.

"How'd you tear your ACL?" Rebecca knelt by Ben's leg and lifted his foot.

Ben sucked in a breath. "Uh. Football with the guys after church. My roommate played semi-pro, so he's always trying to get a game going. I was stupid and caved."

He hadn't been athletic at summer camp, either. It had to be him. Did he recognize her? He wasn't acting like it. Though it wasn't as if she expected him to be overjoyed anyway. Not after the way she'd vanished after camp. Would he understand if she explained? "Did you at least have fun for a little while?"

"First play."

She winced, biting back a laugh. "Oooh."

He shrugged. "I've never been particularly athletic. I figured I'd get injured one way or another, but I hadn't banked on it being this bad. At least it gets me out of having to play football again. Ever."

"Go ahead and put your foot down. Feeling okay?"

Ben nodded.

"Ok, straighten your leg again, let's see if we can go a little farther this time. While you do, tell me about yourself."

"To help take my mind off the pain?"

"Yeah. Plus we're going to spend a bit of time together while you recuperate. Just pretend I'm your hair stylist."

"Getting my hair cut doesn't hurt like this." Ben ground his teeth together. "Um. Let's see. I work for a hunger relief agency, primarily helping to allocate money and organize food drives that churches arrange throughout the year."

Maybe not exactly what he'd been planning in college, but definitely close. "That sounds like a worthwhile job. Fulfilling. Go ahead and lower your foot."

"It is. I like knowing that what I do makes a difference for people in countries where food isn't as abundant as it is here."

She nodded. Making a difference had been her dream, once. "Let's go one more time and then we'll do ultrasound therapy for the soft tissue, and spend some time working on that swelling. And I'll get you some instructions to supplement what the surgeon probably sent home with you."

"Okay." He cocked his head to the side. "You look familiar. Have we met before?

Rebecca tossed her keys into the bowl by the front door and dropped her backpack under the small entryway table. Home. She'd moved to the townhouse in January, but nine months later, she still got a tingle when she walked through the door. Her own space. No neighbors above and below, no roommates. Just the one shared wall, since she'd managed to score an end unit, and the older lady who lived next door was a dear. Maybe it got a little loud when all her grandchildren came to visit, but that wasn't too often, and more often than not, they invited her over anyway. Best of all? She'd done it all on her own. Mom had offered her a loan for a down payment when she'd moved out here... but it was so much better having saved up her own money rather than taking a handout.

Her cell phone rang. She dragged it out of her pocket and crossed the living room to the kitchen as she answered. "Hey, Mom. How'd you know I was just thinking about you?"

Her mother's laugh made her smile. "Mothers know these things. Plus, it's Monday and you just got home from work, so you knew I'd be calling."

Rebecca took a bottle of sparkling mineral water out of the fridge and twisted off the top. "There's that, too. How are things at home?"

"Oh, you know your father. He's absorbed in editing his latest book and planning a big speaking tour around its launch. They've asked him to be the keynote at four regional youth rallies this spring as well."

"He must be in heaven." Rebecca took a long drink of water. Why did it still bother her? Especially now, when the illustrations he used were completely made up?

"Pretty close to it. The first one is in D.C." Her mom's voice lifted at the end, asking an unspoken question.

Rebecca placed her hand over the phone's speaker and huffed out a breath. It had to happen sooner or later. "You know I'd love you to stay here. I have plenty of room."

"Oh. No, that's not it. We'll stay at the hotel they're using for the convention. But... do you think you could squeeze out some time to come down..."

"And let people ogle the bad-girl-turned-good?" Rebecca set the water down on her coffee table. "Mom... I'll come take you sightseeing, have dinner, we can hang out, whatever. But please... please don't ask me to be the poster-child again."

"Ah, Becky, I'm sorry. I promised your father I'd ask. But I also warned him that I didn't think you'd agree."

"How'd he take that?"

"About as well as you'd expect. He'll get over it."

Probably use it to fabricate some new story about her misspent life. "You sure?"

"Of course. You haven't appeared with him since you left for college. Honestly, I'm not sure why he thought you would just because we were going to be in your new hometown. I think, maybe it's his way of trying to reconnect with you."

Rebecca scoffed. "He has my phone number."

Her mother sighed. "I know, Becky. And you have his. I hate being caught in the middle between you two."

"Mom..."

"Don't get me wrong, I understand why you did what you did. I think, in his heart, he does too, now. But it's too late to undo the damage without ruining all the good he's done—and continues to do. Which isn't fair to you. I'm sorry, Becky."

Heaviness settled on her chest. Had she done the right thing?

"Let's put that aside and talk about something more pleasant. How did your date on Friday go?"

Rebecca gave a mirthless laugh. "I thought you wanted to talk about something more pleasant?"

"No second date in the works, then?"

"He might think so, but no." Ben's face flashed into her thoughts and her heartbeat accelerated. She cleared her throat. "Mom... do you remember when I worked at the camp in Colorado Springs for the summer?"

"Of course. Right after your freshman year of college. That's when you got the bright idea to change your name and step away from the notoriety your Dad was forcing on you. Why?"

Rebecca reached for the bottle and took a long swallow of the fizzy water. "Did I ever mention Ben?"

"Hmm. I don't think so. Why?"

She hadn't told her mom about him? She told her mother everything. Now. It hadn't always been that way. "Ben Taylor was the counselor for our brother cabin, so he and I ended up doing a lot together over the course of the summer. Even when we had time off, we gravitated toward one another."

"You had feelings for him. I can hear it in your voice. What happened?"

Rebecca squeezed her eyes shut. "I never told him who I was. That summer at camp, I was just Marie Fischer. Not Becky MacDonald, infamous daughter of the famous pastor-turned-parenting-expert."

"I didn't realize you used your middle name in addition to my maiden name."

"I wanted a clean break, with no way for anyone to connect me to bad-girl-Becky."

"Oh, sweetheart. No one called you that."

Rebecca gave a sardonic laugh. "Mom. They still do. Every time Dad's in the press there's the big 'where is she now' debate about me. Last one had me tucked away in rehab in Switzerland."

"They didn't."

She shook her head. Mom was Dad's biggest supporter, but she stayed out of his business entirely too well. "They did. I think that was about the time you were in Ghana supervising the opening of the new orphanage. I still don't understand how you manage to keep Dad from writing his name across everything the foundation does."

"Give your father a bit of credit, Bec. I know the two of you have your differences, but you know he's a good man."

Rebecca winced at the steel in her mom's voice. "All right, you're right. Sorry. I just wish..."

"I know, honey. Me too. I should have stepped in sooner."

That would've been nice. But at this point there was little point in playing the what-if game. And, all things considered,

Rebecca had made a good life for herself. One where Becky MacDonald had no place and cast no shadow.

Her mother cleared her throat. "So...Ben?"

"He's my newest physical therapy patient."

ELIZABETH MADDREY

2

"I'm telling you, I know her from somewhere." Ben groaned as he propped his leg on the coffee table and set his crutches aside.

"What'd she say when you asked?" Jackson held out the bag of frozen peas Ben used as an ice pack.

Ben situated the peas on his knee. "That she has one of those faces. I guess she gets it a lot. But honestly, it didn't feel like that. There was something in her eyes... I dunno."

"Ah, a mystery woman. Maybe she's the one who got away? What was your camp girlfriend's name again?" Jackson sat on the couch and grabbed the game console controllers, offering one to Ben.

"Marie. But no. She's not Marie. Marie had long, jet-black hair and piercing green eyes. Rebecca's hair is strawberry blonde and cropped almost as short as mine. I'll give you that her eyes are also green, but really, it's not like there are only three people in the world with green eyes."

"I was kidding. But..." Jackson frowned and dug his phone out of his pocket.

"What are you doing, looking up game cheats already?" Ben navigated the home screen of the console and selected their current zombie shooting game.

"Twelve percent, give or take." Jackson dropped his phone on the arm of the couch and settled in.

"Huh?"

"That's how many people, roughly, have green eyes. They're not as common as you'd think."

Ben frowned. "Okay. So they're not as common as brown. What about her hair and general build?"

"Hair's easy. Come on, man, you have sisters. How many different colors has their hair been in your lifetime?"

That was a point. His youngest sister, in particular, loved to change her hair color. And she didn't stick to the hues naturally found in hair. The last time he went home, her hair had been an eye-searing pink that, strangely enough, suited her. Hopefully she'd keep it that way for a while. It was better than the black she'd toyed with in high school. "Fine. Hair is changeable. But Marie was one of those almost too-skinny girls. I was a little worried about her, honestly. Rebecca is... curvy."

Jackson swiveled his head to look at Ben. "Fat curvy or well-endowed curvy?"

"Not fat. Just... shaped like a woman should be, you know? Not like some kind of pre-adolescent boy in a dress. Marie wasn't that bad, but she was close. She was addicted to running. Every chance she got, she was running."

"Does that mean you ran, too?"

"All summer long. Worst torture of my life."

Jackson laughed. "The things we do for love. And you let her slip away, after all that?"

Ben scooted the peas off his leg. "I'm not really in the mood to play right now. I'm going to head to my room and do some work."

Had he let her slip away? Was there more he could have done to keep in touch? But how did you pursue a relationship when she gave you a fake phone number and never managed to remember to write down her address? At some point, didn't you have to let it go?

In his room, Ben scooted his chair closer to his desk, angling so that his leg could stay straight, and bumped his mouse to wake up the laptop work had issued him. He really needed to upgrade the machine he had for his personal use. The comparison between it and the work computer emphasized how slow it had gotten. He opened his email and then, frowning, opened a web browser and typed in "Marie Fischer."

So many results. How did you even start trying to sort through them? The links that had photos would help some. Even if she dyed her hair or wore colored contacts, she couldn't change her ethnicity. Besides, what was he supposed to say if he *did* find her? *Hey Marie, remember me? I've been carrying a torch for you for the last ten years?*

Ben snorted and closed the browser. Not likely. Move on. Just move on. Maybe he'd ask Rebecca out. Could you do that? Could you ask out your physical therapist? He cracked his knuckles and yawned. Was he always going to be attracted to the impossible women?

"It's less crowded today." Ben gripped the side of the chair as he raised his leg. The pain was less today. Progress?

"Mondays are always our busiest day. The people on a once-a-week schedule all seem to like to come at the start of the week. Get it out of the way, I guess." Rebecca grinned. "You're doing great. Let's start working on flexion a little."

"Flexion?"

"Bending your knee. Go ahead and lower your leg, then see if you're able to bend at all. Don't stress about getting to ninety-degrees, let's just see what we're working with."

Ben gritted his teeth and bent his knee. Or tried to. "Well...it's not straight."

She chuckled. "It's a start. We're not going to push it just yet, but I wanted to see a baseline. Keep giving it a shot though, just stop when it starts to hurt."

Ben nodded and cleared his throat. What was it they said about not having because they hadn't asked? "I was wondering if you had time for lunch after this?"

Her eyebrows shot up and she held his gaze for several heartbeats, her face unreadable. What was she thinking? "Don't you have a ride coming for you? You shouldn't be driving yet."

Heat crept up his neck. "I... might have mentioned that I was planning to ask you to lunch and told him to come at one."

She let out a short bark of laughter. "What if I say no?"

He shrugged. "Then I guess I hobble next door and eat at the sandwich shop by myself."

"I'm pretty sure the practice discourages dating patients."

"I'll let you buy your own. You can even sit at a different table, if it makes you feel better. Then it's just two people striking up a conversation while eating their lunch."

Rebecca's lips twitched. "Do you always get your way?"

"Is that a yes?"

She offered a slight nod.

Ben grinned. "Then yeah, usually."

Glancing at her watch, Rebecca pushed to her feet. "Do ten more extensions, try to bring your foot back under the chair a little farther with each one. I'll go get my wallet."

3

What was she doing? Rebecca jiggled her wallet. On the one hand, she had to eat. There wasn't anything intrinsically wrong with the sub shop next door, though the staff ate there so often it was usually a last resort. On the other hand...this was Ben. The longer she was around him, the harder it was to stay silent. He suspected. Or he had. He hadn't said anything today, and had seemed to accept her dodge the first time he asked. So maybe her brush off had worked. Her stomach sank. That's what she'd wanted, wasn't it? But if he didn't suspect, why had he asked her to lunch? He couldn't possibly have trouble finding a date, why would he hit on his physical therapist?

This was ridiculous. She'd go out there and tell him she changed her mind. Then she'd go get lunch...somewhere else. Anywhere else. She took a deep breath and strode into the lobby. Ben smiled.

"Ready?"

Rebecca shook her head. "Actually..."

His smile faltered. "It's just lunch."

She squeezed the wrist strap of her wallet. Her stomach growled.

"I heard that. You can't say you're not hungry now."

The excuse died on her lips and she checked her watch. "All right. You're right. I've got thirty minutes. You get twenty of them."

"I'll take it." Ben jerked his head toward the door. "Can we walk together or do we need to meet over there accidentally?"

She pressed her lips together to suppress a smile. "We can walk over together. I'll even sit at your table."

He chuckled and picked his way across the room, hitting the door assist button. "After you."

"I see chivalry isn't dead after all."

"Not since they started putting these accessibility buttons on the doors. Though having crutches helps, too. No one's going to get angry at me for hitting the button when it's obvious I need it myself. We'll see if that trend continues once I'm rid of them or if I end up being accused of benevolent sexism again."

Rebecca snorted out a laugh. "Benevolent sexism?"

"That's what one lady called it. She was really angry with me. I guess I was supposed to let her fumble around with the door when her hands were full of bags and she was trying to hold on to a toddler as well as her dog's leash." Ben shrugged. "I can't seem to help myself."

He hadn't been able to in college either. Several of the girls at camp had remarked on it, though they'd all considered it sweet, if a bit old fashioned. It had made Rebecca feel special. Still did. "Don't change. I'm going to go out on a limb and say that the broad majority of humans, regardless of gender, appreciate a show of respect. And if they don't, well. Phooey on 'em."

"Phooey. Strong words, there, Ms. Fischer."

Rebecca pulled open the door to the sub shop. "Sadly there's no button here, and, as I have a vested interest in you not reinjuring yourself, I hope you'll allow me?"

Ben crutched through the door. "I'll even say thank you."

She followed behind him, lips pursed. He was still babying his knee. "You should be putting a bit more weight on that leg when you walk."

He stopped and frowned over his shoulder. "I don't want to reinjure it."

"Nobody wants that. But it's not going to get stronger if it never gets used. The crutches are there to keep your full weight off, not all of it. If it hurts, back off some, but try to start using it." Rebecca offered a bright smile in return for the glare he shot her. But the next few steps he took looked better. Should she offer to carry his food for him?

Ben stood at the counter directing the creation of an enormous sandwich. He couldn't possibly eat like this all the time unless he was one of those annoying people whose metabolisms hadn't changed since they were twelve. As soon as the thought occurred, she got a flash of him in line at camp, his tray piled high. "Ugh. You probably haven't gained an ounce since college, have you?"

He laughed. "One of my roommates has started getting into sustainable eating, thanks to his new girlfriend. It's not horrible, but sometimes all the vegetables leave me craving processed deli meat and cheese slices that are closer to plastic than actual dairy products."

Rebecca wrinkled her nose. "You actually crave this stuff? I consider it make-do food."

"There's only so much 'healthy' a person can handle, you know?" Ben shuffled down toward the cash register.

She walked the clerk through a bare-bones vegetarian sandwich and moved to pay. "I don't think most normal people know that, actually. Most of us are just trying to keep from becoming part of the obesity epidemic."

Ben scoffed. "You buy that?"

She paid for her sandwich and combined his food with hers before she picked up the tray holding both of their subs. "You don't?"

"I'm not sure. Obviously, if you look around, you can see that there are people in America who could stand to lose some weight. But if you keep your eyes open, you'll see there are people right here without enough to eat as well."

That was true, though it was surprising he realized it. "Don't you work in *international* hunger relief?"

"Yeah. Doesn't mean I'm oblivious to the situation closer to home though. In fact, we're trying to put together a project with one of the homeless missions downtown." He named one of the Christian organizations in the city and continued. "They do a lot for families that aren't homeless but who have trouble providing enough

23

food for their families on a daily basis. Hunger isn't just a problem for third-world countries."

"I volunteer down there—no one's said anything about a joint project."

"We're in the early stages yet. Honestly, I probably shouldn't even have mentioned it." Ben angled his head. "Can we say grace?"

Rebecca lifted her brows. As far as he knew, he barely knew her, yet he wanted to pray before their meal? Definite bonus points. She nodded.

Ben said a quick prayer for the food and their time together before grabbing his sandwich and taking a huge bite.

She pulled her small sub into two pieces, wrapped up half and nibbled on the corner of the other.

"You're only eating half? Of a half?"

Rebecca sighed. "I quit running a few years ago. It's a long story, but the end result is that I don't have the regular exercise that I used to love. I still work out, but going to the gym or taking a walk isn't the same. Thus a closer eye on my diet. I'm scheduled at the mission tonight, as it happens, and their dinners are hearty and delicious. Most days I help out downtown, I try to skip lunch."

"That seems rather poorly thought out for someone in healthcare."

"Maybe." Not that it was any of his business. Time to turn this conversation around. "Have you been off work since your injury?"

"Nah. They gave me a laptop. I can do most of my job as long as I have the Internet and a phone. I'm getting so spoiled working at home, it's going to be tough to get back to the office full-time." He set down his sandwich and took a long pull on his soda. "Any idea when that might be?"

"It's really up to your surgeon. Typically it's at least two weeks before you're comfortable off crutches and able to drive. There's a little wiggle room, depending on how your PT progresses."

Ben nodded. "That's about what I figured...This is going to sound crazy, but I can't stop wondering so I'm just going to ask: have you ever gone by the name 'Marie'?"

Her heart jumped into her throat. Rebecca finished chewing the bite in her mouth, swallowing despite the sudden metallic taste that pervaded everything. He recognized her. Not only that, he remembered her. Was it possible he thought about her as often as she thought about him? But even if he did, what was she supposed to say? She managed a weak smile. "It's my middle name."

"You disappeared. Just...poof. I sent you letters through the camp office, 'til they asked me to stop. What happened?" Ben flipped the paper over the remainder of his sandwich and pushed it away.

Rebecca's heartbeat thundered in her ears. She'd only gotten one letter. By the time she decided to go ahead and answer it, she hadn't been able to find it. He deserved the truth. Could she afford to give it to him? "That's another long story. I'm sorry I never wrote you."

He looked across the table at her, saying nothing.

She wasn't going to say any more. It was too much to get into right now...she needed to figure out how much she was going to tell him. Wasn't it enough, for now, that he'd connected her to Marie? Did he have to know all the details of her quest to separate herself from her family and the stigma her father had wrapped her in? Even if Dad hadn't meant to, he'd turned her life into a nightmare. Being Marie for a summer had shown her that it was possible to have a normal life.

"All right. Well. I guess I should let you get back to work." Ben stood, wobbling until he arranged his crutches correctly. He made it two steps from the table before he turned and held her gaze. "I fell in love with you that summer...and I've never really recovered."

Rebecca swallowed, tears burning the back of her eyes as he made his way to the street. She stopped herself from calling out or following him. She'd fallen for him, too. But when you were living a lie, regardless of the reasons behind it, you didn't deserve a good man. She'd expected him to move on. His words echoed in her head. He wasn't the only one who'd never recovered.

"Hey, Rebecca, come meet a new volunteer."

Rebecca stuffed her bag into a locker and closed it. She snapped on a combination lock and moved across the room to where Jerry Christensen stood next to a slender girl, probably in her late teens. "Hi. I'm Rebecca."

"Kira, nice to meet you."

Jerry grinned, hands in his pockets. "Kira's a college student, but she's taking a semester off. Rather than loafing around, she decided she'd like to volunteer here as much as she can."

"That's wonderful. I know it's often hard to find folks to lend a hand during the day. Most of us are after-work and weekends, but the people here need help all the time. Speaking of which..." Rebecca glanced toward the door. "I've got a handful of kids waiting on me to help them with their algebra."

"I was wondering if you'd mind having Kira shadow you? She's studying creative writing, so she could help with English homework."

Kira offered a soft smile. "Or whatever. I've got a pretty good memory and have always enjoyed school. I even like algebra."

"You're hired." Rebecca grinned. "I don't mind math, but I don't think I'd ever go so far as to say I like it. Come on, the kids are great." Why was Kira taking a semester off if she liked school?

With Kira trailing in her wake, Rebecca strode down the hall to the room designated for quiet activities like reading and homework. Eight kids sat at a conference table. Some hunched over books, scribbling intently, others flipped pages, and yet others reclined, eyes closed and earbuds firmly embedded.

Rebecca knocked on the table to get everyone's attention. When they all looked up and removed at least one earbud, she gestured to Kira. "Everyone, this is Kira. Kira, the kids."

Groans chased around the table. A prim, well-dressed girl straightened in her seat. "We're not kids, Ms. Rebecca. We're in high school."

Rebecca laughed. "Fair enough, Latoya. I stand corrected. Regardless, Kira's going to help tonight, too."

A young man jerked his chin. "What she good at?"

"I'm studying creative writing in school." Kira pulled out an empty chair and sort of collapsed into it.

"Tha's cool. I'm wit' her, she can help on that dumb poem we have to write for math."

"You have to write a poem for math?" Rebecca sat between two of the kids who were busily working on their homework. "Why?"

The boy shrugged. "Mr. Wilson said it was something about finding new ways to remember sh—stuff."

Rebecca shot him a pointed look.

He held up his hands. "Hey. I caught it. I should at least get credit for that."

"All right, I'll only charge you half."

The boy frowned but stood and jammed his hands into his pockets. He tossed a nickel across the table to Rebecca and dropped back into his chair. "I ain't never gonna win nuthin."

"Who'd want to win nothing?"

Rebecca bit back a snicker at Kira's response. If the girl wanted to explain double negatives to D'Andre, more power to her. She watched as Kira coaxed the poetry assignment from the boy and they began to discuss their options.

"Ms. Rebecca?"

She turned at the quiet voice by her elbow. "Yes, Tina?"

"Mr. Jerry asked if you'd come back to the office? I can help out here."

Everything looked like it was under control. Not that it hadn't been before she appeared. By and large, these were good kids. They didn't need her. Not really. But it felt good to be here. It wasn't

27

saving the world, but maybe she could make a little difference here or there.

Rebecca stood, leaving her chair out for Tina, and went back to Jerry's office. She tapped on the door frame. "Tina said you wanted to see me?"

"Yeah. Come on in and shut the door, would you?"

She pushed the door closed before sitting in the chair facing Jerry's desk. "Everything okay?"

He nodded. "Mostly. First, I thought I'd give you the background on Kira...I don't think she'd want it getting out too much, but since I'm hoping you'll keep an eye on her, it's good if you know."

Rebecca cocked her head. "Sure. She seemed to connect pretty well to D'Andre. If she can get through to him, she'll be fine. She wants to hang out with the tutoring crowd?"

"She needs something that will let her sit. She has leukemia. That's why she's taking time off school and," he paused, swallowed, "the treatment isn't going well. We're not sure how long she'll be able to stay out of the hospital. She wanted to do something to make a difference in the meantime."

"You know her." It wasn't unusual for friends and family to pitch in around here, so why did it rub her the wrong way? Was it because he hadn't introduced her that way? Was she really that easily annoyed?

"She's my goddaughter. Her mother was Meredith's roommate in college. Our families have been close since the beginning." His voice caught. He took a sip from the large mason jar of water he kept on his desk and cleared his throat. "Anyway. If you can help keep an eye on her, keep her from overdoing, I'd appreciate it. She has such a heart for God, I don't want to deny her any chance to use it."

Rebecca nodded, her heart aching. Why did things like this happen to people so young? All the "right" answers flitted through her head, but they didn't make her feel any better. "Was that it?"

"One more thing." His gaze flicked over her shoulder. She turned to look. Nothing but a closed door. "I know you like to keep your monetary involvement quiet."

Rebecca's brows shot up. "You know about that?"

Jerry held up a hand. "Don't get irritated. I pieced it together. I don't think anyone else has, or will. Few people have access to all the information that would allow the dots to connect. But since you are our biggest donor, by far, I thought I'd ask if you were interested in being part of a collaboration that Bread of Heaven has approached us about?"

She rubbed the back of her neck. "Depends, I guess."

"On?"

Rebecca blew out a breath. "If you pieced together that I'm a donor, then I suspect you've also figured out who my parents are?"

Jerry gave a brief nod.

"I'd like to keep that part quiet. I enjoy being Rebecca Fischer, that's why I changed my name legally. It's not like it'd be hard for someone to do a little digging and figure it out, but so far the media hasn't felt like bothering. I'm content for them to speculate on the whereabouts and shenanigans of Becky MacDonald."

He leaned back in his chair, a smile at the corner of his lips. "I can't imagine that would be a problem. How much is made up?"

Rebecca shook her head, shoulder slumping. "With the exception of forging a note to get my ears pierced when I was eleven and I did sneak out of the house once in high school, all of it."

Jerry grimaced.

"So you understand why I'm happy enough to leave her behind."

"I do. As it's the truth, it's easy enough to say you're the most faithful of our volunteers and that's why I've asked you to be part of the project. We'll leave it at that. I can't imagine it being an issue, but if it becomes one, we can address it then. Sound good?"

"Yeah."

29

Jerry pushed a fat folder across his desk. "Here's the initial information we have. The board's basically given the okay and then stepped back for me to take care of it. I was hoping someone would step up and spearhead the thing but so far, no luck."

"No one?" She pulled the folder into her lap and flipped it open. The cover letter had Ben's information at the top and his bold scrawl across the bottom. Her stomach clenched. Of course he was involved. He'd even mentioned it this afternoon. Why had she said yes before her brain kicked in?

"Nope. So if you're on board, I'm going to make you primary. I'll help out as needed, but my hands are full enough with all the day-to-day stuff around here. As much as I'd love to see this project take off, I just don't have the ability to handle it personally."

"Can I pray about it?" Maybe God would make it clear that she didn't have to do it. Certainly spending even more time with Ben was a bad idea. Wasn't it? Or was this God's way of telling her that she and Ben had some kind of future together after all these years?

Jerry frowned. "Of course. But...if you can't, or won't, take it on, we'll probably have to let them know that we're not able to work with them."

Lead settled in her gut. No pressure there. Rebecca took a deep breath. "All right. Let me take the folder home, read through it, pray about it, and I'll let you know tomorrow."

4

Ben propped his crutches against the wall and hobbled to the table. What had he been thinking? It was bad enough that he'd asked her to lunch after talking himself out of it on the way to therapy. Jackson had needed the extra time to run some errands—the fib about having asked him to come later was just that, a fib. Still, why hadn't he been able to leave well enough alone and simply start fresh, without worrying about whether or not she really was Marie? He sighed and cradled his head in his hands.

"Spill it."

Ben looked up and couldn't quite stop the half-chuckle as Jackson set down a can of soda, slid another across the table to Ben, and tore open a bag of cheese-flavored corn chips. "Do you think we stop learning as we get older?"

Jackson frowned and shook the bag before dipping his hand in and pulling out a handful of chips. "Nope. If that was the case, Paige would've given up on me completely after that fiasco with Senator Carson instead of giving me a second chance. Plus, I learned enough this summer to realize that no matter how sure I am that I'm in love with her, it was too soon to say anything about it. Even if the dinner at Marilyn's would've been the perfect romantic setting to do just that."

Ben popped the top on his soda. "It's just me, then. Cause that last little bit of discretion would've come in handy at lunch."

"What happened? I thought you just grabbed a sub next door while you were waiting for me."

"I asked Rebecca to come. She said yes."

Jackson crunched on chips, his gaze steady on Ben. "And...you confessed your undying love?"

Ben took a long drink from his can. It wasn't quite like that. But it was close.

"You didn't. You've known her what, two days? That's fast even for me, bro."

"It wasn't exactly like that. In fact, it's kind of your fault."

Jackson sat back, eyes wide. "How?"

"You're the one who got me convinced that she might actually be Marie. So I asked her."

"And it's her?"

Ben nodded.

"Wow. Did she say anything about why she never got in touch with you?"

He shrugged. "Basically that it was a long story. I waited, but she didn't elaborate. It didn't seem like there was any point in pushing. So I got up and left."

"I'm not seeing the problem. At least now you know that it's her. Gives you a place to start, right?"

Ben cleared his throat. "I might have mentioned, as a parting shot, that I'd fallen in love with her that summer."

Jackson shook his head and smirked. "Eh, so what? Shouldn't she have been able to figure that out? Or at least suspect?"

"And then I might have finished it with indicating that the situation really hadn't changed."

"Ah." Jackson reached for another handful of chips. "That changes things slightly. What'd she say?"

"Dunno. I walked out."

"Dude."

"I know, I know. But what was I supposed to do?" Other than keep his mouth shut in the first place. But that ship sailed as soon as he asked about her name. Ben drained the soda and crushed the can.

Jackson pushed the chips toward Ben. "What now?"

"Change physical therapists, I guess. There're a ton who work there. I imagine it can't be too hard to figure out what days she's not available, right?"

"Sure you want to do that? I mean, aren't you upset because she just disappeared after summer camp? But now you're going to do the same thing?"

Ben blew out a breath. Jackson had a point. Not one he really wanted to consider, but a point nonetheless. Was he going to run? "It's not quite the same thing."

"How is it different? Are you going to keep in touch with her another way? Ask her out again?"

"Well, no. I hadn't planned——"

"Then it's the same thing. You're running just like she did. Just like Paige did this summer."

Ouch. Ben frowned. "What do you suggest?"

Jackson shrugged. "Seems to me, if you want someone in your life, you pursue them."

"And if they run the other way?"

"Run faster."

Ben closed his laptop and pushed back from his desk. He raised his leg, extending his knee like he did in therapy, wincing at the tinge of soreness. What should he do about Marie-slash-Rebecca? Jackson's suggestion made sense. But he'd already been down that road once. All that had gained him was a very polite cease and desist letter from the camp and a rejected counselor application the next spring. He didn't blame them for the latter. Sending that many letters probably verged on stalking. But how else was he supposed to have reached her? At least knowing that Marie was her middle name made it clear why he hadn't been able to find her. His Internet skills weren't as sorely lacking as he'd wondered.

It didn't answer the immediate question though. Should he stick with it? See if there was anything there for them to build on? He hadn't been lying when he said he'd never gotten over her. Every woman he'd dated in the last ten years had failed to measure up to his memories of Marie—Rebecca—whatever he was supposed to call her. And even though he hadn't even scratched the surface of who she was today, there were enough hints to suggest that given a little time, he'd be even more in love with the woman she'd become.

So where did that leave him? Could he walk away? Or had God brought her back into his life for a reason? Even if that was the case, maybe it was time to use a little more strategy in his pursuit.

He scowled as his cell rang. It wasn't a number he recognized. It really was too bad the 'Do Not Call' registry didn't work like it was supposed to. Though it was possible this was someone connected with the mission downtown. He hadn't programmed all those numbers into his phone yet.

"Hello?"

Silence, then a throat cleared. "Ben?"

His eyebrows lifted. "Rebecca?"

"Yeah. Hi. Um. I got your home number from your client file. Not strictly allowed...I hope you're not mad. I just wasn't happy with how we left things this afternoon. And...is it too late to call?"

Ben chuckled. The nerves in her voice were something new. Encouraging. "No, it's not too late. And as I'd planned to give you my number this afternoon, I'm glad you looked it up."

"Okay. Good. Look, I'm sorry. About so much, but we can start with camp. I only ever got one letter from you. I don't know if the camp forwarded any others or what, but...I was going through some stuff, it started that summer and took me the better part of a year to wade through. When I finally felt settled enough to write back, I couldn't find your note. I didn't mean to leave things that way."

That explained a little, though not everything. "It's okay. The stuff you were going through...did that have to do with why you were going by your middle name?"

"Ha. Yeah. It's all tied together and not really phone conversation material. It's probably enough to say that I needed to figure out who I really was. Camp was the first step in that process."

That made sense. That was a large part of college, wasn't it? Figuring out who you were, separate from your parents. He'd never felt the need to use a different name, but all things considered, he had a pretty normal family. "When you're ready to talk about it, I'd be interested to listen. So, about lunch..."

"Please don't. I had feelings for you, too. I'm sorry I handled them so badly."

Had? Did that mean they were gone now? "It was college."

"That it was." Silence stretched across the line. "Anyway. I wanted to say thank you for lunch and let you know that I hope you don't feel awkward about me being your physical therapist. But if you do, I'll understand if you need to switch to someone else."

"If you're okay with me staying on, I'd just as soon not rearrange my schedule."

"Great. Then I'll see you on Friday."

"Rebecca?"

"Yeah?"

"I'm going to ask you out again. For a real date, this time. I figure you deserve a heads up."

"Oh. Um."

"Don't say anything. I haven't asked yet. I'll see you at PT. Good night."

Ben ended the call and smiled. Run faster? No. It felt like some subtle stalking might be in order. Time to formulate a game plan.

5

Rebecca set down the phone and pressed a hand to her stomach. She wasn't going to be sick. Maybe if she told herself that a few more times her body would listen. But she'd done what needed to be done and they should be back on professional ground. Except that he was going to ask her out again. The crickets in her stomach started jumping again. She huffed out a breath. She'd say no. She had to. They weren't nineteen anymore and this wasn't summer camp.

She ignored the stab in her heart. It was time to be practical. And realistic. Both of those things meant there was no future for Ben and her. Or her and any guy. As much as she might dream of marriage and kids, that would mean opening the door to her past, and that wasn't something she was willing to do. Let bad-girl-Becky stay in rehab in Switzerland, or jet off to Tokyo to be a flag-girl for illegal street racing. Whatever Becky did, that girl wasn't coming back to the States and intruding on the life of Rebecca Fischer.

Her cell lit up, its cheerful ring tone shattering the quiet. Rebecca smiled at her mother's face on the screen.

"Hey, Mom."

"Hi Becca. It's not too late, is it? I know it's nearly ten, your time, but I didn't want to wait until tomorrow."

Rebecca boosted herself up onto the kitchen counter and swung her legs. "Nope, it's fine. I don't have an early day tomorrow. Everything okay?"

"Oh, it's fine. You remember I mentioned the conference in D.C. this spring?"

"Sure. That's in March, right?"

"Something like that. I don't have my calendar right here."

Rebecca chuckled. Her mother was lost without the fat day-timer she'd been lugging around since the mid-eighties. No amount of cajoling would get her to switch to electronic scheduling.

"Anyway. Your father's decided to join the planning committee on their initial trip to the venue, get a feel for the lay of the land and so forth. So we'll be in town next week. Is there any way you could take a few days off and play tourist with us?"

Next week? "Um."

"I know it's short notice. Will you ask?"

The only new client she had right now was Ben. Everyone else would be fine going through their exercises with minimal supervision. Another therapist could easily handle that. But Ben...they could handle his rehab, too, realistically, regardless of whatever pangs missing him would cause. "I'll ask."

"Thanks, sweetheart. I know it's an imposition to have so little notice. But it'll be great to see you. It's been too long."

"I'll enjoy seeing you too, Mom."

"We're *both* excited about the possibility, Becca. Do you really think your father has any interest in the pre-planning meetings?"

Rebecca sighed. Probably not. Dad was much more of a fly in, give a talk, bask in the adoring adulation of his fans, and then zip off into the sunset kind of guy. Even so, it was a stretch to think he cared about seeing her. "I was home at Christmas. It hasn't even been a year."

"Oh, honey. Your father loves you."

She pressed her fingers into her eyes and inhaled deeply. "I know. I'll let you know if I can get some time off, okay?"

"Do you think you can let us know tomorrow? I suspect your father will want to cancel our flights if you're not available."

Rebecca sighed. "I'll ask first thing and text you. The whole week?"

"If you can."

She had the time. But she'd been saving up her time off for a real vacation. Something with friends or on her own. Something that had the hope of being relaxing. Not that seeing Mom would be bad, she'd been toying with the idea of the vacation being a mother and daughter adventure. But Dad...Dad complicated things. "All right."

"Thanks honey. I'll talk to you tomorrow."

"Right. Bye."

Rebecca plugged her phone into the charger and scooped up the fat folder from the mission. She might as well see what she'd gotten herself into. There wasn't really any way to say no, not after the guilt trip Jerry had sent her on. The mission needed the exposure and the potential new donors that would bring. Not to mention Bread of Heaven was a well-known, respected agency, so being associated with them was only going to help the mission. There was obviously some benefit to the larger charity. Was it as simple as wanting to expand into local missions?

She flipped open the folder, smiling at Ben's confident scrawl at the bottom of the letterhead. Maybe something in here would help her get a better handle on what Bread of Heaven hoped to gain. And maybe, if she was really lucky, she'd get a bigger picture of the man Ben had become.

"Ben, this is Sara. She's going to be working with you next week when I'm off."

Ben frowned, his gaze steady on Rebecca as he extended his hand to Sara. "But you'll be back?"

Rebecca nodded, ignoring Sara's less-than-subtle elbow in her ribs. "My folks decided to come visit."

He nodded.

Sara waved. "I've got another client coming in, but I'll see you next week, Ben."

"Maybe you could meet us for lunch on Thursday?" Where had that come from? Hopefully he'd say no.

"I could probably do that. I'll need to check with my roommates and see if someone can give me a ride."

"Right. I forgot you're not cleared to drive yet. Never mind."
Thank you, Jesus.

He chuckled. "Nuh-uh. You asked. I'm going to see if I can swing it. But this isn't the same as me asking you out. Just so we're clear."

"It's really not..." She trailed off at the stubborn set of his jaw and swallowed. *In for a penny.* "I can pick you up, if that's easier."

"Deal. Do you want me to give you my address, or you just wanna look it up in my file?"

She laughed. "I'll go get you a piece of paper. Do another ten extensions while I'm gone."

Rebecca stared up at the restaurant's sign and frowned. This is what she got for letting Sara choose their dinner spot. Season's Bounty. It even *sounded* pretentious and expensive. They could get salads anywhere, even at a drive through. Why did they have to go to Clarendon, for crying out loud?

"Boo." Sara tapped Rebecca on the right shoulder before peeking around her left.

"Have you been here before? 'Cause I..."

"Oh, relax. It's delicious and not overpriced. You're just upset about having to be near the city on a Friday night like a normal single person instead of holed up in the suburbs like an old fogey." Sara glanced at her watch. "Jen should be here soon. This'll be fun. Trust me."

Rebecca scoffed. "You remember what happened the last time you said that, right?"

Sara waved it away. "Please. How was I supposed to know it was a strip club? My mom's friend said it was the best girls night out she'd ever been to. I had no idea she was that kind of person. Neither did my mom, for that matter. This is just dinner. No show. Promise."

Jen jogged up, breathing heavily. "Sorry I'm late. I had to park practically at the Courthouse Metro."

"There's a garage right there." Rebecca pointed across the street.

"Yeah, well. I didn't want to pay garage prices. I found a meter. One quarter should see me through to when switch to free." Jen shrugged. "I really want to go on the Holy Lands trip the pastor mentioned on Sunday. So pennies are getting squeezed until they whimper. Let's eat, I'm starved."

Sara pulled open the door and gestured for Rebecca and Jen to go in.

Rebecca's stomach growled as the rich, meaty smells assaulted her nose. Maybe this wasn't going to be so bad after all. There was definitely more than salad on the menu.

The hostess smiled. "Do you have a reservation?"

Sara nodded. "Under Reynolds."

"Three?" At Sara's nod, the hostess slid magnets around on the podium before collecting menus and rolled silverware. "Follow me."

Rebecca elbowed Sara. "Look at you, making reservations. I was about ready to mention the taco place down the street."

"I made the mistake of not having a reservation the first time I came here. They get busy on weekends, so I figured I'd call ahead just to be safe." Sara grinned.

"Looks like that was a good call. They're packed." Jen nodded to the dining room. "I don't see any empty tables. Where are they putting us?"

The hostess stopped at a table in the back corner. "Here you go. The soup tonight is cream of mushroom with bacon. Your server will be with you shortly."

Rebecca slid around the table, taking the chair in the corner where she could look out over the room. They really were doing a brisk business. "Food must be good if they're this busy all the time. Of course, you say mushrooms and bacon, and you've got my attention."

Sara and Jen laughed.

Rebecca flipped open the menu. "What else is good?"

Sara opened her menu. The corners of her mouth turned down. "Hmm. The menu's changed a lot since I was here in August. I guess they really do keep it seasonal and local; it's not just a gimmick to get people through the door."

Jen shook her head. "Cynical. Both of you."

"Like you're any different." Rebecca set her menu down. There wasn't any question. She was getting the soup and the stuffed pork chop. It didn't matter one way or the other that the pork came from nearby, or that the spinach and garlic used to stuff them came from the chef's own garden. The description made her mouth water and she didn't have to cook it.

"True. True. That's why we're friends."

"That and we're the only sane single people at church." Sara sighed and closed her menu. "Anyone else getting that pork chop? It sounds too amazing to pass up."

Rebecca raised her hand.

Jen shook her head. "I'm getting soup. And bread. And that's it. Don't let me cave."

"Dieting again?" Rebecca frowned at her eternally ten-pounds-overweight friend. "You need to figure out how to be happy in your skin. You're beautiful. And not fat."

"What she said." Sara jerked a thumb at Rebecca. "Seriously."

Jen hunched her shoulders. "Look, it's not like I'm starving myself. I'm just trying to make better choices and avoid shelling out for jeans that are another size up. If nothing else, I'd like to put that shopping trip off 'til the spring, after the trip to the Holy Lands. Besides, it's kind of rich for the ex-running-addict to be giving body image advice."

The blood drained from Rebecca's face as the barb hit home. She bit back a retort. She'd quit running, hadn't she? And bought a whole new wardrobe as the pounds—and shape—came back. Now she had her mother's hips, whether she wanted them or not. But at least they came with a little more up top. She hadn't been mistaken for a boy in years.

"Bzzt. Foul." Sara made a T with her hands.

"Yeah, okay, sorry." Jen frowned. "I just want..."

"I get it. Don't worry about it, 'k?" Rebecca patted her friend's hand and blew out a breath. "Did I tell you my parents are coming to town this weekend?"

"Um, duh? You're handing off Mr. Seriously-too-hot-to-be-real to be my client for the week." Sara waggled her eyebrows. "Maybe I can take him to lunch after a session and plumb the inner depths of his soul. He looks like someone who has some dangerously deep inner depths."

Jen snickered. "What does that even mean?"

Rebecca reached for her glass. Her entire body had to be flushed. Empty. Where was their server?

"It means he's hot, not wearing a ring, and, given the fire bolts shooting out of Rebecca's eyes, not fair game for anyone but her. Dang." Sara gave an exaggerated sigh. "Woe is me."

"Please." Rebecca cleared her throat. Definitely time to change the subject. "Was the service slow last time you were here?"

"Hang on. I'm out of the loop. Who's the hottie? When did this happen? And I totally agree that he's off limits, cause if looks could kill, you'd be living in past tense, Sara." Jen scooted her chair in and pinned Rebecca with her gaze. "Spill it."

A girl who looked impossibly young appeared at the table. "Hi, I'm Cara. I'll be taking care of you tonight and I'm so sorry you had to wait, it's my first night. Can I take your drink order and maybe start you off with an appetizer?"

Rebecca let out the breath she hadn't realized she was holding. Saved. At least for a minute or two. What was she supposed to tell them? These were her two closest friends. They knew almost everything, though she hadn't said exactly who her dad was. They'd never pushed, which meant they'd either figured it out and were being nice or they didn't care.

43

When Cara left with their drink and dinner orders, Jen focused her attention back on Rebecca. "So? Let's have it."

Sara leaned forward. "I'm interested, too. Cause the look you gave me says he's more than a good looking PT client."

Rebecca shifted uncomfortably in her seat. "It's a long story..."

"So what? We've got all night. Right, Jen?"

"Right."

6

Ben laughed and tossed a balled up napkin across the table at Jackson. "Hey, at the end of the day, I have another lunch date with her."

"Yeah, her and her parents. That's kind of fast, don't you think? Skipping straight to the 'meet the parents' portion of a relationship?" Jackson looked over at Zach. "Am I right?"

"Don't drag me into this. The only reason you haven't spirited Paige off to Florida to meet your mom is her work schedule. As it is, her parents have started joining the big family lunches with your sister and her crew almost every Sunday. So as far as merging families, you're way ahead of the curve. Why shouldn't Ben be, too?"

"See?" Ben grinned and reached for his sparkling water. "Besides, if you factor in carrying a torch for ten years, we could get engaged next week and I don't think it'd be too fast."

"Who's getting engaged next week?" Paige slid a plate into the middle of the table before squeezing into the chef's table booth next to Jackson.

"Hopefully no one." Zach pointed at Ben. "Just because you've reconnected with your long lost love doesn't mean you need to rush your fences."

Ben shrugged and picked up one of the eggroll-like things from the plate. "Mmm. What's in here? It's good."

Paige chuckled. "Maybe I'll wait 'til everyone's had some before I give out the recipe."

Jackson pulled his hand away from the plate.

"I'm kidding." Paige dropped one of the rolls onto the smaller plate in front of Jackson. "It's just chicken and vegetables. I'm trying out a new recipe for the sauce that's in there, but it's nothing weird, I promise."

"You promise?" Jackson poked the eggroll.

"Hey, I said it was good." Ben reached for another and popped it in his mouth. "You've got to be the most unadventurous eater I've ever met. How'd you end up with someone who can cook like this? It doesn't seem fair."

Paige and Jackson exchanged a look.

"Ugh. Stop it, you two. You're going to make me lose my appetite." Zach snatched an eggroll and cut it neatly in half with his fork. He tipped up the cut end and peered at it before forking it into his mouth. "Mm. These are good."

"Told ya'." Ben looked toward the kitchen as voices raised over the clattering and banging of pans.

"And that's my cue." Paige brushed a kiss across Jackson's cheek as she stood. "I'll be back with more food in a few."

"The food's better, I'll give you that. But it's quieter at home with video games and pizza." Zach reached for the last egg roll.

Jackson shrugged. "I guess. It's not like the two of you have to tag along. I can always bring a book to pass the time. But with Paige's schedule, this is what our Friday night dates are going to be like for the foreseeable future. She's worth it."

"She's good for you." Ben shifted. Was it possible to ease the angle of his knee and lessen the ache? Something had to make it stop. "Figure out where you're putting in the garden yet?"

"She wants to come over tomorrow morning and take a look, but I'm thinking we should wait 'til spring."

"Are you still going to be living with us come spring?" Zach gulped down a long drink of water.

Ben waited for Jackson to dismiss the question. When it wasn't immediate, he frowned. "Why is this even a question? You can't leave."

Zach shook his head. "Dude, do you even have eyes? Look at the two of them. If that's not headed toward marriage, I'm a Benedictine Monk."

Marriage? Okay, so sure, Jackson and Paige were a great match. But they hardly knew one another. And yet...sometimes you just knew. Wasn't Marie—Rebecca—a case in point? He needed to get used to thinking of her as Rebecca. It certainly suited her better, but it was still an adjustment. He planted his elbow on the table and rested his chin in his hand.

"I'm not sure any of us will be living in the same house come spring. I got an email from Jason this afternoon. Seems he and Karin are taking a furlough and would like the house. They're not firm on dates yet, so it might be summer, but..." Jackson shrugged.

Just great. Ben glanced at Zach. "Want to look for something together?"

"Sure." Zach grinned. "But I call dibs on the master if there's a bathroom in it. Schlepping down the hall is for the birds."

"That's fine. If we're not sharing, at least I won't be searching for a toothbrush-sized sliver of counter space in between all your hair products."

"Don't do anything rash, all right? He just sent the sort of heads up email. I wasn't even going to mention it until I had more information. Clearly that would've been the smarter choice." Jackson blew a kiss toward the kitchen.

Ben stuck his finger in his mouth and made an exaggerated gagging sound.

Zach snickered.

"Hey. It gets us free food, don't knock it."

"And it was good, don't get me wrong, but are we hitting the movies tonight or not?" Ben looked at Zach.

"Yeah, come on. We'll leave loverboy here to moon over his sweetheart and go watch some buildings explode." Zach slid out of the booth and grabbed Ben's crutches from where they were propped against the wall.

Ben hoisted himself to his feet. "Tell Paige thanks for the food. It was good. And keep us posted on the house, okay? It's better to know sooner than later. All right, Zach, let's scoot."

Zach held the kitchen door open for Ben as he navigated into the dining room. Did you ever get used to using these ridiculous things? They were awkward. And his armpits hurt. As did his knee.

The rubber stopper on the end of one crutch caught on the metal transition strip between the tiled kitchen floor and the carpeted dining room. Ben stumbled, hopping on his good leg as he fought for balance. His hand slipped off the grip and his arm shot out. He lurched to the side, crashing into someone.

"Sorry." Ben's face and neck burned.

"It's fine. Are you okay...Ben?" Rebecca chuckled. "What are you doing here?"

Perfect. "You mean other than tripping over non-existent hazards? One of my roommates is dating the chef. We usually hang out for dinner on Friday. It's better than anything any of us can cook—"

"Hey. I can cook." Zach peered around Ben. "Hi. I'm the other roommate, Zach. Sorry I couldn't catch him completely before he mauled you. Are you sure you're okay?"

"I really am, thanks. I'm Rebecca, Ben's physical therapist. It's nice to meet you."

"Oh." Zach's eyebrows lifted and he shot Ben a look. "The pleasure's mine. I'll go get the car and meet you out front."

Zach clapped Ben on the shoulder as he brushed past, causing him to stagger forward. Idiot. "Excuse him. He's a high school math teacher. His students' lack of maturity rubs off on him."

"All good. So...you eat here a lot?"

"Most Fridays. Paige is a great chef and it beats pizza. Though I guess I should give Zach his due. He can cook pretty well, when he takes the time. Jackson and I are fairly close to hopeless." Ben shrugged. "I should let you get back to your date?"

The corners of her mouth poked up. "Nah. Couple of friends from church. We're finishing up and trying to figure out what to do next."

"Zach and I are headed to the theater to catch an action movie, if you'd like to tag along." Ben fought a wince. Where had that come from? Sure, he was planning to ask her out. But a spontaneous tag along with all kinds of friends wasn't what he had in mind.

"That could be fun. Let me go see if they're game. Is there room for us to carpool with the two of you? It'd be easier that way."

"I don't see why not."

"I see why you like her." Zach tossed his keys onto the kitchen table and sagged into a chair.

"She's something special, isn't she? And she hasn't changed that much since college. Some refinement, maturity, sure. But the sense of humor and quick wit? Those are what lured me in the first time. Her friends seem nice, too." Ben made his way to the couch and sank into the cushions, propping up his leg with a sigh. Elevating his knee was close to heaven. He'd definitely overdone it today.

"Sure."

"That's it? Sure? Neither one caught your eye even the tiniest bit?"

A faint tinge of pink glowed on Zach's cheeks. "I'm kind of seeing someone."

"What? Who? When did this happen?" Ben shifted to stare at his friend. "How did you manage not to mention this?"

Zach lifted a shoulder. "We're keeping it casual right now. Her choice. I'd love to push for more, but I also don't want to scare her off. She's important."

Wow. Zach wasn't usually this serious about anything other than math. "And she is...?"

"Amy."

"Amy-at-work, Amy?"

Zach nodded.

Ben whistled. "That seems...complicated."

"This from the guy who wants to date his physical therapist."

Zach had a point. "But I won't be her patient forever. Presumably, I'll heal before much longer. You'll still be working together."

"Thus the taking it slow. There's no policy against it—I checked—but she's concerned. I sort of see her point, but it's not as if we work for a high school that's turning away applicants left and right. Heck, we're nearly a month into the new school year and we still have five open positions. I don't think they'd fire a teacher unless they had no choice."

And that, right there, was the joy of working at an inner city school. How did Zach manage it day after day? And more than manage it, he thrived on it. Ben was all for helping people. He didn't work to provide food for the hungry because it was the only job available—he believed in what he was doing. But Zach took philanthropy to a whole new level. "You should invite her to join our Friday night mooch dinners at Paige's. Then it's less like a date and more like hanging out with friends."

"Plus you get a chance to pester her with questions?"

Ben lifted a shoulder in a one-sided shrug. "Hey, after the third degree you applied tonight, I think I'm due."

"What? All you'd ever say was she was the one who got away. And maybe you mentioned camp. I've been wanting details for a while now. She was happy to provide them. And seeing as how she's the one who did the talking, I'm guessing they were actually true."

Ben snorted. He didn't exaggerate. Much. At least Rebecca had kept things reasonably factual, though it hadn't hurt his feelings any to see the emotion surfacing as she talked about their runs and hikes. Even the campfires, though they'd been on duty, had been romantic. She remembered. More, her feelings hadn't been something he imagined. After so many years not knowing, the thought had occurred that he'd simply read too much into a summer flirtation.

"Anyway. I don't know about you, but I'm beat." Zach headed down the hall to his room.

Ben dropped his head back against the sofa and closed his eyes. He was tired, but not sleepy. He called up the mental picture of Rebecca laughing during the movie, his heart accelerating from the warmth of just being near her.

He turned on the game console. Sleep wasn't happening anytime soon.

ELIZABETH MADDREY

7

Rebecca pulled up to the curb and forced a smile. Nothing quite like driving for an hour and a half so that someone could save twenty dollars on their plane ticket. She'd gone round with her parents more times than she cared to count since moving to the D.C. area about how BWI wasn't actually a local airport. But there was no persuading them. Not when there was money to be saved.

Her dad lifted a hand in greeting and began walking toward the trunk. She pulled the release, threw the car into park, and stepped out. "Let me help you with that, Dad."

"I've got it, Beck. Thanks." He hoisted the suitcase into the car and wiggled it over to one side before pulling her into a bone-crushing hug. "It's good to see you. Thanks for picking us up."

"No problem. Where's Mom?" Rebecca scanned the crowded sidewalk outside the arrivals area of BWI. "I'm not going to be able to wait here very long."

"She had to run into the restroom. She should be just a second. Let me go get our other bags."

Rebecca kept an eye on her dad and another on the police car inching its way down the loading area, scooting people along who weren't actively involved in picking someone up. Worst case scenario, she could circle and leave Dad here to wait for Mom. Her stomach clenched. Circling gave her a headache. She inevitably missed a turn and ended up making the route longer than needed.

"Here we go, bag number two."

"Do you want to put the carry-ons on top, or in the backseat?" Rebecca moved so her dad could wrestle with her mother's larger suitcase.

"In here is fine. I was hoping we could grab some dinner on the way to the hotel?"

She chuckled. "Of course. Have somewhere in mind?"

He swung an arm over her shoulders. "You know I do. Ah, there's my bride."

Rebecca watched her mom scan the crowd, catching the exact moment her eyes landed on them. Too bad it didn't warm her heart to have her dad's arm over her shoulder. But at least she'd moved past his public displays of affection triggering hives.

"Hey, Mom." Rebecca hugged her mother and nodded toward the car. "We'd best get going before I end up with a ticket. They're pretty strict."

They piled in the car, her dad squeezing into the back while her mom scooted the passenger seat as far forward as it could go. Why hadn't Dad just sat in the front? Probably figured it was chivalrous. Whatever. She'd rather sit by Mom anyway. "Where are we headed?"

With a belly full of Thai food, Rebecca drove into the parking garage under her parent's hotel. The conversation at dinner had, amazingly, not been awkward. Her dad had been subdued, and interested in her work. Two things she hadn't experienced with him in more years than she cared to count. Maybe this week wouldn't be as horrible as she was expecting.

"Let me help with the bags, Dad. You go up and check in. Mom and I will meet you in the lobby."

Rebecca's father studied her for a moment before nodding. "If you're sure?"

"Of course, dear. You go. We'll be right behind you." Rebecca's mom made a shooing motion with her fingers.

Rebecca turned off the car and watched her dad cross the garage to the elevators, his brisk stride covering the distance rapidly. "It's good to see you, Mom."

"You too, Becca. And we're both so grateful you were able to get the week off. You sure you don't want to stay with us at the hotel? We'd love to have you close, and save you that horrible commute every day."

It was tempting, but only slightly. The drive wasn't going to be fun. But it wasn't as if she didn't sit in traffic on a normal day anyway. She was just going a bit farther. On the other hand, being back in her own space, alone with her own things every night couldn't be discounted. It'd be a much needed decompression time after a day with her parents. "Nah. I'll be fine. Besides, this way if meetings pop up, or run long, I can just head home."

"And leave me on my own at the hotel? Gee. Thanks." Her mom smiled, shaking her head. "All right. Can't say I blame you. I'd probably say the same thing. Come on, let's get that luggage and meet your dad. He's probably wondering what's keeping us."

Rebecca lugged the two suitcases out of the trunk while her mother collected the carry-on bags. At least the big bags had wheels. Rebecca pulled them behind her to the elevator. "Have you thought about what you want to do tomorrow?"

"Any of the touristy things. What's most interesting to you? I haven't been to D.C. in years, so I'm willing to see whatever. Your father won't be free tomorrow—he's in meetings all day, from breakfast on. I do have to join him for dinner. You're welcome, of course, though I imagine you'd rather not?"

Rebecca grimaced. "Do you mind?"

"We understand."

"Which isn't the same thing as not minding." Rebecca sighed. "I'm sorry."

"Like I said, we understand." Her mother held the elevator doors open as Rebecca pulled the suitcases into the elegant lobby.

Her father waited by a large potted palm. "There you are. We're all set. You won't change your mind and stay, Becky?"

"No. But thanks, Dad." She fought a yawn. "I'm going to head home, if that's all right? What time do you want to get started in the morning, Mom?"

"Why don't you pick me up at ten? That way you can sleep in a little, maybe miss some of the traffic. How does that sound?"

"Like heaven."

"I'm a little jealous of the two of you, have to admit." Her dad grinned and pulled Rebecca into a tight hug. "I'd much rather sightsee than sit in meetings, but, such is life."

"You thrive on it, Dad, and you know it." Rebecca wriggled out of his embrace, hugged her mom, and eased back. "I'll see you tomorrow. Sleep well."

Back in the garage, Rebecca locked the doors and lowered her head to the steering wheel. Over all, it had been better than expected, but Dad was still Dad. Had she really expected that to change? Still, maybe her mom was right. It did seem like he was trying, though why couldn't he call her Rebecca—or at least Becca, like Mom—instead of Becky? She'd gotten tired of correcting him. Maybe Mom could take a stab at it. She'd ask tomorrow.

She yawned again, turned on the engine, and started working her way back home.

8

Ben hobbled down the hallway to the living room without his crutches. He wasn't technically supposed to be without them, but between the rubbing and weight bearing, his arms needed a break. Besides, it wasn't as if he was going far. He'd grab a bag of chips and hunker down on the couch for some game playing time. His knee started to give. He grabbed for the wall.

"Oof. Ow." Okay, maybe not the brightest move to leave the crutches in his room.

Jackson's head popped up above the back of the couch. "You all right?"

"Yeah, I'm fine. Just stupid, I guess. What are you doing home? Thought you were hanging with Paige tonight?" Ben limped the rest of the way into the room and stopped as his gaze landed on Paige, curled on the couch next to Jackson. "Ah. Sorry."

"It's fine. Why don't you join us? We were going to put on a movie." Paige sat up and scooted over, making room on the couch.

"I don't want to intrude. I'll just..."

"I have a variety of stuffed puff pastries in the oven. I'd love more than one opinion on them."

Ben looked from Paige to Jackson. What was the protocol here?

His expression must have betrayed his dilemma because Jackson laughed and gestured to the empty cushion. "Sit down before you fall over and reinjure yourself. We're here because we knew someone would be home."

"Oookay. If you're sure." Ben eased into the space they'd created for him. "Let me know if I'm in the way. I can watch a movie in my room."

"Get that knee elevated." Paige patted his leg as she stood. "I'm going to check on the food. Why don't the two of you figure out what we're watching."

"If you give me just a minute to rest my leg, I'll get out of your hair. I can't imagine you actually want me to play chaperone any more than I want to be third wheel." Ben propped his leg on the coffee table. "I really didn't know you were here or I would've just stayed put."

"It's all good, man. Paige is pretty strict about not being completely alone together." Jackson frowned down at his hands, which were twisted together. "Realistically, it's good that she's vigilant, but it's still frustrating."

"It's not exactly a picnic for me." Paige grinned and set a plate of steaming hors d'oeuvres on the coffee table before pressing a kiss to Jackson's cheek. "But..."

Jackson grabbed her hand and pulled her to his side. "I know, I know. This way we don't get carried away."

Heat crawled up Ben's neck. He should go back to his room. Even if they didn't want privacy, they should have it. If being in the house knowing he could walk out whenever was enough, he'd give them a little more space. He scooted forward and cleared his throat. "I'll just..."

"Oh no you don't." Paige glared at him until he sank against the back cushions. "You at least have to stay and try the food. I really do need opinions. I'm considering them for the winter menu, but I'm worried they're too frou-frou."

"I'm sure they're delicious. Anything you come up with is tasty." Jackson winked as he selected a pastry and bounced it between his hands. "Hot."

"That's the whole 'I just took them out of the oven' thing." Paige shook her head and offered Ben a toothpick.

Ben speared a morsel. "Do we get to know what's in them?"

"Nope. It's a surprise."

Ben frowned and sniffed. All he could smell was pastry. There couldn't be anything terrible in there with no smell, right? He tentatively bit through the flaky crust and he teeth sank into gooey...cheese? Flavor exploded on his tongue. "Mmm. These are good. Are they all the same?"

Paige shook her head. "There are two kinds. Try the other side of the plate."

Ben stuffed the rest of his first piece into his mouth and reached for another. Jackson still hadn't tried his. "What are you, chicken? Take a bite."

Jackson offered a half-hearted chuckle before putting the pastry in his mouth. He gave a tight-lipped smile while he chewed.

"Well?" Paige scooted over to meet his eyes.

"The thing is, I've never really liked goat cheese. So, I'm not really the person to ask. Don't get me wrong, it's good. It's just..." Jackson shrugged.

Crestfallen, Paige nodded. "Not your thing. Got it. The other one doesn't have cheese. Will you try it?"

"Of course." Jackson laid his hand on her knee. "I'm sorry. It's good."

She held up a hand. "It's fine. You don't have to love everything I make. I value honesty, you know that."

Ben turned his laugh into a cough.

"You all right, bro?" Jackson whacked him on the back.

"Fine. These are good, Paige. Definite menu material." Ben struggled to his feet. "I'm going to take a few and head back to my room. I forgot I needed to do...something."

"You're not going to stay and watch the movie?" Paige frowned. "I promise no chick flicks."

"Nah. You two have fun." Ben grimaced as he put more weight than he should on his knee and made a mental note to follow instructions more closely in the future. When they said he wasn't ready to ditch the crutches, they were telling the honest truth.

"At least let me go get your crutches for you." Jackson stood and brushed past him.

Ben sagged against the wall. He ought to object, for form if nothing else, but the throbbing in his knee pushed his ego aside. He accepted the crutches. "Thanks."

"You sure you have something to do? Paige wanted to know about Rebecca—she's hungry for a female friend and is hoping that you and Zach will find nice girls and deliver them into her clutches."

"I can hear you, you know." Paige knelt on the couch, looking over the back at Ben and Jackson. "But he's not wrong. At least give me a little hope before you go hide in your room."

He wasn't hiding. Exactly. "She's great. In college, she had dreams of helping people—she has an amazingly tender heart. And that's what she does. I've watched her with her other clients when I get to PT early. She's gentle, but tough. Plus she volunteers at the homeless mission we're hoping to partner with."

Paige gave a slow nod. "Sounds encouraging. Is she a super girly-girl?"

Ben scoffed. "No. I don't know if she still does, but the girliest thing she used to do was collect salt shakers."

"No pepper shakers in that collection?" Jackson's brow lifted.

Ben shrugged. "Probably. But it was the salt shakers she cared more about—they were her reminder that we're to be salt and light, and that even the tiniest pinch of salt offered someone the promise of a better life in Christ."

Paige grinned. "A pinch of promise. I like that. I want to meet her."

"I'll see what I can do."

Back in his room, Ben flipped channels on the TV before turning it off. How could you have that many channels and still be without anything entertaining to watch? He dragged his laptop over to the bed and stretched out. Maybe he could get some work done. Scrolling through the email that had collected since Friday he huffed out a breath. When he did manage to get back to the office, it was going to be an adjustment. Did they realize how many pointless meetings they had? If they could keep him in the loop through a two-paragraph email, why not just do it that way to start out?

Ben typed a few responses and sent them before opening the email from the director of the downtown mission. A slow smile spread across his face as he read. Only God would do something that amusing. And perfect. He stopped at the bottom of the email where Rebecca's contact information was neatly typed. His gaze darted to the clock glowing on his nightstand. Before he could over-think, he picked up his cell and punched in her number.

"Hello?"

He didn't bother fighting the grin at the sound of her voice. "Rebecca? It's Ben. Do you have a few minutes?"

"Sure. I just got home and need to unwind a little before bed. I was going to see if there was anything good on TV."

"There isn't."

She laughed. "Alrighty then."

"No, seriously, I just spent ten minutes flipping channels. There's nothing. Unless you're one of those people who watch the food shows. There are always food shows."

"Yeah, that's not really my thing. I cook, but I don't love it so much I want to sit and watch someone else do it. Plus, when they get going fast with their knives, I cringe. I keep expecting someone to lose a finger."

"See, now, that possibility is what makes them interesting enough to watch."

"Gross. Why are guys always gross?"

He let out a bark of laughter. "It's in our DNA, I think."

"Bleh. I'm guessing you didn't call so you could set me up for nightmares about lost appendages though, right?"

"Right. Sorry. Hey, do you still collect salt shakers?"

"You remember that?"

Ben hunched his shoulders. It probably wasn't a good idea to let on that he still remembered all their conversations. Practically word for word. "Apparently."

"I do. I've started getting a little pickier about which ones I pick up, though. Some of the plain crystal ones, even if they're antique...I only have so much room. Why?"

Uh-oh. How was he supposed to explain why Paige was asking about her without giving away too much? "You remember I told you about my roommate Jackson?"

"Dating the chef, right?"

"Right. She's over tonight, they're watching a movie in the living room. It came up when I went in to mooch some food."

"Hmm. A roommate with a chef for a girlfriend sounds like a winning situation. Lucky."

"Definitely. She made these cheese puff type things tonight, and another that was sort of mushroomy. Really good."

"That's just mean. My dad dragged us to a Thai restaurant. It was good, but just not my favorite."

He frowned. She'd loved it in college. Every night off, they'd driven to the nearest place that had passable Pad Thai. "What happened?"

She hesitated. "You remember that, too? I don't know. Overexposure, I guess."

"Hmm. That's too bad. There are some good Thai places in the area. Anyway, still not the reason I called. Sorry. I got an email from Jerry, at the mission downtown and he said you're going to be the point person for our joint effort. I'd been hoping to get together with the folks there at some point this week to get things going. I know your parents are in town, but is there any chance you'll have some time?"

"Maybe. When did you have in mind?"

"I'm pretty flexible. This is the only major thing on my plate right now since I'm stuck telecommuting, unless I can get a roommate to drive me in. Do you know who else will be on your committee?"

"Funny."

He blinked. "What'd I miss?"

"I'm it. They're not what one would term 'over-staffed' at the mission. If I hadn't agreed, Jerry was going to have to tell you guys that they didn't have the personnel to take on the project, regardless of the potential good it can do."

Ben winced. He'd known things were tough for them, but hadn't realized it was that bad. "Hmm. We still on for lunch on Thursday?"

There was a long pause. "That was the plan..."

"Maybe we could take thirty minutes before or after?" Her sigh crackled in his ear. "Or not. I guess it can wait 'til next week when your folks are gone."

"Sorry. My parents just...complicate things. I should have time in the evenings for email though. Or some phone calls?"

That could work. His driving desire for a meeting was to get to know the committee in person, put names to faces, that sort of thing. If she was it...he probably didn't need that, regardless of how much he might want it. "All right. But be warned, I'm known as the email king at work."

She chuckled. "Noted. But I draw the line at calling you 'Your Highness.'"

"What about 'Oh, Great One'?"

"We'll see. I don't remember you being this full of yourself at camp."

Ben chuckled. "I was young."

"You're a goof."

"Guilty as charged. But that hasn't really changed."

Her voice sobered. "Thanks."

"Anytime. Though I guess I'd like to know what for."

"It was a long day. Talking to you was, apparently, just what I needed."

Warmth spread through him. "Get some sleep. I'll send an email tomorrow."

"All right. 'Night."

Ben ended the call and leaned his head back, staring up at his ceiling fan. She'd been flirting, right? He wasn't mis-reading their conversation, seeing what he wanted to see? He replayed their banter. Definitely flirting. With a chuckle building in his chest, he sat up and flipped open his laptop. He double-checked the email address from Jerry and began to type.

9

Rebecca flipped off the bathroom light and ran a hand through her hair, sending droplets of water flying. She really should get back in the habit of wearing a headband when she washed her face, but she'd stashed all her long hair accoutrements away when she'd gone super short two years ago. Did she even know where that box was anymore?

She crossed her bedroom and checked her phone one last time. How did she get an email in the five minutes it took her to get ready for bed? She flicked the screen and poked the app, eyebrows lifting. Well, well, he really was the email king, wasn't he? She tapped the message:

From: Benjamin Taylor

To: Rebecca Marie Fischer

Re: Bread of Heaven/DC Mission Joint Project

Ms. Fischer,

Thank you for agreeing to be a part of the Bread of Heaven (B of H) project with the DC Mission. Please see the attached files for background information on this project. I look forward to working closely with you over the coming months.

Sincerely,

Benjamin Taylor

Oo-kay? She had a file from them already, the one they'd given Jerry. What on earth had he needed to send right away? She dropped to the bed and criss-crossed her legs before tapping the first attachment. Some kind of video? There was a pause as her phone opened a video player and Princess Leia strode down the hallway of, was it the Death Star? Shouting, "I am NOT a committee!"

Rebecca laughed. "Good one, Ben. Though in this case, Leia, I am the committee."

She poked the next attachment. Her heart fluttered as a slide show of photos from camp started up. How did he put that together so quickly? It wasn't possible. But that would mean...

"Not possible." Her voice was a whisper, but even so it startled her. "Great. Now I'm talking to myself."

Rebecca swallowed and eyed the final attachment with suspicion. He'd effectively said he was still in love with her at the sandwich shop, but she hadn't taken him seriously. Ten years was a long time without contact. But the pictures...

Steeling herself, she tapped the last file, laughing as a picture of a debonair, silver-haired man leaning casually against the back of a dark restaurant booth filled her screen. The caption said: I don't always send email right after hanging up the phone...Oh who am I kidding, yes I do. All Hail the King of Email.

Still chuckling, she plugged her phone in and crawled into bed with a book and a silly smile.

"Thanks for meeting me." Rebecca slapped her menu down on the table as Sara slid into the booth opposite her. Her feet were on fire after a day tromping around D.C. with her mom. Thankfully, Mom and Dad had that dinner meeting this evening which meant she could have a little break and relax with her friend.

"Sure. Beats going home to a townhouse full of airheads whose only saving grace is that they pay their portion of the rent on time. Honestly, I'm not sure what I was thinking taking a room with a bunch of college students." Sara made a gagging motion. "Were we ever that young?"

"Probably." Rebecca shrugged. "It's not like we're old now, you realize."

"Yeah, I guess. But working full time and being out of school...it's a whole new world. You know?"

Rebecca nodded. And not having roommates was one of the major reasons she lived in Springfield instead of closer to work. If she had waited until she could afford to live single in Fairfax, she'd still be waiting. "How long is your lease?"

"I've got another six months. They're already pressuring me to at least commit until the end of the school year. Thankfully for GMU that means May, so only two months past when I was planning on bailing. But I don't know."

"Have you even started looking at other options?"

"Of course not. If I was one of those people who planned ahead, I probably wouldn't be in this situation to begin with." Sara unrolled her silverware and aligned them on the paper placemat in front of her. "Doesn't mean I want to sign on for two extra months with the drama queens."

Rebecca laughed. "So how was work today?"

"Mmmmm. I suspect you don't actually care how sweet, eighty-six-year-old Mr. Thompson is doing recovering from his hip replacement or how Melinda managed to create yet another scheduling disaster that took the whole office to unravel."

"Again? How many second chances is she going to get? I have house plants that could run the appointment desk better than she does."

Sara snickered. "Probably true. And yet, none of those houseplants are the niece of owner's wife."

"I forgot about the family connection. She's never going anywhere, is she?"

"Unlikely. Though I don't think she's going to be on appointments much longer. She was in the back organizing the supply room after lunch. Worst case there is it takes us longer to find things."

"Let's hope she gets stuck there. That room could use some consistent management." Rebecca opened her mouth to ask about Ben, but snapped it shut when the server appeared at their table. The hole-in-the-wall Mexican place was a favorite for the two of them on nights Jen couldn't join them, so they rattled off their orders. "Now..."

"All right, all right. He's fine."

Rebecca scowled at her friend.

Sara laughed. "You should see...hang on a sec." She picked her phone up off the table and snapped a picture, flipping the screen around so Rebecca could see. Definitely needed to remember not to make *that* face again. Ever. "I take it that means you need more details than fine?"

"Why do I hang out with you?"

"Because of my sparkling wit and personality, coupled with the fact that Jen is Mexican food intolerant, so if you want chips and salsa and don't want to eat alone, I'm it?" Sara gestured to the basket and bowl that the server deposited, along with their drinks.

Rebecca dunked a chip in the thick red puree and crunched down. Heat singed across her tongue. Oh, yeah. This just might let her forget that she had four more days of sightseeing with her mom looming on the horizon. "Probably part of it. Don't make me beg."

Sara drummed her finger on the side of the glass. "He's a nice guy. Of course, I figured that out on Friday when he invited us along to the movie. And I say 'us' because, while it was clear you were who he's interested in, he didn't make me, or Jen, feel like an imposition. There were no veiled hints or attempts to get you to move somewhere else with him. It was just a group of friends hanging out at the movies together. And honestly, for that alone, I'm already jealous of you."

"I...but..."

Sara held up her hand. "I didn't say it was reasonable. But if you don't scoop him up, you're an idiot and, after a day or two to mourn you, I'll totally be moving in on him."

Rebecca's eyes widened. "Hey. Who said I wasn't scooping him up?"

"Aha." She grinned. "I wondered if you were as nonchalant as you've been acting. He's wondering too, in case you were curious."

"He said that?" Rebecca dropped the chip she held back into the basket. Empty calories. Delicious. But still empty.

Sara lifted a shoulder. "Not in so many words. He's in love with you."

"He's in love with ten-years-ago me." Rebecca shook her head. "There's a difference."

"I don't think so. It might have started out that way, and that definitely fed the attraction, but it's not *just* that anymore."

Rebecca clasped her hands in her lap, her fingers twining together. Her throat went dry and raspy. He might have moved from loving Marie to loving Rebecca...but he still didn't know who she was. Not really. "What am I supposed to do?"

"Unless you're an idiot, you love him back, get married, have babies, and live happily ever after. Preferably sooner than later, 'cause he's a keeper." Sara frowned. "Why isn't this making you happy? I thought for sure this would have you giddy with delight."

Rebecca gulped half of the contents of her water glass. This wasn't supposed to happen. She was supposed to change her name, establish a life, and only deal with her past when she went home once a year for Christmas. "Do you know, really know, who my dad is?"

Sara pursed her lips. "I have my suspicions."

"Yeah, well, Ben doesn't even have those."

"So, where are we headed today?" Rebecca's mom adjusted the strap of her purse across her chest and offered an expectant look.

The morning of her third straight day of touring, and her mom still looked perky and ready to go. If Rebecca's mirror was any indication, neither of those adjectives described her. A little break from walking around all day would be welcome. Rebecca pulled her lip between her teeth. This was either going to be a great idea or a horrible one. Her gut said it was more likely to be the latter. "Um. Would you like to see the homeless mission where I volunteer?"

"Sure. But honey, you told me you hadn't told them." Eleanor pointed at her chest. "I'm not as recognizable as your father but it's not like I have a low profile. Especially when it comes to something like this."

"As it turns out, Jerry, he's the director, already pieced it together. He's promised to keep it quiet and since the Board shouldn't be around...I can't imagine anyone else who's there is going to notice or care. Particularly since the reason we're going is Jerry sent out a 9-1-1. Most of their staff is down with some kind of flu-like thing. They're really shorthanded today."

"In that case, let's go. Or should I change? I don't mind getting grubby in this, but if you think I should...?"

"You're fine. Thanks, Mom."

Rebecca took the scenic route, if you could call it that, to the mission, pointing out the few statues along the way. It wasn't fair to drag her mom along, but if she'd begged off, Rebecca knew Mom would have just spent the day in the hotel room waiting for Dad. And Jerry had been desperate, so saying no wasn't really an option there, either. She probably would've used a sick day to come down and volunteer if she hadn't already taken vacation.

Eleanor tapped on the window. "This is lovely. It's a little slice of green in the middle of broken."

Rebecca followed her mother's gaze to the fenced in lot the mission set up as a garden. They did a lot of gardening to supplement the donations and reduce the cost of food they had to purchase. "This was one of the projects they started shortly after I came on board. They'd been getting donations of fruit and vegetables that the markets deemed unsalable, but it didn't seem right that people couldn't have fresh now and then, too."

"Do they own the block?"

"They were able to get a good deal from the city. It'd been derelict for so long, they really only objected for form." Rebecca's attorney had handled the purchase, using funds from her trust to complete the transaction. Once she owned it, she sold it to the mission for a fraction of what she paid. Jerry and the board thought they'd snared a deal from the city. With no one the wiser, everyone was happy. It was so little in the overall scheme of things.

Her mother shot her a look from the side of her eye but nodded. "I see. The residents work the gardens?"

"The ones who are interested do. Sometimes we end up using a little friendly coercion on the less interested, but generally speaking there are enough folks who enjoy spending a couple hours out there that it hasn't been an issue. And it's never a bad thing to look at the meal on your plate and know you contributed to it. Come on, I'll take you to meet Jerry and we can find out where we're needed."

Rebecca led her mom into the shelter, waving to the harried woman at the reception desk on her way back to Jerry's office. She gave a quick rap on the door-frame and poked her head in.

"Oh thank goodness." Jerry rounded his desk, hand extended. "I've got everyone I could rope into it scrubbing the common areas to do what we can to ensure those germs cease flying through the shelter and infecting everyone. We really can't afford to spread something like the flu to the people who come to us for help. But that's left Kira on her own with all the pre-school kids. She's doing okay, she loves kids, but..."

Rebecca shook her head. "Aren't there close to thirty kids here during the day? We'll head right over. I wanted you to meet my mother. Mom, this is Jerry, the mission's director. Jerry, Eleanor MacDonald."

"Call me El, please. It's a pleasure to meet you. I hear so much about the wonderful things you're doing here." Eleanor extended her hand.

Jerry shook it, offering Rebecca a curious glance. "The pleasure's mine. I didn't realize...?"

"They're in town for the week. We were going to hang around the museums. This seemed more important."

Jerry's face fell. "You shouldn't have..."

"Don't be ridiculous. My only goal was to spend time with Becca. This is just as good—maybe better." Eleanor rubbed her hands together. "Now, where are those kiddos?"

ELIZABETH MADDREY

10

Ben scowled at his laptop. It was Wednesday. He'd sent Rebecca two or three emails a day and she hadn't responded to any of them. Not all of them were frivolous, though he could admit that the trailer for the latest Star Wars movie probably didn't merit her hitting reply. Was she even reading them? Some of the questions about the joint fundraiser were actually semi-time-sensitive. Sure, okay, she was doing the tourist thing with her parents this week, but hadn't she said she'd have some time in the evenings?

He sighed and scrubbed a hand over his face. If he was honest, it wasn't the email that was bothering him. He missed her. Sara was nice, and she certainly seemed to know about physical therapy, but she wasn't Rebecca.

Before he could talk himself out of it, he punched her number into his phone and hit send. He was just confirming plans for lunch tomorrow. That was reasonable, right?

"Hey you. I was just thinking about calling you." She sounded tired. And a little sad.

"Hey yourself. You okay?"

"Yeah. Just a long day."

He chuckled. "Sightseeing can do that to you. See anything good?"

"We actually ended up at the mission today. All the usual day workers came down with the flu. Jerry's goddaughter was the only person available to work in their day program for kids, and she's in the late stages of leukemia and probably shouldn't have been there with all those germs anyway. But she's the sweetest, most wonderful girl and it doesn't seem fair that the way things are going she's not going to see Christmas." Rebecca sniffled.

Ben closed his eyes. He ached to have his arms around her and let her lean on him the way she had after a bad day at camp. She hadn't had many of those, having always been an upbeat person, but that just made the times when she needed to lean on him more memorable. "I'm sorry."

"Don't be. I'm just being silly. Honestly, Kira is like this shining beacon, taking it all in stride and simply resting in Jesus and I barely know her and I don't want her to go. Mom was the same way."

Ben furrowed his brow. "Is your mom sick?"

She gave a watery half-laugh. "No. Sorry. Mom went with me to the mission today. She fell in love with Kira, too. It doesn't seem fair."

"Ah. Fair...that's one of those things..."

"I know, I know. Sorry. Like I said, most of this is exhaustion talking. I'm sure I'll be better tomorrow after a good night's sleep. So how has your week been going? Sara treating you well?"

"Sure. Though I'm not sure any of the torture you people devise and call physical therapy can be called nice treatment. Still, she seems to think the doctor will let me ditch the crutches next week. Then maybe I'll be able to drive and start being a productive member of the workforce again."

"Whoa there, Ben. Don't rush things. How's the range of motion?"

He chuckled. "Good. It's good. I can bend and straighten almost like normal."

"Any swelling?"

"Nope. And the pain's basically gone too. Unless I push myself too hard."

"I recommend not doing that."

"Gosh, thanks. I'll keep that in mind." Ben shook his head. At least she didn't sound quite as sad anymore. "So...we still on for lunch tomorrow?"

"Can I ask you a random question?"

"Uh. Sure?"

"Do you keep up with celebrities at all?"

"Only when they're in the news for something ridiculous. You know, the big stuff that hits the front page—like when that singer had a mental breakdown and started sewing clothes out of bubble gum wrappers? I knew about that. But otherwise? I'm really more of a video game kind of guy. Video games and baseball. Why?"

"Oh, no reason."

Ben frowned. That wasn't very convincing. No one just spit out a weird question like that without some kind of compelling reason. "Uh-huh. Wait, don't tell me. You're a physical therapist by day and a gossip blogger by night. You're worried I'll uncover your secret identity and accidentally share it with the world, making it impossible for you to use your adorable, unassuming manner to get any more of the ungettable interviews."

"Please."

"Hmm. Okay, not that. Then...oh, I know. You have a gossip column habit that you're desperately trying to break and you needed to know that I'm not going to drag you down with my own inability to resist researching and discussing the latest scandal in detail."

She snorted out a laugh. "Stop, okay? It was just a question."

"Mmm. And it has to do with lunch tomorrow because...?"

"It doesn't, all right?"

He grunted. "And now you've neatly sidestepped lunch twice. Should I be hobbling down to the kitchen to make sure we have peanut butter?"

"You don't have to do that. I'll pick you up at ten-thirty."

He grinned. "Perfect. See you tomorrow."

Ben ended the call, stood, and stretched. He reached for his crutches and headed down the hall toward the living room. Jackson sat on the couch, flipping through the channels. Zach had books and papers spread out on the dining room table. Typical night...why had he been holed up in his room?

"Given any good F's today?" Ben pulled out a chair at the table and sat, peering at the papers Zach was grading.

Zach grinned. "Not today, but I'm not finished yet, so there's still a chance. Honestly, I'm kind of surprised at how good some of these are."

"Good? They're math problems. Aren't they either right or wrong?"

"Usually, sure. But I assigned a poem."

Ben put a finger in his ear and jiggled. "Come again? I swear I heard you say you asked your math class to write poetry. But I know that can't be right."

"Nope, you heard me. I've been reading some studies that suggest a connection between creative writing and mathematical ability. Figured it was worth a shot."

"You want them to hate you, don't you?" Ben crossed his arms and slouched in his seat, easing his knee straighter. He was trying to keep it bent for longer periods of time when he sat, but by the end of the day, the aches just weren't worth the minimal progress that contribute to.

Zach shrugged. "It was extra credit. Still, almost everyone turned something in. Some of them are really quite good. Amy liked the idea."

"Aha." Jackson clicked off the TV and moved to join them at the table. "Now we get down to it. Impressing the girlfriend is always a good plan."

"She isn't my girlfriend. She's just a friend."

"Who happens to be a girl." Jackson tossed out the words, an impish gleam in his eye as he turned to Ben. "Have you ever heard anyone deny a relationship as much as Zach?"

"Not unless they were running for office." Ben laughed at Jackson's expression while Zach raised his hand for a high five.

"Low blow." Jackson shook his head. "Just for that, maybe I won't invite you to dinner on Friday at Paige's. Even if she has a new ravioli dish that she wants us to try."

Ben's stomach gurgled. How long had it been since he'd had good ravioli? Too long. "That's just mean. You know ravioli is my favorite."

Jackson shrugged.

"Don't worry, Ben. If the overly sensitive lobbyist won't invite us, we'll go on our own and sit in the dining room. Let him swelter in the kitchen by himself." Zach lifted the stack of papers and tapped it on the table, neatening the edges, before setting it aside.

That might not be too bad. Maybe he could ask Rebecca along...though he'd really rather their first date be alone. Doing things with a group was fun, but he was itching for some time with just the two of them sans knee exercises. Had she said when her parents were leaving? He'd have to ask at lunch. "That's a plan. Or at least the start of one."

"Come on, you know I'd never leave you two hanging. I was kidding." Jackson drummed his fingers on the table. "Can I get your opinions on something?"

"It's better to ask if we'll withhold our opinions when you don't want them. You know that, right?" Ben rubbed his knee absently.

"What he said." Zach flipped open another file folder full of papers. "Let's hear it."

Jackson swallowed and dipped his hand into his pocket, tossing a small velvet box into the middle of the table.

Ben eyed it then looked over at his friend. "Is that what I think it is?"

Jackson nodded.

"Wow." Ben ran his tongue over his teeth. "How long have you had this?"

"I went shopping this afternoon on my way home from work." Jackson stood and paced. "You still think it's too soon, don't you?"

Zach reached for the box and pried open the lid. Ben's eyebrows shot up and he let out a low whistle at the sparkling diamond. Celtic knots formed the sides of the ring with bands of pave diamonds continuing the sparkle all around. "Dude."

"What?" Jackson threw himself back into a chair. "I thought I was unique but still mostly traditional. And the knots are Trinity knots, so kind of referencing the cord of three strands thing..."

Zach held up his hand. "Stop. It's gorgeous. I can't think of a woman who wouldn't love to wear it. Are you sure it's the right size?"

"Mostly. I asked her dad to dig around a little, see if he could figure it out. This is what he told me." Jackson's shoulders relaxed. "You're sure it's okay?"

"Better than okay." Ben drew the box closer and eyed the decorative details. He'd always been a fan of the simple gold band with a stone at the top, but this might have him rethinking when the time came. "Is that white gold or platinum?"

"Platinum. It'll stand up to washing better. She washes her hands a lot. And that's why the diamond isn't up high, but fairly inset. I thought maybe there was a chance she'd be able to wear it when she worked." Jackson shrugged. "Maybe not. But she certainly wasn't going to be able to wear something with a high prong setting. It'd collect all kinds of food and stuff."

"When are you going to ask her?" Zach filched the box and ran a finger down the side of the ring before snapping the lid closed and sliding it back across the table.

Jackson caught it and clutched it with both hands. "Not sure. Maybe Sunday? I know it's fast. But it's right. I want her in my life forever. Even if she wants to be engaged for a long time to give us more time to get to know each other, I'm okay with that, as long as we're moving forward."

Ben tapped his fingers on the table. "I'm assuming since you asked her dad about the ring size, he knows what's going on?"

Jackson nodded. "He and her mom are excited about the idea. Honestly, that's why I went ahead and looked at rings today. I hadn't actually planned to buy something, I haven't done nearly as much research as I normally would for a purchase this big but this one...it whispered her name. With them in the know, I'm not sure how long I can hold off before they spill the beans."

"You don't think she's expecting it?" Zach leaned back in his chair, absently pushing aside the papers in front of him.

"I don't know. Eventually, sure. We talk about being married all the time. But the timing of it is nebulous. Still, it's understood between us, I think." Jackson puffed out his cheeks. "You think..."

"No, I don't. I was wondering. That's all." One corner of Zach's mouth lifted. "Chill. Sounds like you've got it covered."

Ben nodded. "I agree. She's lucky to have you. And you her. We still get to come over to your house and eat though, right? Even when you have kids running around the table wreaking havoc?"

Jackson laughed, his death-grip on the ring box loosening. "Of course. The kids will look forward to their meals with Uncle Ben and Aunt Rebecca."

Zach snickered. "I'm kind of surprised you're not asking where he got it and what else they have."

"Har-har. We haven't even been on an official date yet. You might be rushing things a tiny bit." Though he had made a note of the jeweler, that wasn't something he planned to share anytime soon. "Besides, Zach's the one holding out on us. How many of his late 'faculty meetings' are really dates with Amy?"

Red crept up Zach's neck and onto his face but he kept silent.

"I rest my case." Ben shook his head. "Not even the tiniest denial. Which makes me suppose they're all dates. What is that, two, three a week? And your best friends and roommates haven't even met her yet."

"What's up with that?" Jackson frowned across the table at Zach. "You know what? We're having a triple date on Sunday. Ben, tell Rebecca. Zach, tell Amy. No excuses."

"I'm not sure she'll be free..." Zach trailed off when Jackson nailed him with a look. He hunched his shoulders. "I'll ask."

Jackson looked at Ben, eyebrows raised.

"Yeah, sure, I'll see if she can swing by. But I'm not calling it a date."

"I don't care what you call it. Just make sure she's here." Jackson stood, tucking the ring back in his pocket before striding down the hall.

Ben glanced at Zach. "He's gotten bossy, hasn't he?"

11

Why had she agreed to this? Rebecca looked over at her mother who was smiling out the window of the passenger seat. At least Dad had a last minute lunch engagement crop up. Mom's face wasn't splashed all over the papers or the backs of books that got lots of press like Dad's was. Maybe, just maybe, she could pull this off without Ben realizing who she was. Used to be? No, was. It didn't matter how much she tried to avoid it, Becky MacDonald was part of who she was. If it hadn't been for her, Rebecca Fischer, physical therapist, wouldn't exist.

"Okay, one more time just to be sure we're on the same page."

Eleanor turned with an amused smile. "Honey, I've got it. No mention of MacDonald as a last name, or your father in general. The only name changing you've done is go by your middle name one summer during college. Though I will, one last time for the record, register my complaint. If you love this man, and my mother's intuition says you do, he needs to know everything. You can't build a future based on lies."

Rebecca's forehead wrinkled. "I know, Mom."

"Mmmm."

How could her mother pack so much censure into a simple hum? And really, what else was she supposed to do? Just walk up and say, 'oh, by the way, my names are complete lies but I promise everything else you know about me is true'? That'd go over super well. Not. She bit back another sigh. Sometimes having a mom you told everything to was a pain. Her GPS dinged and announced their arrival at the destination, a well-maintained mid-century modern home. "Wow. Even with roommates, this is a nice place. How much does a charity pay?"

"You can ask during lunch. Why don't you run up and ring the bell to let him know we're here?"

She shot her mother a look. "I'm not asking how much he makes."

Her mother grinned.

"Oh, good grief. It was just a comment. I would've loved to be able to afford a single-family. But it would've meant roommates. Lots of them. And even then we wouldn't have been this close to everything." That wasn't precisely true. If she'd dipped into the trust she could easily have lived in this neighborhood. But she wasn't using the trust for personal things. Not if she could help it.

"Just go get your friend." Eleanor shooed her toward the door.

Rebecca wiped clammy palms on her jeans as miniature rabbits started up a game of racquetball in her stomach. Mom would stick to the plan. She had to. With a deep breath, she pushed the doorbell, smiling as La Cucaracha played inside. Would anyone other than a group of guys have that as their bell tone?

The rhythmic clomping of crutches grew louder before the door creaked open. "Hey. Right on time."

Saliva pooled in her mouth as Rebecca took in his sharply creased khakis and green polo. There ought to be some kind of law against looking that good in such a simple outfit.

"Did I drip toothpaste on my shirt again?" Ben looked down, wiping his polo.

Oh great, caught staring. Rebecca swallowed and shook her head. "No. You look amazing. Perfect."

Ben's eyes sparkled as he maneuvered down the step and stopped to pull the door closed behind him. "Tell me more."

Fire burned across her face. "I just meant you hadn't spilled anything."

"Uh-huh." Ben winked and gestured for her to go ahead of them down the walk. "If it helps, I often think the same about you. Even in scrubs."

She fought the urge to fan herself. Shouldn't it be fall by now? Cool temperatures? Leaves dropping? That sort of thing. Oh, who was she kidding? Being around Ben always left her overheated in one way or another. Rebecca cleared her throat. "Thanks. Do you mind sitting in back?"

Ben worked his way around the front of the car. He peeked in the window then straightened with a grin. "Who's the hottie in the back seat?"

Rebecca chuckled and shook her head. Of course Mom moved. "That's Mom."

"Cool." He opened the back door and transferred both crutches to one hand. "Mind if I join you?"

"Don't be ridiculous. As soon as I saw your crutches, I realized you needed to be up front. I'm Eleanor, Becca's mom, and I'm really looking forward to getting to know you a little during lunch."

"See if everything she's said is true?" Ben stepped backward, closed the rear door and opened the passenger door.

Eleanor nodded. "I have a hard time believing someone can be *that* wonderful."

"Mom." Rebecca glared over her shoulder as she slid behind the wheel, heat that had just dissipated returning full force. She must look like a tomato.

Ben laughed and patted Rebecca's shoulder. "Never fear, Mrs. Fischer. It's all true."

Eleanor's head dropped back as she laughed.

Rebecca's hands tightened on the steering wheel. What had she gotten herself into?

"So, Becca tells me you work for Bread of Heaven?"

Ben set down the spoonful of soup that had been half-way to his mouth and nodded. "I do. I've been there since I finished college. Actually started as an intern over the summer and that morphed into a full time position. It's a great organization and I love knowing that what I'm doing positively impacts the lives of the less fortunate. Had you heard of B of H before?"

"I had, actually. I do some work in Africa through Homes of Hope." Eleanor's gaze slid to Rebecca.

Rebecca gave a slight nod. They'd agreed not to talk a lot about her mom's work, but it was natural that it came up. At least she hadn't come right out and admitted that she started the charity. Particularly since Mom had used her married name and, so far at least, had been content to let Ben call her Eleanor.

"Oh, they're fabulous. I haven't had the opportunity to coordinate a project with them yet, but I'm hopeful that maybe I will with the next international focus I head up." Ben scooped up some soup.

Eleanor furrowed her brow. "I thought B of H was only international?"

Ben grinned. "They have been in the past. I'm working to try and change that, at least on a small scale. I think our primary focus will stay abroad, but we're doing a test partnership with the local downtown mission. Actually, I get to work with your daughter on that."

Eleanor turned to Rebecca. "You never mentioned that."

Rebecca hunched her shoulders. "Sorry. I just got put in charge of the project last week. I didn't want to bore you and Dad with the details. Plus...I don't really have all the details yet. Ben and I need to figure out a time to get together and go over some questions I have after reading through the proposal we got from B of H."

"Hmm." Eleanor studied Rebecca for several heartbeats. Had her mom figured out that she didn't want Dad knowing the details? She'd have to mention it after they dropped Ben off. Her work at the mission was hers, not something for her dad to exploit in one of his talks. Eleanor returned her attention to Ben. "What prompted you look at domestic projects?"

Ben shifted in his seat. "It's...complicated."

"Which means it has to do with money, right?" Rebecca handed the server her empty soup bowl and took the salad she'd ordered. When everyone had their entrees, she raised an eyebrow at Ben. "Am I wrong?"

"Not entirely, no. Though I'm not sure why you sound so annoyed about it. The fact of the matter is, even non-profit organizations need to have money. We have expenses and salaries to pay, just like everyone else. The difference is that we work very hard to ensure that that vast majority of any income goes directly to benefit the people we help." Ben frowned. "Why *are* you upset?"

Rebecca's stomach clenched. It was a good question. She didn't have a particularly good answer, either. But it was still as if tiny bugs were crawling under her skin, leaving her itchy and irritated. "I just want to be sure that whatever partnership the mission enters is for their benefit, not a publicity stunt for Bread of Heaven."

Ben jolted like he'd been slapped. "Where would you get that idea? You said you have questions after reading the packet we sent over, but a statement like that leaves me wondering if you've actually looked at anything in that folder."

Rebecca drew in a breath. Eleanor laid her hand on Rebecca's arm. "Why don't we change the subject? Becca said you two first met at summer camp. Have you continued doing work with youth, Ben?"

Ben angled his head, his gaze lingering on Rebecca for several heartbeats before he turned and offered Eleanor a strained smile. "I teach Sunday school to middle school boys."

Rebecca sat back as Ben continued to talk about his work with kids both at church and through short-term international mission trips. Of course, those were through his job, so it was unlikely he could get out of them if he wanted to. Still, he was doing more than offering a few hours a week like her. But unless she wanted to live off her trust fund, there was no way to do more. And if she was living off the trust, she'd have a lot less money to give to the mission. Besides, she liked her job. Maybe she wasn't saving the world, but she did good, honest work and helped people live better.

"I like him." Eleanor leaned back in the passenger seat as Rebecca backed out of Ben's driveway. "I think you father will, too."

"What do you mean 'will'? I have no intention of Ben ever meeting him."

"But..."

"Nope." Rebecca shook her head. It meant nothing serious could ever happen, but hadn't she acknowledged that when she officially changed her name? If she was going to get away from Becky MacDonald, it meant she'd be alone. A high price, maybe, but worth it.

"Well, that'll make the wedding awkward." Her mother crossed her legs at the ankles and turned to stare out the window.

Rebecca snickered. "Mom. You know I'm not planning on getting married. That ship sailed the first time Dad did his talk on abstinence with me as the shining example of what a high school slut looked like. It was bad enough that every guy who asked me out for my last two years of school expected me to sleep with them on the first date, but it only got worse when they realized I wasn't going to. And everyone in the teenage world knows about it because he still trots out that little speech. How can I tell anyone my real name, introduce them to Dad, and not have them wondering if they need to have me tested for STDs before proposing? And if I can't tell them who I am, you're right, there's no future. Not a long-term one at least."

Eleanor frowned. "So you don't ever plan to settle down and have a family? Really?"

Rebecca rubbed a hand over the dull ache in her chest. "I just don't see any other way around it."

Ben slammed his laptop shut and pushed away from his desk. What was wrong with her? They'd been having a nice conversation and then *wham*, out of the blue came...whatever that was. Sure, okay, Bread of Heaven was hoping to get more donors from their partnership with the mission, but the mission stood to gain new donors as well. And they'd been completely open about that in all of the documentation. The fact of the matter was that many people who gave to international hunger relief had no idea that many Americans went hungry every day. The reverse was true as well, though those who gave locally tended to know about the international problem. They just didn't necessarily see it as their responsibility to do anything about it. Maybe seeing a joint effort would help them change their minds. So what, exactly, was Rebecca's problem?

Zach poked his head in the door. "Hungry? I was going to throw together something dinnerish. Easy enough to make two plates instead of just one."

Ben shook his head. "Thanks though."

"How was lunch?" Zach leaned against the jamb.

"Food was good. Her mom is great. But we touched on the fundraiser and then things got weird, like she shut down. I don't know."

"Huh. Gonna call her?"

Should he? "I was thinking of giving her a day. See if she needed some time. I mean, if she's not excited about working together...I don't want to push."

Zach nodded. "If she doesn't call tomorrow, you'll call her?"

"I don't know. Probably. Why?"

"'Cause Amy's nervous about Sunday and I kind of promised she wouldn't be the only one there who hadn't met everyone else yet.

Plus, as much as we've been spending time together, it really has been work-related at this point. I haven't quite figured out how to bridge that friend-slash-coworker gap. So, anyway, I kind of made it sound like just a group of friends hanging out."

Ben gave a sardonic laugh. "I didn't even remember to ask about Sunday. I'll do that for sure tomorrow. I still think she needs an evening to collect her thoughts."

"All right. But if you can possibly avoid making me a liar, I'd appreciate it."

"I'll do my best."

Ben stared at his phone. He wasn't going to call. That didn't mean he couldn't text, right? He grabbed the phone and put in her number. What to say?

Had fun at lunch, thanks for inviting me. I like your mom.

That should do. His phone buzzed with a response. She had fast fingers.

Glad you could come. Mom liked you, too.

Hmm. Ben's stomach clenched. Something was off. He tapped in another text.

But...?

Minutes ticked by without a response. Should he call after all? Or should he just leave it alone? He shouldn't have even texted. Why did he always do this? He plugged his phone into his charger and grabbed his crutches. Maybe there was a ridiculous monster movie on that he could sucker Zach or Jackson into watching with him.

Paige bustled around the living room, lighting candles and adjusting the trays of bite-sized munchies she'd put in various locations.

Ben frowned, his brow creasing. "I'm confused. I thought it was just you and Jackson, Zach, Amy, and me? It's not like it's going to be a standing room only cocktail party."

Paige crossed her arms. "Men. Doesn't this seem friendlier than dumping everything on the kitchen table and making people circle it for food? Now there's something delicious wherever they are."

Or wherever they aren't. Ben bit back the retort. He was either going to have to con people into bringing him things or do a lot more walking without crutches than he was supposed to. Even if he was expecting to get clearance tomorrow that would allow him to drive and ditch the torture devices, he wasn't going to take any chances today.

"Wait. What about Rebecca? Why'd you leave her off the list?" Paige crossed the room and perched on the edge of the sofa. "Isn't she coming?"

Ben lifted a shoulder. "I'm not sure. She wouldn't commit one way or the other, I wasn't comfortable pushing super hard, and so she'll either show up or not. But I don't think I'd count on her. She said it was a long week with her parents in town."

"What's going on? From what Jackson said, things were going great with the two of you, once you figured out that she was your long lost romance."

"Yeah, well. I don't know." Ben raked a hand through his hair. "I thought so, then I had lunch with her and her mom and she's been dodging me since."

The doorbell rang. Ben smiled in spite of himself. Paige groaned. "Why haven't you guys changed that? Seriously, are you twelve?"

"There's some part of every guy out there that stays twelve. Don't you know that? Relax, it's just a doorbell." Jackson stopped and squeezed Paige's shoulder on his way to answer the door.

Ben hauled himself to his feet when he spotted Rebecca standing there, her hands clasped in front of her. "You made it."

"You must be Rebecca. Come on in." Jackson opened the door wider. "I'm Jackson. This is Paige, and you know Ben already. Zach—you met Zach, right?—went to get Amy. She lives downtown and doesn't have a car. So he was meeting her at the Metro."

"Hi." Rebecca's gaze flitted around the room before settling on Ben. "Sorry I didn't let you know I was coming for sure."

"As you can see, Paige made enough food for a party of thirty, so we were covered either way. But I'm glad you made it." Ben sank back onto the couch. "Come on in and have a seat."

Paige nudged Jackson in the belly with her elbow. "We're going to grab the last of the food from the kitchen."

"Can I help?" Rebecca ran her palms down her jeans.

"No. We're good. You sit." Paige pointed to the couch before grabbing Jackson and heading into the kitchen.

Ben chuckled. "I think she's giving us privacy. There can't possibly be anything left in the kitchen to bring out. Except maybe the stove and refrigerator."

"Ah." Rebecca crossed the room and sat, angling toward Ben. "Look. I'm sorry about Thursday. I'm protective of the mission. I know that sounds silly, but I got worried that this was all just a big publicity stunt for Bread of Heaven, something designed to steal our donors and get them involved in international ministry. Not that they can't be doing both, but so many have a limited budget and..."

"Stop. That couldn't be more wrong. I really believe that this project can help both agencies. If I didn't, I wouldn't have suggested it. Local ministry is just as important as international. And that's part of the point I'm hoping people will see when they see us partnering together."

"Okay." Rebecca blew out a breath. "Sorry. Maybe we do need to go ahead and plan that meeting. I guess I'm not as proficient with email as I thought."

Before Ben could comment, Zach and Amy, trailed by Jackson and Paige came in from the kitchen. After introductions were made, Ben eyed at the food scattered around the room. "All right, let's eat."

Ben leaned against Rebecca's car, his heart pounding. "I'm really glad you decided to come."

"Thanks. I am too. Look, I'm sorry about Thursday. My parents being in town was stressful. It's complicated. Anyway, I shouldn't have jumped down your throat about the project. I looked back through the information and it's a solid plan. Getting people out to see the mission and interacting with the people who stay there is good."

He cleared his throat. "Are you free on Friday?"

"Um. I can probably make time if that's easier for you."

Ben frowned. "For what?"

"Were you thinking of getting together to start work on the project? I have some ideas for how to word the invitation..."

A slow smile spread across his face as he shook his head. "That's not really what I had in mind, no. Though maybe we can talk some about the project, too. I was thinking more along the lines of dinner. Just you and me."

"I don't...Ben...." She took a step back.

He reached for her hand and pulled her close. Fire—the good kind—burned along his leg and side where they touched. "Rebecca. Tell me you don't still feel it. There hasn't been anyone I've really cared about since camp for me."

Rebecca's tongue darted between her lips. Her voice was husky. "I feel it. I—you said at the sandwich shop—I never stopped loving you, either. But, Ben...I can't...it just isn't possible."

He jolted, the air catching in his lungs. "Why?"

She eased back, severing their contact, and crossed her arms. "It's complicated."

"You say that a lot. But complicated problems still have solutions. Let me help you find one."

Her eyes glistened in the streetlight and she shook her head, blinking. "I can't. Just let it go. Let me go, Ben."

"Rebecca..."

She wrenched the car door open and darted in. "I'll see you at PT tomorrow. I had fun tonight. Thanks for the invite."

91

Ben stepped back as she slammed the door, shutting him out. The engine revved to life. He stared, numb, as she backed out of the driveway and turned down the street, her car's taillights disappearing. What now?

Zach pulled up next to the curb and hopped out of his car, hands in his pockets, whistling merrily. His night had apparently ended better than Ben's.

"Hey man, Rebecca on her way home?"

"Yeah." Ben blinked and pulled himself back to reality. "Amy seems nice."

Zach grinned. "She is. She liked Rebecca and Paige, too. Still not sure if she understands how interested I am in her, but there's time for that to develop, right?"

Time. Was time the problem? Was ten years too long apart for them to rekindle what they had? He sighed.

"You okay?"

Ben shook his head. "I asked her out."

"'Bout time. Where are you going to take her?"

"Nowhere. She said no—it's 'complicated.'" He made air quotes. "I don't know what to do with that."

Zach pursed his lips. "You know what they say about eating an elephant, right? Seems to me that applies to any complicated proposition. Come on, I'm pretty sure Paige said there were leftovers in the fridge. A snack'll help you sort it out."

Ben turned and followed in Zach's wake. A snack wasn't likely to hold any answers. But it probably wouldn't hurt, either.

13

"You did what?" Sara thumped back against the bank of lockers in the employee lounge. "Are you insane?"

Rebecca pressed her fingers against her eyes. It was a distinct possibility. She hadn't slept at all. She'd been too busy replaying the disastrous conversation with Ben. Over. And over. And over. She'd wanted him to kiss her. Desperately. He'd acted like he was thinking about it. And then she'd pulled out the 'complicated' line again. She moaned. "I'm an idiot, aren't I?"

"Let's see. Gorgeous man from your past who also happens to be a strong Christian, gainfully employed in a job where he helps the less fortunate and, oh yes, still in love with you ten years after you disappear without a trace asks you out on a date. You tell him no and that you can't get involved with him at all. Um. Yes. You're an idiot." Sara threw her hands in the air. "I mean, seriously, Bec, what were you thinking?"

Rebecca winced. "When you put it that way, I'm not sure. But ten years, Sara. It's been ten years. I'm not the same girl I was back then."

"Get real. He's not expecting you to be. He's not the exact same guy, for that matter. But the only way to find out how much those changes matter, if they do, is to go out with him a few times. And I do mean a few. No more of your one date then dump philosophy."

"I don't..." Rebecca snapped her mouth shut at Sara's glare. Okay, so maybe she did. But how was she supposed to get close to someone—anyone—when a future was out of the question? There's no point.

"Why can't you just explain it to him? Do you really think he won't understand?"

"He might. But what if he doesn't? What then? Then I'm completely out of luck and he'll be out of my life forever."

"As opposed to...?"

Rebecca pulled her lower lip between her teeth. "Maybe you have a point."

"I know I do." Sara grinned. "Now get out there and help him get that knee back up to snuff so the two of you can go dancing."

Rebecca snickered. "I thought I was trying to keep him around, not scare him away."

Sara waved Rebecca toward the door.

He'd already started his exercises. He looked up, the blue of his eyes icier than she'd ever seen them. Her heart stuttered and she swallowed as her stomach began to churn. "Morning."

"Yep."

"Ben."

He paused in his leg extensions and quirked a brow. "If you're going to tell me it's complicated again, you can save your breath. I understand that. What I don't understand is why you won't try explaining it to me. Maybe I could help uncomplicate things."

Her lips twitched. The last thing he was going to do was make things simpler. Her dad had been distraught that he'd missed lunch, and a chance to meet—and grill—Ben. If she came clean, Dad would descend like a hyena to a fresh kill. She could hear the new parenting speeches already. "That's...unlikely."

After a long look, he nodded. "All right. Well, the doc cleared me to drive and ditch the crutches this morning. He also said I could cut back to twice a week on the PT. So I guess that makes things easier."

"Why would it?"

He shrugged. "I'll switch therapists. Since I have to reschedule everything anyway. That way you can go back to uncomplicated and I can try to move on."

"Just like that?" Sara dipped her spoon into the dish of frozen yogurt and assorted toppings that sat on the table between them.

"Yeah. Here I am taking a deep breath, getting ready to ask him out on Friday, where I plan to spill the whole sordid story and he says don't bother, he'll just move on." Rebecca dragged a hand through her hair. "It's probably for the best."

Jen tapped her spoon against her lower lip. "How can you think that, let alone say it? You've been hung up on him since college."

"No I haven't." Rebecca frowned as she dug around a gummy bear. Seriously, who put gummy bears in frozen yogurt? They just got hard and gross.

"Oh, okay. Remind me of the names of everyone you've dated in the last ten years. And by dated, I don't mean went out with one time. I need at least three dates for these people to count." Jen scooped the gummy bear out and popped it in her mouth.

Rebecca opened her mouth, but no names came to mind. "That doesn't prove anything. It just means I haven't found the right guy yet."

"Or it means you found him, ditched him, and then ruined a second chance with him." Sara shot her a disgusted look. "Honestly. You're hopeless. And now, since he's yours, even though you've messed it up, neither of us can take a shot with him. Which is seriously unfair."

Rebecca tried to swallow around the lump in her throat. "Sorry to inconvenience you."

"That's not what she meant." Jen frowned at Sara. "Though he is yummy, you have to admit that, objectively speaking of course. Still, he's also a toad, 'cause he gives up too easily."

A smile tugged at the corner of Rebecca's lips in spite of herself. "Thanks. I really blew it, didn't I?"

"Seems like it. But...maybe there's still hope. You're still working on the joint project at the mission, right? So it's not like he can get completely away from you." Sara scraped the bottom of the yogurt container. "We'll just have to strategize."

"What are you doing here?" Jerry strolled into the common room of the mission where Rebecca was sitting with a few of the teens who were busy with their homework. Since no one needed her help, she had her e-reader out and was trying to work her way through a research paper on new rehabilitation techniques, but her eyes kept glazing over.

"It's better than being at home. I was hoping I could actually make some headway on this professional development reading but I'm not having any luck with that." Rebecca shrugged.

"Ah." He pulled out a chair and sat. "What's wrong with being at home?"

"I don't know. I love having my own space, but maybe I need a cat or something. When my girlfriends headed home after dinner, I just kind of ended up here. Not that I'm needed. Kira's been doing a great job keeping everyone on track with their studies. Where is she?"

"You must have just missed her. I sent her home, she wasn't looking good. I think she's overdoing. I love that she wants to spend as much time as possible serving the Lord, but not if her efforts mean she has less time overall. She never complains, though I can see the treatment's leaving her exhausted. Her parents say being here is the best medicine so I try to keep my worry to myself." Jerry rubbed his neck, his own exhaustion evident. "Anyway, how's the work with Bread of Heaven going?"

"It's all been email so far. Lots and lots of email. I had no idea planning a donor open house could involve quite that many words. I mean really, what's to plan? You choose a date and time, figure out the food, send invitations. Done. Right?"

Jerry chuckled. "You're asking the wrong person. You notice we've never done events, right? They're simply not my forte. Honestly, the Board was so excited that B of H wanted to combine efforts, I think they would've agreed to participate even if we lost money on the prospect."

Rebecca frowned. Losing money was a valid concern, and not something to joke about. "Well, they may still get their wish. B of H doesn't do anything half-way. The list of caterers they sent is way, way out of the realm of reasonable as far as I'm concerned. I don't understand why we can't just get boxes of frozen, bite-sized things from the warehouse store and cook 'em up on site. You've got a reasonably talented kitchen staff who could handle that."

"It's the marketing mindset. You don't impress the big donors with reheated mini-quiches."

She scoffed. "Assuming any big donors even come. Besides which, I can think of one big donor who'd be more impressed with an event that cost less than five grand to host. And that's on the low end."

Jerry winced. "At least we're splitting the cost with them."

"That *is* the split cost."

He coughed. "Oh. Wow."

"Yeah. I'm not sure how they think fancy food and a tour through our gardens is going to open pockets. Are there really people who don't know we're down here?" Rebecca crossed her arms. If people paid any attention, they had to know something like this was around. Then it was a simple matter of an Internet search or asking around at church. It's not like it's hard to find places to give.

Jerry watched her quietly.

"What?"

"What else is going on? You're as close to angry as I've ever seen you, and I've seen people go out of their way to try to annoy you."

She blew out a breath. Why did the open house bug her so much? "I guess I'm just annoyed that it takes a big international hunger relief agency to draw attention to the fact that there are families within ten miles of the nation's capital who go to bed with growling stomachs every night. Are they at the same level of poverty as kids in Africa? Okay, maybe not, but they have just as little assurance of their next meal as those kids. Why is food insecurity considered less important at the local level? We shouldn't need a big open house and fundraiser to get attention; people should be looking for ways to help that go beyond dropping off the extra can of pumpkin puree at the food bank on Thanksgiving."

Jerry fought a smile. "We do get an awful lot of pumpkin puree. And spinach. I'm not sure who decided canning spinach was a good plan, but if the food bank shelves are any indication, the primary reason people buy it is to donate it. And we do find ways to use it—it's better than nothing. As to why people aren't more proactive, I can't help you with that. I think most of us spend our lives focused on the minutia of day-to-day living and don't think about the fact that one in eight families downtown aren't sure where their next meal will come from. It's easier to focus on the global problems and the fact that, as a whole, America's wealthy and well-fed. I think people feel selfish if they give locally, like somehow they're letting Jesus down. And that's simply because they don't recognize the need is as big as it is."

"Which is the point of the open house. All right. I get it. I can't say it sits well, but I understand at least."

"As for the expense? That I can't really speak to, but I do know Bread of Heaven gets a lot of support from all over, so it's probably safe to say they know what they're doing. I'm inclined to trust them."

Rebecca nodded slowly. Bread of Heaven certainly had a huge budget, the majority of which went directly into their programs. She'd spent time digging around online and found only positive ratings by financial accountability watchdogs. Jerry was right. She needed to trust them. Trust Ben.

And that, right there, was the kicker.

14

His knee was throbbing. Was it a good throbbing that indicated healing or a "wow, you really overdid it today" kind of throbbing? Probably the latter. But being back in the office for a full day had been nice. And driving. Gosh he'd missed driving. Paige might try to convince Jackson to cut back on his driving and bike to the Metro, but Ben didn't see that ever working for himself. Thankfully, Rebecca didn't have those same sustainability-focused tendencies that Paige had. Not that Rebecca was a going concern in his life anymore.

The reminder was a fresh knife through his heart. But she'd been pretty clear that whatever her complications were, keeping them secret was more important to her than letting him help her unravel them. And there wasn't a future with someone who didn't trust you. There just wasn't. Couldn't be. Maybe if he kept reminding himself, he'd start to believe it.

Jackson tapped on Ben's window. "You coming in, or planning to sit in your car the rest of the night?"

Ben pushed the door open. "I was getting there. The thought of walking was making me cringe though."

"Come on, I'll get your bag of peas out of the freezer and you can prop your leg up. Wanna split the pizza I ordered?"

His stomach gurgled. "Yeah. I could go for that`. Any chance you put mushrooms on half?"

"I do mushrooms now, but I draw the line at olives." Jackson held out his hand. "Give me your laptop bag. No sense in you hauling more than you need to."

"Thanks, man." Ben eased out of the car. At least there weren't shooting pains when he put weight on his knee. But it wasn't comfortable, that was for sure. After locking the car, he hobbled after Jackson.

"So other than overdoing it, how was it being back at the office?" Jackson set Ben's laptop bag down at the edge of the couch and tossed Ben the bag of frozen peas he'd snagged on their way through the kitchen from the car port.

Ben sat and arranged the make-shift ice pack, sighing as the cold seeped through his pants to his aching knee. "It was good. They're a great bunch of people, and email and video chat isn't quite the same. What about you? Anything earth shattering in the world of political lobbying these days?"

"Not really. Still kind of feel like I'm in the newbie phase, even though I've got plenty of projects that are solely my responsibility. They believe in chucking you into the deep end and seeing how well you do. Did you see Senator Carson may be resigning?"

Ben winced. "I honestly haven't paid attention since you quit working for her. Frankly, I didn't pay a ton of attention when you did. But I'm sorry to hear it."

Jackson nodded.

The garage door slammed shut and Zach strode into the living room. "Please tell me someone will go in on pizza with me."

"Already on the way." Jackson grinned.

"Finally, something goes right. It's been an insane day." Zach's gaze landed on Ben's knee. "Overdid it?"

Ben laughed. "Yes, Mom. Sorry. It won't happen again."

"Whatever. You're the one with peas on your leg." Zach pulled a chair from the dining room table closer to the couch and stretched out, resting his feet on the coffee table.

"Why was your day insane?" Ben shifted the peas to a different angle on his knee.

"Just the joy of working in an underfunded school system, probably. But they're trying to 'encourage' staff to volunteer for extracurriculars. Like I have nothing better to do. I love my students, don't get me wrong, and I'll do whatever it takes to help them succeed. But I'm a math teacher. I don't need to be coaching a sport or doing theater or whatever madness they're dreaming up for me to do. By the time I teach, plan, and grade, I've already put in twice the hours they pay me for." Zach stood and paced to the kitchen, then back. "And yet when I say something along those lines—more tactfully, mind you—people treat me like I'm evil and trying to take advantage of the school by not pitching in."

"By people, you mean Amy?" Jackson arched a brow.

Zach sighed. "Yeah. Primarily."

"That's a tough place to be." Jackson stood when the doorbell rang.

Ben snorted. "Like he has any idea, Mr. Perfect Relationship over there. You can join me on the 'why bother' side of the couch."

"Right. Do you not remember my summer?" Jackson set the pizza down on the coffee table and flipped open the lid. An amazing aroma, a mix of spicy sausage, mushrooms, and oregano, filled the air.

Zach offered Ben and Jackson plates before sliding a slice onto his own, tendrils of cheese stretching nearly a foot before he managed to break and scoop them on top of a piece. "I'm not moving to bitter and jaded land just yet. But save me a spot, just in case."

"I'm not bitter and jaded." Ben dragged pizza onto his plate and leaned back. "I just don't understand women. I think that part's incredibly clear. I mean, seriously, if you have a complicated problem, wouldn't you talk about it and try to get it figured out instead of just yammering on about it?"

"You really don't get women, do you?" Jackson sucked in air around his bite of pizza. "They don't want solutions, they just want to vent. You're supposed to say 'there, there' and pat them on the back. Then, if they ask, you can suggest how to fix it. But you never offer. Ever."

"Women ought to come with instruction manuals." Ben crammed a wedge of pizza, dripping with cheese, in his mouth. Was there anything more frustrating than women? How was he supposed to know that all he was supposed to do was sympathize with her? When you mention how complicated something is that many times, it sounds like you're looking for a solution. It just did.

Zach snickered. "I imagine they think the same about us. Nothing new on the Rebecca front since yesterday then, I take it?"

"Nope. She sent a few caustic emails about my catering suggestions for the open house at the mission downtown. Otherwise, she hasn't said anything. Speaking of that, though...do you think Paige would have any interest in putting together a proposal?"

Jackson shrugged. "Ask her. Things seem pretty stable at the restaurant now, so she might have time to pick up catering again."

"Should I call the restaurant?" Ben eyed the pizza. The slices were huge, but awfully tasty. One more wouldn't hurt. He slid a second slice onto his plate.

"Nah. I'll shoot you her email." Jackson wiped his fingers on his jeans and reached for his phone. "When the pizza's done, who's up for a game?"

"Read my mind." Ben caught a drip of sauce with his tongue. "You in, Zach?"

"Oh yeah."

"Thanks for meeting me. I really hate doing this kind of consult over the phone if I can help it." Paige spread papers out in front of her on the table. Two chefs worked in the kitchen, their banter barely audible over the music playing. "Do you mind sitting in here? I want to be close in case there're any issues with prep."

"This is fine." Ben shifted in the booth, trying to find an angle that didn't make his knee throb. He was going to have to talk to the doctor about that sooner than later. Or maybe his physical therapist on Thursday. Would he see Rebecca? He steeled himself, pushing away the dull ache in his chest. If he did, he did. He and

Rebecca were still working together, after all. He'd have to see her again at some point. "I really appreciate you doing this."

Paige grinned. "Hey, business is business. And since the transition seems to be pretty well under control, catering is back on the menu, so to speak. Not that we've had a ton of potential clients banging down our door, mind you, but I did turn a few people away right at the start. Needed to be sure I could handle it. Or that I had enough staff who could."

"Makes sense." Ben flipped open the folder he'd brought along and offered Paige the top sheet. "This is what I've been giving the other companies I've asked for bids, but I'm open to suggestions. I know you probably have your own take on things, and since you have such a unique twist on food, I get that you'll need to make adjustments. But it should be a general guideline, I hope."

Paige scanned the page and nodded. "Yeah, this is great. You're better prepared than I expected." She glanced up and met his eyes. "Sorry. That came out wrong."

"No, it's fine. I understand what you're saying. But, unlike my roommate, fundraisers are part of my bread and butter. And, in the interest of friendliness, I'll let you know that what's come in so far has seemed incredibly overpriced. So I'm hopeful that your bid will be more in the realm of sanity."

Paige let out a short laugh. "All right, I'll do what I can. I did bring a few sample menus for you to look at—that might help get me pointed in the right direction."

Ben took the pages and skimmed them, his mouth watering as he read the descriptions.

"While you read, can I ask if Rebecca said anything about Sunday? I really enjoyed getting to know her and...well, Jackson can tell you, I don't make friends all that easily. I was thinking I might see if she wanted to hang out again."

What should he say? It was a good idea. The two of them—honestly, all three ladies—had appeared to have a great time. But with things the way they were, could he give out Rebecca's number without her getting annoyed? Still, a new friend was always a good thing. Right?

"I think you should definitely get in touch with her. Did she give you her number?"

Paige nodded. "She gave me her card and put her email on the back. You think she'd be open to it?"

At least he wouldn't be on the hook for giving out her info. She'd said she had fun. Ben nodded. "I do."

"Cool. What about those menus? See anything that whets your appetite?"

Ben flipped the papers down on the table and tapped the one that was most interesting. "I like this one. And it seems...upscale but not pretentious?"

She laughed. "That's a good description. I might have to start referring to it that way in-house. All right, that gives me everything I need. I'll email something today—though it might be later tonight, after we close. So don't look for it 'til tomorrow."

"Great. Thanks, Paige." Ben stood, his knee practically singing with relief as it moved out from under the table.

"My pleasure. Say hi to Rebecca for me. And let her know I'll be getting in touch?"

Ben offered a tight smile. Hopefully she'd take that as assent. And if Rebecca was open to getting together, then maybe neither of them would key in to the fact that he hadn't said anything in advance.

"Why is Ben on my client list for today?" Sara slapped her schedule down on the table in front of Rebecca and crossed her arms.

Rebecca shrugged and prayed her voice would stay steady. And that the tears prickling her eyes wouldn't show. "I guess he needed to change things around."

"Did you forget who you're talking to? I thought you were going to work things out."

"Yeah, well. I chickened out. If he doesn't want to work with me, I'm not going to force the issue. Besides, it's not like we spent a whole lot of time connecting on any kind of deep level during therapy. It's all about strengthening his knee. You know that."

Sara sighed and propped a hip on the table. "So you're letting him go? Just like that?"

Rebecca swallowed, though it did nothing to ease the acidic burn creeping up her throat. "I don't see another choice. If I want to have something—anything—with him, I have to tell him the truth. I can't—"

"Won't."

Rebecca glared. "Fine. Won't do that. So where does that leave me?"

"First place trophy winner for most pig-headed person I've ever met, that's where. Do you really think you're the first person in the world whose dad is a class-A jerk?"

"He's not a jerk...not really."

"Even better then. How many people do you know who don't have issues with one or both of their parents at least some of the time? Perfect families only happen in books. You deal with it and move on. Besides, I thought you said your dad was coming around."

"Doesn't erase the damage or the stigma." Rebecca reached into the backpack sitting by her chair and pulled out the current issue of a Christian living magazine that more churches than she cared to count gave out for free. Let alone the people who actually subscribed. She thumbed it open and dropped it on the table, gesturing to the half-page photo of her parents at the start of an article concerning her dad's upcoming book and speaking tour. She tapped the sidebar. "Read that. Aloud. Go ahead."

"Where is she now? Though Dr. MacDonald has made a name for himself as a parenting expert, it wasn't his degree that got him there. It's hard to forget the troubled teen years of his daughter Becky that formed the basis for his expertise. His quiet, unassuming manner as he discussed the heartbreak he and his wife encountered in the face of their daughter's escapades is what earned him his place on our bookshelves and our hearts. In the last several years, the tales of Becky have faded from prominence as Dr. MacDonald has returned to more generic examples of misbehavior and suggestions for coping. However, speculation still runs rampant that Becky hasn't reformed from her tempestuous ways. Sources suggest that, at the time of this printing, the troubled young woman is, in fact, residing in Switzerland at an extended in-patient rehabilitation and mental health facility as her parents, yet again, work to return their lost sheep to the fold."

Sara snorted, her cheeks flushed, eyes sparking. "Honestly? This proves my point."

"How? How does that prove anyone's point but mine? Apparently, the only way I could possibly turn out was to become an insane druggie. You know this magazine is everywhere, so who's he going to believe?"

Sara cocked her head to the side and studied Rebecca. "The woman he loves. If she'll let him."

Rebecca licked her lips and closed the magazine. "Pretty sure that ship has sailed."

"So call it back to port. What do you have to lose?" Sara squeezed Rebecca's shoulder. "Think about it, at least. Okay? In the meantime, if you feel the need to swap clients, just swing by. I like old Mr. Phillips, even if he does try to pinch your booty when you're not looking."

Rebecca trudged from the parking lot into the homeless shelter. It wasn't her night to volunteer, but yet again she couldn't face the prospect of her empty townhouse. What had been her haven now felt empty and dead. She really should look into getting a cat. A dog would be better, but they needed more regular hours than she could promise at this point. Cats, at least, could survive pretty well independently. And, if she was lucky, she'd get one that was willing to cuddle now and then. Maybe she'd swing by the shelter this weekend and see if they had any likely candidates.

She waved at Jerry as she walked by his office. He shook his head, though a smile tugged at his lips. It wasn't as if he was going to turn a volunteer away. The common room was busier tonight, lots of folks gathered around the television watching, she craned her neck to see, a game show? Not their usual choice, but maybe the news was too depressing. Onlookers hollered out answers before the contestants, going for funny instead of accurate. She grinned. Many of the folks who came to the mission had a wicked sense of humor.

Rebecca pulled out a chair at the table on the far side of the room where Kira sat with D'Andre.

"Maybe you can settle this for us, Rebecca." Kira smiled as she looked up from the text book on the table. "D'Andre says that as long as you get the right answer, it shouldn't matter how you got it. I think it's just as important—maybe more—to have the right process, even if you make a little mistake along the way and get the answer wrong."

"Um. Math?"

D'Andre nodded and slid a paper over to her. "Mr. Wilson graded me down because I didn't show my work. I did it in my head, cause this is easy, so why spend the time markin' up a paper?"

Rebecca studied the math test, eyebrows lifting as she saw the answers with minimal work. She puffed out her cheeks. "I'm going to side with Kira and Mr. Wilson on this one. Showing your work is important. He needs to know that you really understand how to get from A to B, not just that you're a lucky guesser."

"Or that I cheated? You can say it. I know that's what everybody thinks." D'Andre crossed his arms and jutted out his chin. "But I didn't cheat. This is just easy."

"I've seen enough of your work to know you didn't cheat, D'Andre. You're a bright kid, smarter than you let on. And I suspect that's why you didn't want to show your work, in case someone else noticed that you're smart. But you've gotta let your teachers see it— I'm guessing they already know. But they can't grade you fairly if you don't do all the steps." Rebecca tapped the paper before sliding it back. "Is Mr. Wilson tall and skinny, with sort of a skater haircut?"

D'Andre snorted out a laugh. "Yeah, that's my boy. You know him?"

What were the chances that Zach was the math teacher in question? Was she going to spend the rest of her life running into connections that tied her to Ben? "Just met him. He seems pretty cool though. I bet if you had a talk with him, explained the situation, he might help you find a way to save face and still get full credit."

"Maybe I'll do that." D'Andre took the book and paper and stuffed them in his tattered backpack. "I gotta' bounce. Mom needs me to watch the little ones. She's got a job interview. Might give her better hours. Thanks for the help. I'll hit up Mr. W tomorrow."

Rebecca waved. She should probably text Ben and see if she could get Zach's number to warn him. Nothing quite like being put on the spot by one of your students. But she could do that later. That gave her a chance to figure out some other way to get in touch with Zach without having to text Ben. She looked at Kira and smiled. The girl was wan, and looked like she'd lost weight since the last time Rebecca had seen her. "How're you doing?"

"He told you?" Kira propped her elbows on the table.

"Yeah. Sorry. I'm supposed to try and make sure you don't overdo. He loves you a lot—like you're his own."

Kira grinned. "That's Uncle Jerry. He takes on everyone's problems. But it's what makes him good at this. I'm doing okay. Tired. The treatment...it takes a lot out of me. I'm not sure how much longer I'll be able to convince my folks that I can still come down here, so I'm trying to get in as much time as I can."

"Isn't there something else you'd rather be doing?" In a similar situation, would she keep coming here? Keep working and serving? Or would her focus be more selfish? She wanted to say she'd still concentrate on serving...but the truth was, she didn't believe she would.

"Not really. God's given me so much to be thankful for. I have a great family, wonderful friends, and so many experiences that most people don't get. The time I spent at college was amazing and even if I don't get to go back, I'll always be grateful for the chances I had when I was there. Why wouldn't I give back while I can? If God calls me home, I want to know I was faithful when I had the chance."

Wow. Rebecca sighed. What would it be like to have that kind of conviction about your calling? And to be able to act on it? What little clarity she'd had herself had disappeared quickly once it became obvious no one was going to take her desire to make a difference seriously. That's why she'd switched majors and gone on to get her master's in physical therapy. But it wasn't like she made a difference for God. Not really. Sure, she helped people get better, but what eternal value was there in any aspect of her life? None.

"Just be sure you aren't setting your health back. I know you've made a big impact on the kids, D'Andre especially, but if you work too hard and can't come in at all, you defeat the purpose. Plus Jerry'll kill me."

Kira laughed. "I'll do my best."

Rebecca crawled into bed. Was it too late to text? Surely Ben turned his phone off or set it to vibrate or something when he went to bed. Didn't everyone?

Hey, when you get a minute, could I get Zach's #? Need to ask a math
?

She hit send. He probably wouldn't see it until tomorrow. So she'd just hope she got to Zach before D'Andre did. She opened her email program and shook her head. Did the man do anything other than send email?

Rebecca skimmed the first message. Was she supposed to care about tablecloth colors? Why did it matter? She sent back a quick reply letting him know that the suggestions sounded fine, archived the message and moved to the next. Her phone buzzed with a new text.

Sure. 7035550117 but I'm good at math, can I help?

She smiled. That was friendlier than he'd been at the clinic today, when she'd gotten the barest wave from him while she escorted Mr. Phillips back to the weights. And the crazy old man had pinched her butt three separate times. Honestly, he was sweet, but someone needed to remind him that behavior didn't fly anymore. If it ever had.

Nah – it's about a student of his. Thx tho.

She opened a new text and warned Zach about D'Andre's desire to keep his cool status while still making a good math grade. Hopefully, Zach was able to see the boy's potential and would be willing to figure something out. He'd seemed pretty reasonable, but that'd been in a social setting. And he'd been trying to impress that other girl—Amy? So who knew? Maybe he was one of those strict teachers who never bent a rule in their life. In which case, she'd owe D'Andre an apology.

Her phone buzzed again.

Missed u today. Sara is a good PT. But she's not you.

Tears pricked her eyes. If only she deserved a man like Ben. But how could she? If she told him the truth, would he believe she wasn't what her dad painted her to be? What if he didn't? She'd rather live without him, knowing that he thought she was someone special, someone worth knowing, than to still be without him and have him think of her the same way everyone else thought of Becky MacDonald.

Sighing, she powered off her phone and plugged it in. She'd reply tomorrow. Or not at all.

16

"Scoot down one more. Paige is coming today." Jackson pushed against Ben's shoulder.

Ben shook his head and slid down the pew a bit further. "That enough room, or do I need to move up a row? Honestly, why can't the two of you just sit on the other side?"

"'Cause I like the aisle. You know that. And I don't think Paige is coming to our church instead of hers so that she can sit by you and Zach."

"Listen to the guy with a steady girlfriend getting all high and mighty." Zach rolled his eyes and sat next to Ben. "Maybe the two of us should find the loser section of the sanctuary."

"Hey, guys."

Paige's perky voice brought an involuntary smile to Ben's lips. It wasn't hard to see what Jackson saw in her. Though what she saw in him...that was a whole other story. Ben filed that away to use later when it was time to rag on Jackson some more. The truth was, the two of them were perfect together and, when he wasn't dwelling on his aching heart or the fact that he hadn't heard from Rebecca since Thursday, he was happy for them. "Happy Sunday. What'cha got there?"

Paige grinned. "Your church has all those Christian living and family life magazines for people to take. Mine quit doing that last year. It was getting too expensive and people didn't really take them. So I snagged the ones I've always enjoyed. That's okay, right?"

Ben shrugged. "I'd imagine so. That's why they're there, right?"

"That'd be my guess as well. If it makes you feel better, you can just pretend I grabbed them and you took them before I could look at them." Jackson slipped his arm around Paige's shoulders.

"I'll do better than that. When I'm finished with them, I'll leave them at your place so you really can read them. Who knows, you might find out something interesting."

Ben snickered. The chance of Jackson actually reading any of those magazines was slim to none. None of them were likely to read the things. The few times he'd browsed the display, they'd all looked like mommy mail. Why would Paige even be interested? Maybe there were recipes or something. Who knew? He pulled his attention back to the service that was starting.

When the singing was over, he pulled out his phone and opened his Bible app to follow along with the pastor as he read. His finger hovered over the text icon. Should he make sure Rebecca was okay? Two days with nothing...though admittedly it was the weekend, so it was unlikely she'd be working on the plans for the open house downtown. Not that there was much to do anyway. Paige's catering proposal had been so much better—and more affordable—than any of the other options he'd sent her, she'd jumped on it. With that done, all they really needed to do was get the invitations printed and mailed. He still needed the donor list from the mission for that—or did they want to mail their own? That was something to ask...but not during church.

Zach's elbow in his side dragged him out of his thoughts and, after a quick glance at Zach's Bible, he navigated to Matthew 25. One of the things Ben loved about Pastor Brown's sermons is that he didn't shy away from the hard topics. This looked like it was going to be another to download once they got it on the church website. Practical ways to give a cup of water to the least of these—maybe they should see if the pastor would speak at the open house. Not everyone wanted to believe that the food and water in the passage could, in fact, be taken literally.

Sure, it was good to help in less concrete ways, too. But how many people stopped at taking their castoffs to the thrift store or sending Bread of Heaven a check? Not that a check was a bad thing, but they could use bodies, too. People who would go overseas for a week or two and help with the food distribution, or assist in digging a well and building a shelter for livestock. Or, if leaving the country was too scary, why not go downtown and help organize the shelves at the mission or man the desk on distribution days? Hmm. That was something they should add to the open house—tangible ways to help both organizations that went beyond money. In fact, maybe that should be their primary focus? If they tied it in to being Jesus' hands and feet, instead of just being His checkbook...he'd run it by his boss. If he was on board, he'd see what Rebecca had to say.

Ben eased his leg up onto the coffee table and stretched his head to one side, then the other, letting out a soft "Aah" when the bones in his neck cracked. What a day. Bread of Heaven wasn't typically a place where meeting after meeting ate up your time, but today it had been. And very few of them had been worth the time. He hadn't even had five minutes to catch up on his email from the weekend, and that just wouldn't do for the self-proclaimed Email King. Maybe he'd spend some time later tonight doing that. Jackson was at a campaign rally all evening and Zach said he'd be at a late faculty meeting. So he had the house to himself. And he was going to work? Lame.

What else did you do on a Monday night though? He drummed his fingers on his knee. Should he call Rebecca? See if she wanted to grab a bite? It would probably count as the date he'd been threatening to ask her on—and that was a mark in the negative column. He wanted their first official date since college to be memorable. But...given her reaction to the idea of dating, he wasn't positive there was ever going to be a first official date. At least not one that heralded the start of a relationship. He pulled his phone from his pocket and stared at it, then dialed.

"Hello?"

"Hi, Sara?"

"Yes. Who's this?"

"It's Ben. Ben Taylor? From Phys—well, Rebecca's friend? You gave me your number when we were meeting at the theater, in case we couldn't find one another?"

"Oh, sure. Hi. What's up?"

He wiped damp palms on his pants. "This feels a little high school...but I was wondering if you had a minute to talk about Rebecca?"

"Just a *little* high school?"

He scrubbed a hand over his face as his stomach clenched. "Yeah, okay, maybe more than a little. Look, this was a bad idea. I'll let you go."

"No, no, no. I was just teasing you. I love Rebecca and am happy to tell you all about how wonderful she is. Though I won't promise I'm not going to tell her you called."

Ben mulled that over. It was fair. Probably. He hadn't planned to ask her not to say anything. "All right, seems reasonable."

"Excellent. So...shoot."

He cleared his throat. "I'm guessing you know about summer camp?"

"Maybe not the whole story, but pieces, yeah."

Hmm. He'd assumed Rebecca would've told her friends every last detail. Though maybe since they weren't friends at the time it was happening she'd only shared a basic overview? Did it matter? "Okay, so I get that she went by Marie that summer instead of Rebecca. I'm not really clear why she did it, but I don't necessarily care beyond curiosity. So I thought that once we figured all that out and realized that our feelings were basically the same that we could move forward. But now she's just backing away and telling me it's complicated."

"Is there a question in there?"

Ben gave a short laugh. "What am I supposed to do? My mom always said if a woman tells you to back off, you back off. But I really don't want to let her go. I've tried that—tried to move on, find someone else. It always feels like I'm settling for second best. At the same time...I don't want to be with someone who's only around because it was either go out with me or get a restraining order. You know?"

Sara snickered. "Yeah, that's never a good thing. Look. Rebecca has reasons for brushing you off. I'm not sure I'll go so far as to say they're good ones, but they are to her. On one hand, she'd pull away from any guy she cared about with the same reasons. She's convinced they're insurmountable. On the other hand, too many people have given up on her too easily in her life. So my advice? Do what you can to stay part of her life, even if it means letting her friend zone you for a while."

Ben winced. The friend zone. The ultimate kiss of death to any relationship.

"I know you're thinking you can't get out of there once you've been put in the zone, but I promise, with Rebecca, you're better off starting over as just friends than trying to push for more right now."

"You're sure?"

"As sure as I can be. I'm not Rebecca. And sometimes she does things I'd never predict but...it's the course of action I'd take, if I was you."

That was probably as good as he was going to get. Even if it wasn't the assurance he was hoping for. "Do you know details about whatever it is she thinks is so complicated?"

There was a long pause before Sara spoke. "I do. But it's for her to explain. Even if I disagree with keeping it quiet, it's not for me to tell."

"I wouldn't expect you to. But it helps to know she's told someone. So...maybe there's hope that down the line she'll decide to tell me after all. Thanks, Sara."

"Sure. Have a good night."

"Yeah. You too." Ben ended the call and dropped his phone on the coffee table. Friend zone. That probably ruled out calling her up and asking if she wanted to grab a bite to eat. At least for now. He got up and rooted around in the kitchen, finally giving up and putting together a sandwich from assorted leftovers in the fridge. Carrying his plate, a bag of chips, and a big glass of iced tea, he went back to the living room.

He took a bite of the sandwich, d tugged a magazine out from under his plate, and flipped it open. Might as well see if there was anything of interest, since they were sitting here.

"What are you still doing up?" Jackson draped his suit jacket over a chair and sagged onto the couch next to Ben. "I figured everyone'd be in bed by the time I got home."

"Zach just headed back. He's probably still up. Let me ask you something." Ben slid the magazine with the article about Dr. Roland MacDonald and his latest parenting book so Jackson could see it and tapped the photo. "Does this look like an older version of Rebecca to you?"

Jackson frowned and studied the picture. "I don't know. Maybe? Why?"

Ben sighed and slapped the magazine shut. "I'll admit I could be losing my mind, but that woman looks a lot like Rebecca's mom. I thought at the time how Eleanor and Rebecca shared a striking resemblance."

"Yeah, but a lot of women look like younger versions of their moms. My sister could definitely be confused with some of Mom's younger pictures. What does that have to do with anything? That photo is of the MacDonalds. Isn't Rebecca's last name Fischer?"

"Yeah. I just—you know what, never mind." Ben rolled the magazine into a tube and stood.

"Nuh-uh. Spit it out."

Ben wet his lips. He'd been thinking the words all night, since he first read the article. Saying them aloud though...that made it more real somehow. "What if she changed her last name too?"

Jackson's eyebrows arched. "That's...a stretch, don't you think?"

"I don't know what to think. All she'll tell me is that it's complicated. We're over before we really have a chance to start because it's 'complicated'." Ben made air quotes. "Makes me wonder."

"Okay, sure. I'm still not seeing the relationship to the MacDonalds though."

Ben unrolled the magazine and flipped back to the article. He turned to the next page and tapped the sidebar. "Read this."

Jackson skimmed the page before pushing it back toward Ben. "Huh."

"That's it? Their daughter is named Becky. You don't think—"

Jackson held up a hand. "I'm not sure. There are some possible coincidences, certainly. And seeing this, I think Dr. MacDonald spoke at one of our youth rallies when I was in high school. If Rebecca really is his daughter, then...well, she's got some issues. Serious, serious issues."

"What do you mean?"

"Dude. All I remember is leaving his speech thinking I'd made it easy on my mom my whole life. The guy went on about the various problems they'd had with her—finding guys in her bed, staying out all night, that kind of thing."

Ben frowned. That didn't sound like the same girl he'd met at camp. They'd talked for hours every day, about all kinds of deep things. Including the fact that they were both virgins and were committed to staying that way until they were married. That didn't necessarily preclude having someone in your bed all night, but it seemed unlikely. Her conviction on the topic was even stronger than his own. "What if...what if it wasn't true? If he made it up just to have a good lesson to share?"

Jackson scoffed. "That's reaching, man. Look, if you think there's something to it, why don't you poke around online and see what you can figure out?"

"I'm not a computer guy, you know that. I email, that's it. Sometimes I can find what I need with a search engine, but even that's iffy. I tried hunting for Marie for the last ten years and came up with nothing. What makes you think I'll have better luck now?"

"Hmm. Tell you what. I'll email my friend David. He's into computers. Maybe he'll have some ideas of how to look or, if he's bored at work, maybe he'll do some digging for you." Jackson shrugged. "Worth a shot, right?"

"Yeah. Thanks, man."

17

"Guess who called me last night." Sara plopped into a chair at the sandwich shop next to the PT office and unwrapped her sub.

Rebecca pried the lid off the so-called salad they'd made her—essentially a huge pile of shredded lettuce with the rest of what would normally go in a sub dumped on top. Still, she couldn't face their soggy yet somehow dried out bread today. "No idea. The President?"

Jen snickered and pulled open a bag of chips. "Good one."

"Do you even want to know?" Sara flipped up the top piece of bread and frowned. "Why do they always put on mustard? I didn't ask for mustard. It's like they hate me."

Rebecca offered Sara her plastic knife. "Scrape it off. You know they confuse easily. Why do we come here again?"

"'Cause the two of you can walk. Why I drive thirty minutes to meet you, now that's a reasonable question." Jen took a long drink from her soda. "But I was going to have to stay late today anyway, so I might as well have a long lunch. Just tell us, Sara. Who called you?"

"Ben."

"My Ben?" The words flew out of Rebecca's mouth before she could think. She blinked. "Not that he's mine. Obviously. But Ben Taylor? That Ben?"

Sara smirked. "I think you were right the first time. *Your* Ben. And yes, that's the one."

Rebecca stabbed her fork into the bowl until it was loaded with more than would comfortably fit in her mouth. She wedged it in anyway. She wasn't asking why he called. Was. Not. Asking.

Jen pursed her lips and studied Rebecca before turning to Sara. "I'll bite. What'd he want?"

Sara finished removing the offending mustard, wrapped the knife in a napkin, and set it aside. "Mostly he wanted to know if he should let Rebecca here push him away, or keep after her. The way I heard him, he's unhappy with her attempts at a brush off but also is enough of a gentleman to let her go if that's really what she wants."

Rebecca's heart leapt but she feigned disinterest as she swallowed. "What'd you say?"

"I'm not sure I'm going to tell you that. I mean, I can see you're not really uninterested. But at the same time..."

Rebecca reached across the table and grabbed Sara's arm. "Just tell me."

"Aha." Jen elbowed Sara. "That got her."

"All right, all right. I told him to keep trying, but to let you put him in the friend zone for a while." Sara shook her arm loose and picked up her sandwich. "You're welcome."

"That's all he asked?" Rebecca stabbed at the salad again.

Sara sighed. "He did ask if I knew what was so complicated."

The blood drained from Rebecca's face and her fork clattered to the table. Her voice stuck in her throat, coming out like a croak. "What did you tell him?"

Sara's eyes widened. "Really? We've been friends how long and you have to ask me that? I said it was your story to tell, but that he should keep after you to tell it. Sheesh, Rebecca. What's wrong with you?"

Heat flooded her face and she dropped her gaze to the table. "Sorry. I'm sorry, you're right. I just..."

"Yeah, well. You need to trust your friends." Sara wrapped up her sandwich and strode from the restaurant.

Rebecca watched her go, her mouth hanging open. She snapped it shut as the bells on the door jangled Sara's exit.

"She's not wrong, you know." Jen frowned. "Sara and I have your back. You know this. But I also think Ben would, if you'd give him a chance. Besides all that? It's been what, ten years since your dad said anything about you in his talks? Think it might be time to let it go? The only person you're punishing by holding on to all of this is you."

Jen's words echoed in her head the rest of the day. She wasn't trying to punish anyone. She was just trying to protect herself. She'd tried to track down Sara and apologize, but her friend had managed to keep busy the rest of the day. And then sneak out before Rebecca could corner her. She'd just have to track her down tomorrow. At this point, she was going to go visit the cat shelter where she'd put in an online application and then go home.

Her phone rang as she pulled out of the parking lot. Rebecca hit the button to transfer the call to her car speakers and answered.

"Hello?"

"Hi, sweetie, it's Mom."

Rebecca smiled. There was no need for her mom to say who it was, yet she always did. Habit, probably, but it made her warm inside. "Hi, Mom. What's up?"

"Just checking in on you, seeing what you're up to."

Let's see, annoying her friends, brushing off the one man who'd ever managed to get past her defenses and into her heart...probably better not to lead with any of those. "I'm on my way to an animal shelter. I think I'm going to get a cat. They have this adorable medium-haired tabby on the website who I can't get out of my head. They emailed to say my application had been approved and I could come and meet the cats tonight, see if any of them were a good fit."

"Oh, that sounds like fun. Will you get to bring it home tonight?"

Rebecca slowed and took the ramp onto the Beltway. "No. Maybe this weekend. The application is preliminary. Once you have a particular cat that you're interested in, they have some kind of process they go through. I didn't get a full explanation. Probably when I'm there they'll give me more detail."

"Aw. That's too bad. But I guess it gives you time to change your mind, too?"

That was a thought. Did they have people back out after they took a cat home? Was there some kind of return policy? "Huh. Maybe that's it. A waiting period to make sure you're serious. Dunno."

"Are you looking at a kitten or a grown cat?"

"I wanted a kitten, initially, but they basically insist you adopt kittens in pairs. I'm...not sure I'm ready for two cats. Though maybe it's easier? I don't know. I guess we'll see how it goes when I'm there. The tabby is almost a year old, so I think he's able to go solo."

"Hmm. Two cats would give them companionship while you're away from home. It's something to consider. It's not like you spend tons of time there."

That was true. Rebecca drummed her fingers on the steering wheel as she inched forward in the bumper-to-bumper evening traffic.

"What's Ben think?"

Rebecca frowned. "What does Ben think about what?"

"Getting a cat. When the two of you get together, the cat, or cats, will be part of the deal, right? You wouldn't take them back to the shelter?"

"No, of course not. But...Ben and I aren't going to end up together, Mom. We talked about that."

"I'd hoped you'd come to your senses about that. Becca, honey, don't you think it's time you moved on?"

"You too, Mom? Jen—and Sara for that matter—gave me almost that exact speech at lunch today." Rebecca sighed. Was this God trying to tell her something? Why didn't He just talk, in a real, audible voice, like He did to the heroines in the Christian novels she read?

Her Mom's sigh echoed her own. "Your dad's sorry, sweetheart. He's told you this more times than even I can count. And beyond that, once he realized the predicament he'd put you in, he stopped using the stories. What more, really, do you want him to do?"

"I don't know, Mom. But you saw the sidebar in the magazine that just featured his upcoming release, didn't you? It's not as if the problem has gone away just because he stopped making it worse."

Her mom's end of the line was quiet. Had she hung up?

"I understand it's hurtful, Becca, but really, what else are they going to print? They ask about you—they always have—and for ten years, your father has respected your wishes and simply ignored the question and asked that the interviewer return to the subject at hand. What he'd like to do is tell them how incredibly proud of you he is. How he admires the fact that you've completed a Master's degree and are a successful and sought-after physical therapist who spends her off time tutoring homeless and disadvantaged children. He'd love to talk about the foundation you set up for your trust fund and all the good that does. But to try and make up for the harm he caused you, he stays quiet because you asked him to. And so the reporters speculate."

"How...how did you find out about the foundation? That's confidential. Or it's supposed to be." Apparently her attorney did a bad job securing her privacy like she'd asked him, since Jerry put it together too. Was her true identity that easy to discover? She did Internet searches fairly regularly, trying to see if there were any connections and never came up with anything. But maybe she should hire someone who really knew what they were doing. Just to be sure.

"We set up the trust fund. Just because you're able to draw on it now doesn't mean we aren't still informed about how you use it. The fact that you saved up to buy your home with your own money, and that you don't use the trust for personal purchases makes both of us incredibly proud. No matter what your father might have said about you when he was fabricating examples for his speeches, he's the first to admit that you've made us proud."

Rebecca flicked on her turn signal and eased onto the exit. Traffic on the back roads was just as heavy as the highway, though this was at least moderated some by traffic lights. Her parents were proud of her. The words were foreign, even in her head. "Okay."

Her mother laughed. "That's it?"

"I don't know, Mom. It's a lot to take in. And I'm here so, I'm going to go pet some cats."

"Do that. And Becca, while you're at it, think about what I've said. Your father and I love you. We're proud of you. And we want you to have a full, fabulous life, not this empty half-life you've constructed."

Rebecca swallowed. Her life wasn't empty. She had friends. And a job she was good at. Maybe she wasn't changing the world like she'd always thought she would, but sometimes you had to adjust your dreams to suit the reality of life. Didn't you? "I love you, too."

"Text me a picture of your kitty."

She smiled. "All right. Bye, Mom."

Rebecca ended the call and pulled into a parking spot in front of the shelter. The fact that her parents loved her wasn't news. And yet...something was different this time. She shook her head and grabbed her purse. She'd go and pet some cats and maybe she'd figure out why her skin was too tight and prickly.

18

Ben pulled his car into a spot near the Annapolis waterfront and cut the engine. Traffic had been...horrendous. There was really no other word to use. How did people commute into DC from here? There was no way the lure of waterfront living was worth that kind of insanity day after day. And it was Thursday. It wasn't like this was the weekend, with everyone and their cousin flocking to the water for the weekend. He grunted and shook his head. Took all kinds.

He eased out from behind the wheel and stretched his leg. His knee was stiff, but, amazingly, not sore. *Thank you, Jesus.* Maybe it was healing after all. PT this morning with Sara had been awkward. Even after having been her patient on Tuesday, it was clear their conversation on the phone made her feel cornered. Which was not what he was going for. Probably needed to figure out a way to apologize. Of course, if this was the friend zone in Rebecca's book, he was probably better off recognizing she was a lost cause and moving on. 'Cause she barely returned any of his email, let alone his attempts to talk to her. At least she'd agreed to use Paige's restaurant for the open house catering. That was something.

A brief stroll down the block and Ben stopped in front of the Irish pub Jackson's friend, David, had given him directions to. It was a strange place to meet a computer consultant, but this whole business was strange. Who changed their name as an adult unless they got married? And why the secrecy? Assuming that was really what Rebecca had done. But if she had, how much of what he thought he knew about her was a lie?

Ben stepped through the door. The place was busy. A few empty tables were dotted throughout the dim room. Decorations consisted primarily of wood—wood booths, wood floors, wood beams in the ceiling. Ambiance oozed around him as the quiet strains of a folksy love song reached his ears.

"Can I help you?"

Ben smiled at the frazzled looking server carrying a tray overloaded with plates heaped with food as well as drinks that were nearly sloshing over their rims. "I'm meeting Colin O'Bryan?"

"Sure. He's in the middle of his set right now, just grab a table and someone will be by to get an order soon. I'll let him know you're here."

She zipped off before Ben could formulate the questions that zinged around in his brain. He spotted an empty booth in the corner and angled that way. What had she meant by a set? He inhaled and his mouth watered. Plucking the menu from between the salt and pepper shakers shaped like a Leprechaun and a rainbow, he skimmed the offerings. Fish and chips. That had to be what he smelled. The shakers brought a smile to his lips. Rebecca would love them. Or at least, the Rebecca he thought he knew would. Did she really like kitschy salt and pepper sets, or was it one more fabrication? The same server stopped at his table, took his order, and assured him Colin would be with him in a few minutes.

The music ended. A smattering of applause had Ben looking around. Was it not a recording? There wasn't an obvious stage for a live musician. Maybe the doorway in the middle of the wall led to another room, rather than the kitchen as he'd assumed. Moments later, a tall man strode into the room, heading straight for Ben's booth.

"Hi. You're Ben Taylor?"

Ben blinked. He hadn't given his name. Though David had probably passed everything along. He extended his hand. "I am. You're Colin?"

Colin grinned, gripped Ben's hand, and sat. "Yep. Thanks for making the drive. The pub keeps me busy enough, even on the days we're closed, that getting into DC is a challenge. And I try to keep Sundays free to spend with my fiancée."

Ben frowned. "I guess I'm confused. You work here? David said you were a computer expert?"

Colin chuckled. "The quick summary is that I was the co-founder of a software company several years ago. I got bought out, became a musician, met my Rachel, moved here and purchased a pub. But I do computer consulting on the side as I have time and interest. The little I have from David about what you're looking for shouldn't take too long and it's kind of like a mystery, so it's intriguing."

"You're a musician and you own a pub. This pub. That was you on the guitar?" Ben paused while the server set his well-portioned plate in front of him along with a glass of soda. His thoughts struggled to keep up with the conversation. "David said unraveling the truth was outside his skill set...but you don't think it'll take long?"

Colin shrugged. "David's a great coder, but he's not a researcher at heart. Maybe I should've said it wouldn't take me long to either get your answers or determine that I wouldn't be able to. Though the little digging I did after I got David's email makes me think I'm more likely to turn up the truth than not."

Ben cut into the flaky fried fish and leaned back as savory steam rose into his face. If it tasted anything like it smelled, this was likely to be his best meal all week. "Why's that?"

"I've already dug up the fact that Rebecca Fischer isn't the name she was given at birth. So finding and sorting out her name change should be a pretty straight forward task, particularly since you suspect her initial last name was MacDonald. It gives me a place to look. And it was much easier to determine that Eleanor MacDonald's maiden name was Fischer. So that lends some credence to the idea that you're on the right track. And this is a more recent photo than the magazine used." Colin swiped his phone a few times before turning it around for Ben to see.

The face smiling back at him was absolutely Rebecca's mother. She was even wearing the same blouse she'd worn to lunch.

"Well. That's her. And since Rebecca said it was her mom, I can't see any reason why I wouldn't..."

"What?"

Ben gave a half-laugh. "She asked me if I follow celebrities at all. I'm guessing she was trying to figure out if I'd recognize the MacDonalds. If her dad had come along, I might have. But her mom keeps a lower profile."

Colin tucked his phone back into his pocket. "Do you want me to keep digging?"

Did he? It seemed pretty clear-cut. What would digging give him besides concrete proof? And did that matter? "Nah. I think you've gotten enough proof that I know the answer. If she's not going to tell me the truth...I guess I have to figure out what it means for us, or the possibility of us."

"Sorry. Relationships can be tough."

"That they can. I appreciate the time you took to poke around."

"Happy to do it. I'm just sorry I made you come all this way when I apparently could've sent an email. I thought I'd need to get more info from you."

Ben shrugged. "I'm getting some pretty excellent fish and chips out of the deal, so it's hard to complain."

"I'll let the cook know. He's new and nervous. Rachel's uncle runs a pub in Ireland and he and Rachel's aunt were out for a visit last week. I think Patrick taught the guy a few tricks of the trade—his cooking's gotten a lot better—but now he's looking over his shoulder in case Patrick hops out from behind the counter."

Ben chuckled.

"I'll let you get back to your dinner, then. And if you talk to David, tell him he needs to come up and meet Rachel before the wedding."

"Sure. He's really my roommate's friend, but I can pass it along."

With a nod and a wave, Colin stood. He stopped to chat with various patrons at the tables as he walked past them. Before long, music once again drifted through the space. The guy had talent, there was no denying that. But what made someone give up what sounded like a lucrative software company to be a musician? Then again, what made someone cling to the memory of a summer romance even when the evidence was mounting that it had all been a sham?

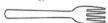

"What are you going to do?" Jackson stretched his legs out and crossed his ankles.

"I'm not sure. On the one hand, reading about Becky MacDonald, it's like I'm reading about a completely different person. Someone I've never met. I just have a hard time seeing the woman I know—even the young woman I knew at camp—doing half of the things her father talks about. And that's the other thing, if you read carefully, other than sneaking out of the house one time, Dr. MacDonald never explicitly says she did these things."

Jackson frowned. "Then why do people still warn kids with horror stories about Bad-Girl-Becky? Why the sidebar in that magazine?"

"That's the question. Or one of them, at least. And, I'll be honest, I only picked up on it because I was looking for proof that he wasn't talking about Rebecca. The implications are there, and very clear. So if you're not focusing on the words, you'd just assume he was talking about his daughter."

"That's...horrible." Jackson reached for the glass of iced tea sitting on the coffee table. "What kind of father does that?"

Ben shrugged. "Dunno. Maybe he had reasons that sounded good in his head. I know I've done things that, looking back, have me shaking my head. I imagine parenting only makes that happen more often. Not that that's an excuse. What he did was...awful. And it does make her name change a little more understandable. When you look through the articles that were published when her dad was doing a lot of speaking...they were brutal to her."

"Okay. But why not be honest about it once you know someone isn't going to lump you into that camp? Why the secrecy?"

Why indeed? From talking to Sara, Ben figured she knew the truth. Probably the other girl they'd been hanging with—what was her name? They seemed pretty close knit. So why would Rebecca tell her girlfriends, but not him? "I wish I knew."

Ben parked in the tiny lot in front of the mission and eyed the building. It was a standard brick, been-here-forever relic of the shabbier parts of D.C. Though it was apparent they tried to keep it looking as good as possible, the building showed its age. Or perhaps it showed simply that the external appearance wasn't the focus of what they did here. Tall stalks of...it had to be corn...speared up along one side of an enormous garden. Other plants were growing closer to the ground and a handful of people moved between the rows with watering cans and flat baskets for harvesting. He'd have to mention the garden to Jackson, it was just the kind of thing he'd enjoy passing along to Paige.

Ben checked his watch and climbed out of the car. He was meeting Jerry, and hopefully Rebecca, to finalize the invitations and get a feel for the layout of the building. Maybe it would give him a chance to be back on some kind of friendly footing with Rebecca, too. He hadn't seen her beyond tiny glimpses during the week. And he missed her. It was like losing her all over again.

The door swung open as Ben reached for the handle. He stepped back, muttering an apology as a tall teen pushed past, his eyes glistening with tears, despite the low riding jeans, sports jersey, and ball cap that pegged him as one of the more macho crowd.

"D'Andre, wait." Rebecca ran down the hall and Ben grabbed the door, holding it for her as she chased after the youth. Tears ran unfettered down her cheeks. Ben swallowed, fighting the urge to catch her arm and find out what was wrong. "D'Andre!"

The boy stopped at the edge of the parking lot, shoulders hunched and arms crossed, the posture more defeated than belligerent. Rebecca caught up and slipped an arm around his shoulders as she said something Ben couldn't hear. After a moment, the boy turned and buried his face in Rebecca's shoulder. She wrapped her arms around him and patted his back, her own tears increasing.

Ben hesitated. Should he stay? Offer to...do what? Help somehow. But how? Or should he go in and pretend he hadn't seen whatever this was? He ran a hand through his hair. If he didn't know about her past, Ben wouldn't question his response. He'd just go try to help. So that was the right answer. Regardless of what he'd discovered, a long, sleepless night had confirmed that he wanted her to be part of his life. No matter what name she used. He didn't believe the stories attributed to her. Wouldn't. There had been too much sincerity in their conversations at camp for it to have all been a lie.

Rebecca and D'Andre turned and headed back toward the mission. Ben grabbed the door and held it open. D'Andre broke free from Rebecca's arm and hurried down the hall.

"Is there a way I can help?"

"Ben? What are you...the meeting. Right." Rebecca sniffled and wiped her eyes. "It's been a rough day. Come on inside and I'll tell you about it."

Fighting the urge to pull her into his arms, he followed her down the hall. The faces he glimpsed in offices were subdued. When they emerged into a large multi-purpose room, groups of people were huddled together, talking in hushed voices and crying.

Rebecca went to a counter that ran down the far wall and poured hot water into a mug. "Tea or cocoa?"

"Tea is fine. What happened?" All sorts of scenarios ran through Ben's mind as Rebecca dropped a tea bag into the mug and then made a second, identical beverage.

Wrapping her hands around the mug, Rebecca glanced around. "We have a volunteer working here, Kira. She hadn't been here long, but you couldn't not love her. The light of Jesus shone through her more than anyone I've ever met."

Ben's stomach sank. This wasn't going to end well. He set his tea down on the counter.

"She...she's got leukemia. The treatments aren't working this time and today she collapsed. They've taken her to the hospital but...it's not looking good. She probably won't make it through the weekend." A fat tear rolled down Rebecca's cheek.

Ben reached up and wiped it away with his thumb before opening his arms. Rebecca stepped into his embrace, silent sobs shaking her body. He rubbed her back and laid his cheek on her hair. "I'm sorry. That's hard."

Rebecca sniffled.

"Should I come back another day? I can just take care of the invitations. This is so much more important."

She shook her head and stepped back. "No. No, you're here. Being busy will help me. Probably help Jerry, too. Grab your tea and let's go see what he wants to do."

19

Rebecca looked over the invitation samples Ben spread out on Jerry's desk. They were fairly standard invites, though each included a slightly different wording that drew attention to the problem of food insecurity in the U.S. and Washington, D.C. in particular.

"Where'd you get these numbers?" She tapped the statistics on the paper.

Ben arched an eyebrow. "I do a lot of research in my job. Adding on those stats was a pretty simple thing. There are national organizations out there that focus on inward reaching hunger abatement, you know. It's not all up to grassroots projects like the mission."

Rebecca bristled. "That wasn't what I meant. I'm just surprised..."

"That I have any idea about hunger and poverty that isn't in Africa. Yes, you've made that clear. And I keep trying to tell you that I'm hoping to expand Bread of Heaven's horizons and help others—including the people who work for us and our donors—realize that the problem is widespread and closer to home."

"Why?"

Ben frowned. "Why what?"

Jerry cleared his throat. "I hate to interrupt, but...can we just choose an invitation and whatever else needs to be done? I'd really like to get to the hospital. Melissa, the night manager is on her way and as soon as she gets here, I want to be ready to leave."

Rebecca swallowed a snide retort for Ben. "Why don't you go, Jerry? I can hold things down 'til she gets here."

"You're sure?" Jerry opened a desk drawer and started tossing files from his desk into it.

"As long as you don't mind me making the decisions for the open house."

Jerry shook his head. "This was supposed to be all you anyway. You don't mind, Ben?"

"Not if you don't. I'm happy to run with things if you've all got too much going on here. I understand..."

"I want to be involved." Rebecca put her hand on top of the invitations and managed a smile. Hopefully a sweet one. She still needed to hear his answer to her question, but that could wait a minute or two more until Jerry was on his way.

"Even better." Ben returned her smile and leaned back in his chair. "I'll be praying for your god daughter, Jerry."

"Thanks. I—we all—appreciate that. I'll let you know if anything happens, Rebecca." Jerry gave a terse nod and disappeared into the hall. He bid good night to the people he bumped into along the way, their brief conversations echoing into the office.

Ben cleared his throat. "Can we get back to the invitations?"

"No. I want to know why Bread of Heaven is doing this. They've been around for years and always focused on international aid, specifically in Africa. So why suddenly shift their focus?"

"Haven't I gone over this with you already?" Ben combed a hand through his hair. "One, it's not sudden. We've been partnering, mostly behind the scenes, with local food banks in major cities across the country for the past eighteen months. This is our first foray into a more visible partnership, I'll grant you, but it's not out of the blue. Two, we chose the mission because we're based here in D.C. and we didn't want to spend time and money flying to other cities. If our open house is a success here, then we might talk about expanding down the road, if we can get the volunteer force we need to make it work. Three, none of the above would apply if it wasn't for me pushing to get this initiative started. I love that we're making a difference internationally, but I drive through the city and see the many struggles of people who live less than forty miles away. How can I not want to help?"

136

Rebecca pressed her lips together. Could she believe him? "What about the money, the donors Bread of Heaven is hoping to gain from this? What if we lose donors to the mission because they catch a vision for international aid instead? We can't afford to have that happen."

Ben shrugged. "What about the Bread donors who realize they need to be making a difference at home and can only afford to support one charity? There's a potential for both of us to lose. But I really believe that everyone is going to win."

It was possible. But wasn't it just as likely that the big, well-known group would win? Sure, Rebecca was the biggest donor to the mission, and she wasn't planning on switching her donations, but the trust fund could only go so far, and there were so many people who needed help. Which meant that any additional donors would be worth having. She sighed. "All right. I guess we're both going to have to trust God to provide."

He smiled. "Right. He's the only one who never lets us down. And since I firmly believe that both organizations are doing what He'd have us do, spreading salt and light in our own ways to Jerusalem, Judea, Samaria, and even the ends of the earth, then it stands to reason that He's going to equip us to do that work."

Objections raced through her mind. It wasn't as if everything always worked out perfectly for people who were trying to do God's will. On the other hand, worrying about it didn't fix anything. Trust. That was cropping up a lot these days. Trusting God wasn't as hard to swallow as trusting Ben. Or her dad. One step at a time. "All right. What do we need to do next?"

"You're all set." The woman behind the desk at the animal shelter smiled and tapped the completed, and signed, paperwork together before filing it. "If you have any questions or need suggestions for a vet, that sort of thing, please give us a call. Don't be surprised if it takes a week or two for them to settle in."

Rebecca peered in the cat carrier where two six-month-old kittens were curled together, resting. "Thanks. Come on you two, let's head home. I hope you'll like all the presents I got for you."

The woman's chuckle followed Rebecca through the door. She set the carrier on the seat and frowned. Would it slide off if she had to stop suddenly? She didn't want the darlings to go flying. There wasn't much room between the backseat and the front but...she tugged the seatbelt down and around the carrier. That should help.

She shut the door and slid behind the wheel. "All right Lucy, Mr. Tumnus, let's..."

Her phone rang and she sighed as she shifted back into park. No sense driving while on the phone if she didn't have to.

"Hello?"

"Hey. It's Ben. Is this a bad time?"

Was it a bad time? She couldn't honestly say yes. But she wasn't ready to talk to him. Last night at the mission had been all business and, as such, straightforward. But if he was calling on a Saturday morning...that had to be personal, didn't it? "No. Not really. I just picked up two kittens from the animal shelter and was getting ready to take them home."

"Ah. Did...do you have plans for the rest of the day?"

"Just spending time with the cats, watching them acclimate. That kind of thing. Why?"

"I was hoping you might be interested in getting together. We could go for a walk or to dinner. Just friends, hanging out."

"Are we friends, Ben?" Rebecca squeezed her eyes shut. What was she doing? Oh, to be able to pull those words back into her brain where they didn't sound quite so stupid.

He sighed. "I hoped so. We were once. I'd like to be again. Is that possible?"

Friends. They had been friends. In love, yes. But also friends. And even without knowing the truth, they'd had a deep, solid friendship. For the summer. Would it have continued if they'd kept in touch? She wanted to say yes. So. "Yeah. Maybe it is. Look...I don't know about leaving the cats alone on their first day. Do you want to come over?"

"Okay."

"I'll text you my address. Give me two hours?"

"Done. See you then. Thanks, Rebecca."

She ended the call and banged her head on the steering wheel twice before shifting back into reverse. Maybe in two hours she could figure out how this was going to work.

Rebecca smoothed a hand over the light-weight lavender sweater she'd changed into. She'd resisted the urge to put on khakis, or something even dressier. This was friends hanging out. She didn't need to dress up. But the holey long-sleeved t-shirt she'd worn to the animal shelter was too ratty even for Jen and Sara. She just hadn't been sure how messy getting the cats into the carrier was going to be. It had been relatively anti-climactic.

Mr. Tumnus hopped down the stairs and scampered around her feet, batting at the frayed edges of her jeans. She laughed. Sweet little boy. She reached down, scooped him into her arms, and scrubbed his head. He gave a low, throaty purr. Lucy, the white patch of fur on her neck gleaming, ran through the room, skidding to a stop just before colliding into a wall. She let out an annoyed meow as she reversed direction. Mr. Tumnus squirmed and Rebecca let him jump down. He pounced on Lucy and the two tumbled together across the living room as the doorbell rang.

Rebecca pressed a hand into her stomach. Friends hanging out. Right. A memory of one of their kisses after the staff campfire ended flitted through her mind, setting her nerve endings on fire. They had chemistry, that was undeniable. But that was then. She pulled open the door and her mouth watered. A cornflower blue polo stretched across his toned shoulders and was tucked into jeans that fit like they'd been made specifically for him. Chemistry certainly wasn't going to be a problem now, either. She cleared her throat. "Hi. Come on in."

He grinned and slid his hands into his pockets as he followed her into the living room. "This is nice. Not too far from everything, but you're also not in the thick of all the traffic all the time. You can probably even get to the grocery store without sitting through multiple traffic light cycles, can't you?"

"Depends on which store I decide to go to. But sometimes, yeah." Rebecca glanced around the room. Had it really been so long since she had guests that she'd lost the ability to be a hostess? "Um. Can I get you something to drink? Or snacks? I probably have some snacks."

"I'm good. Thanks." Ben's gaze traveled around the room. "Can I meet the cats?"

"Oh. Um, sure. Though I'm not positive where they are. They were running around exploring a minute ago. I can go look for them?"

"Don't do that. If I know cats, they'll be running through here before too long and I'll get to meet them then." He frowned. "Are you okay?"

Rebecca chuckled. "I'm nervous. I don't know why, well, I do know why, but it's silly. And now I'm rambling. I'll stop."

"Take a breath. Do you want to sit outside? You have a deck or something, right? Would that make you more comfortable? Or we could go for a walk around your neighborhood or head to the mall? I haven't been to Springfield Mall in forever. Didn't they just redo it?"

He was trying to put her at ease. It was helping. A little. "No, that's silly. I do have a deck, but no furniture on it yet. I was hoping the end of season sales would finally have something that I liked and could afford. That combination is proving strangely elusive."

Ben snickered. "No white plastic chairs from the nearest discount store for the low, low price of five dollars? That's mostly what we have. And since they're so cheap, when they inevitably break or get covered in that weird green not-quite-moss, not-quite-mold that happens to them, we don't feel bad about sticking them on the curb for the recycling guy."

"And that right there is the difference between men and women." Rebecca shook her head and pointed to the couch. "You can sit, if you want. I didn't mean to keep us standing here."

Ben sat, stretching his leg so his knee was mostly straight, and sighed. "You mentioned you stopped running and said it was a long story..."

She pursed her lips. There was nothing inherently wrong with that story, though she'd leave out a few pieces. Like how it was a well-known fact that Becky MacDonald was a distance runner and so it was yet another thing that had to go. "It's probably not as long as I made it out to be. I started developing stress fractures. I thought at first it was just shin splints. I tried different shoes, orthotics, you name it. I went to coaches and had my form evaluated, none of it helped. Finally got some x-rays done. I had to stop for several months and then eased back into things, but within six months, I was in agonizing pain again and the fractures were back. The doctor said I should consider giving it up. Do you still run?"

"No. I was never really a runner. I just wanted to hang out with you."

Her eyebrows shot up. "I never would have guessed that. You always kept up fine. You're joking with me, right?"

He shook his head. "I didn't want to do anything that would make you think I was a wimp. So I pushed through it. Then when I'd go back to my cabin to shower, I'd stand under the hot water and try not to cry. It did get easier after the first month, but I never liked anything beyond it being time with you."

Heat spread across her cheeks. He'd done that for her? "Oh. Well. Thanks."

"Sure. And hey, now that neither of us run anymore, we can go for a not-run sometime."

"I believe they call that a walk."

He shrugged. "Tomato."

"Potato." She laughed. "I haven't thought of that in years. I...oh, there's Mr. Tumnus."

The silver tabby bounded into the room and pounced on Ben's leg. He laughed and reached down to tousle the kitten's fur. "He's adorable. But not a faun."

"Yeah, well, he's got those markings on the top of his head that look like little horns. It seemed to fit. Plus, I love Narnia. Just the idea that there's a whole other world lurking in the back of a wardrobe, that Aslan might pull me into it at any point to come and help, or just be with him?"

Ben ran his hand down Mr. Tumnus' back and up his tail. The cat purred before darting off again. He shook off the cat hair and wrinkled his nose. "Make sure you brush him or he's going to get hairballs if he keeps shedding like that."

"They mentioned that at the shelter. But apparently he loves to be brushed, so that's good. The other is a tuxedo—she's a little shier, so we might not see her. But I named her Lucy."

"You had to, didn't you? I mean, if you've got Tumnus, you must have Lucy. Then the two of them can sip tea while you're away at work."

She grinned. She'd missed this. Unlike the handful of other guys she'd dated, he'd always seemed to "get" her. "Exactly. You know what? Let's go for that walk."

20

"How was your date?" Zach hit pause on the controller, freezing the military assault on the TV in the midst of what promised to be a gory battle for honor.

"Wasn't a date. We're friends, hanging out. She only drummed that into the conversation twelve or thirteen thousand times." Ben shrugged and dropped to the couch, propping his feet on the coffee table. "But it was good. I *like* her. She's fun and interesting and even with the years since camp, it still seems like we have a lot in common."

"So if you get stuck in the friend zone?"

Ben made a face. "I don't know. If that happens, then presumably God will show me someone else He has for me, right?"

"Don't look at me, man. I don't have any answers. I'm stuck in the friend zone with Amy right now, too. Despite my efforts to the contrary. She was ticked that the dinner over here was all couples. She thought it was going to be a big party and told me I'd taken her out on a date under false pretenses."

"Wow." Ben grabbed the second controller and powered it on. "Two questions."

"Shoot."

"If you knew that someone had changed their name to hide their past, would you trust that they really were the person you were in love with?"

Zach cleared his throat. "Is the second question easier? Because I don't know how to answer that one without falling back on the old chestnut of needing to pray about it and trusting God to make it clear one way or the other."

That was the same conclusion Ben had come to on the drive home. Why couldn't it be easier? Something cut and dry. He nodded.

"Yeah, that's what I thought. Second question: is this game multiplayer?"

Zach grinned. "Of course. Let's hit it."

Ben stared at the ceiling. There were really only two options. He could give up, and move on. That seemed to be what Rebecca wanted him to do. Certainly it was she expected him to do. Was she used to people walking away so easily? Was that the problem? There was a certain appeal to that solution. It would mean he didn't have to figure out where the line between fact and fiction lay when it came to the many exploits of Becky MacDonald. If even half of what Dr. MacDonald said she'd done was true...he huffed out a breath. It didn't seem possible. He couldn't reconcile the stories with the girl he'd known at camp. Or the woman he knew now. But what if it was true? If she'd changed, truly changed, and wasn't still living like that, could he love her? Forgive her? That was, at least, easier. It wasn't as if he was perfect. So yeah, Christ had forgiven her. He could too.

Which left the other option. Persevere.

He sighed and rolled to his side. Did he do that on his terms or hers? Could he do it on hers? If she had her way, wouldn't he simply walk away? Sure, they'd had fun together today, almost as if the years between camp and now hadn't happened. But there was still a distance. A huge distance. At camp, he would have taken her hand or slipped an arm around her shoulders. And she would've welcomed that, reciprocated. Today, whenever their hands bumped, she moved away or crossed her arms. It was possible that she'd come around to see things the same way at some point. But how old would they be? They'd already wasted ten years because he hadn't been able to track her down.

Okay, maybe it wasn't wasted. He'd dated during that time. And those experiences had made it clear, to him at least, that Rebecca was the woman he wanted. That she was the woman God had for him. He scoffed. Was that presumptuous? It wasn't as if there'd been some voice booming from heaven telling him, "Ben, here is the woman I want you to marry." Just quiet, subtle things that made him realize no matter who he was with, Rebecca was a better fit. And that all rested on the assumption that the woman he knew—and the girl he'd known—was, in fact, who he loved. She used a different name, sure, but her heart was the same now as it was then. So did it make sense that what he knew was the true person, regardless of label?

He could confront her with the truth. There was definitely an appeal to that. Just lay all the cards on the table and see what she did. His gut twisted. She'd run. And at some point, when someone ran away that many times, didn't you have to let them go? No, confrontation wasn't the right option. Not with her.

So where did that leave him?

"You look rough." Jackson pulled another mug down from the cabinet and offered it to Ben.

"Thanks." Ben grabbed the coffee pot and poured. "Long night."

"What's going on?"

"Just trying to untangle this thing with Rebecca, figure out what I'm supposed to do." Ben stirred half-and-half into his mug and carried it to the table.

"Any luck?" Jackson pulled out the chair across from him.

Ben blew across the top of his coffee. "I have a plan. I'm not sure it's right, but praying about it hasn't given me any ideas beyond this one. So...I'm going with it."

"Going with what?" Zach shuffled into the room and grabbed a banana from the bowl in the middle of the table before dropping into a chair.

"His plan for wooing Rebecca."

"Wooing?" Ben shook his head. "What century are you from? Wooing."

Jackson shrugged. "Paige has been choosing these Jane Austen movies to watch. Once you get past the costumes, they're not half bad."

Zach laughed. "Dude. You might as well trade in your pants for frilly dresses. No guy admits to liking those things. Just propose already, she's taken possession of your man card anyway."

"Spoken like a guy whose efforts to evade the friend zone have been thoroughly thwarted." Jackson sipped his coffee and jerked his head toward Ben. "You were getting ready to tell us your plan."

"I wasn't, actually. It's not a plan, really. I'm going to ask her out. Officially. Take her on a real date and make it clear that it's all or nothing. Because that's where I am. I want her in my life. Permanently. And if she isn't willing to be there, then there's no point in torturing either of us."

"Wow." Zach took a bite of banana. "What if she walks away?"

Ben hunched his shoulders. It was the worst-case scenario, but a plausible one. "Then I trust that God has someone else for me. But let's be honest. If she's not the woman I'm going to marry, there's no point in having a solid friendship with her, that's just going to be misunderstood down the line by the woman I am supposed to marry. Once you're involved with someone, you can't be best friends with someone of the opposite sex. Maybe you can be couple friends, if they have a significant other too, but that's the best you can hope for. So if Rebecca isn't willing to consider a future with me, then for both of our sakes, I'm going to have to move on."

"You think you can?" Jackson snagged an orange from the fruit bowl and tossed it from one hand to the other.

Ben rubbed his hands across his face as his chest tightened. It wouldn't be easy. He'd had ten years of failing miserably to do just that. "I don't know. But I'll have to."

21

Rebecca crossed her arms and stared at the crowded foyer. Her heart raced in her chest. So many people. How did that many people all decide to go to the same church? She looked at Sara. How was she so calm? "Remind me why we're doing this."

Sara laughed and slid her arm through Rebecca's. "Because none of us are happy where we usually go. So it's time to look around and see if there's a better fit."

"When did choosing a church become about being happy?" Rebecca let her arms fall to her side. "And where's Jen? For all we know she's here, just hidden somewhere in the enormous throng. Honestly, she could be getting trampled to death and no one would ever know until half-way through the service when this crowd finally thins."

Sara snorted. "I'm sure the crowd thins *before* the service actually starts, and Jen is right there, worming her way through the clumps toward us."

Rebecca followed Sara's pointing finger and spotted Jen talking to...her stomach plummeted. "He goes here. Let's go. There's another church just down the street we can try."

"What? We agreed to try here. What is your..." Sara's eyebrows shot up. "Aha. Well, I'd say this church just got a little more interesting. Try to smile. They've spotted us."

Right. Smile. She forced her lips to curve. Yesterday had been a mistake. Spending time with Ben only made her realize how much she wanted a future with him. She'd almost blurted out the truth ten different times during the afternoon. And each time their hands had brushed, the electricity sparking through her had made her want to twine her fingers through his and hold on forever. But how did she trust him when her own father hadn't given a second thought to destroying her reputation? If Dad—the first man who was supposed to love her unconditionally and always keep her best interest in mind—could do that, what would keep someone else from doing the same? Or worse?

"Hey." Ben grinned, his eyes sparkling. "Why didn't you tell me you were coming here today? I would've given you directions to the best meeting places—you know, the ones that don't get quite so crowded."

Rebecca glanced around the area. "Is that possible here? What's the typical attendance on a Sunday?"

"I don't really pay attention to that. It's probably on the website somewhere though if you really want to know." Ben shrugged. "I don't love how busy it gets, but I don't blame people for wanting to come. Pastor Brown is amazing. And there are some good people who come here, too."

Probably some not-as-good people as well. Though that was the case at any church, really. The problem with churches, overall, is that they were filled with sinners. Sinners saved by grace, sure, but still sinners. Herself included. Rebecca fought the urge to roll her eyes. Here she stood, judging everyone in the building simply because she was uncomfortable. "Should we go stake a claim on a seat? Pew? Chair? Whatever they use here?"

Ben laughed. "Pews, if you can believe it. They haven't migrated to the pew chair yet, though every so often it gets brought up as a possibility. So far, we've managed to vote it down. I don't imagine we'll succeed forever, but for now, you get the pleasure of a padded pew. Come on, I told Jackson and Zach to save extra room so the three of you could join us."

Rebecca started off after Ben, but Sara grabbed her arm. "Seriously. He is the cutest thing in the world. What is wrong with you?"

"Haven't we been over this?" Rebecca swallowed the lump in her throat. Sara was right, but rubbing it in didn't help. A relationship wasn't possible. No matter how much she wanted it.

Jen drilled her elbow into Rebecca's side. "Listen to Sara. And to me. You're making a huge mistake. He's the epitome of a keeper. And, aside from that, it's time for you to stop living a lie."

Living a lie? She wasn't doing that. She followed numbly after her friends. Is that really what they thought? They didn't see how necessary her choices had been? Rebecca hauled in a deep breath and let it out slowly, widening her eyes and willing back the tears. How could you be in such a huge crowd and still feel abandoned?

"Come on, let's go to lunch." Sara leaned against the driver's side door of Rebecca's car, blocking her.

Rebecca shook her head. "I just want to go home. I don't feel well."

"Baloney." Sara crossed her arms, frowning. "You're trying to pull away because Jen and I think you need to be honest with Ben. What are you going to do? Change your name and move again?"

She ducked her head. The thought had occurred to her, but it probably wasn't a good idea to mention it. Besides, now that she owned a house, moving was a more challenging prospect. You couldn't just give notice to your landlord and move on. "No. Of course not."

Sara scoffed. "You think I didn't see your wheels turning just now? You're a piece of work."

"Awesome. Between Jen thinking I'm a big, fat liar and you saying I'm a piece of work, exactly why am I supposed to want to go to lunch with you? Seriously, if I'm such a horrible person, why would you bother hanging out with me? Just go away and leave me alone." Rebecca reached for the handle of the car door.

"Cut it out, Bec. We're your best friends and whether you want to believe it or not, we really do have your best interest at heart. Ben is amazing. And the two of you deserve a chance." Sara tossed her hands in the air and stepped away from the car. "Whatever. If acting like a petulant child makes you feel better, I can't stop you. But if you change your mind, we're hitting the Afghan place on Little River Turnpike."

Sara strode across the parking lot to her car. Rebecca sagged against the door. This is what she wanted, right? They were leaving her alone, no pressure. Except the pressure was still there and now it was mixed with the vague sense of, yet again, being a disappointment to the people who mattered most in her life. Why couldn't she simply put on a happy face and go eat a gyro with her friends? But if she did, they'd want to know what she was going to do about Ben. And she didn't have an answer.

Her cell rang. Rebecca fished it out of her purse, frowning at the number. She could let it go to voicemail and...what? Be forced into a decision about what to do for lunch. Better to answer and hope for a reprieve.

"Hello?"

"Rebecca? It's Jerry from the mission."

She straightened. She'd never heard Jerry this upset. "Yeah, of course. Hi Jerry."

"I'm sorry to bother you on Sunday. Is there any way you could go downtown and keep an eye on things? I can't reach any of the other staff and I don't want to leave the hospital. Kira," Jerry paused, his breath hitching, "she probably won't make it much longer. I need to be here with her parents."

Tears pricked Rebecca's eyes. She hadn't known the girl very well, or for very long, but she was a solid, gentle presence at the mission who would be missed. "Of course. I'll head down right now."

"You're a life saver. Melissa said she'd stay until I found someone or made it in myself, but she was supposed to be off at eight this morning. Thanks."

"You're welcome. And Jerry...if you get a chance, tell Kira I consider it a privilege to know her."

Jerry sniffed. "I'll let her know."

Rebecca dropped her purse and keys on the kitchen counter and shook the bag of cat treats. Mr. Tumnus and Lucy came running, bringing the tiniest smile to her face. At least someone was having a good day. A good life. She sank to the floor and pried open the zip seal—did they really need to make these things that hard to open? It wasn't as if cats had thumbs—as the cats swarmed into her lap, meowing.

"Mmm, sounds like a pretty good day." Rebecca stroked the soft tabby as she held out a treat for the more restrained, tuxedo-coated Lucy. "And one for you, Mr. Tumnus."

Why couldn't her life be as simple as theirs? The mission had been overloaded today. The chillier temperatures at night were sending more people to the shelter side of things. Before too much longer, they'd be at capacity. Jerry tried to avoid turning people away, but there were only so many beds. And fire codes had to be observed. Since it was Sunday, the overnighters hadn't cleared out as quickly as they did on the weekdays, or so Melissa had said. Rebecca didn't really know what the weekend days at the mission was like. She tended to be there after work, during the week. Should she be spending more weekends there? Jerry said they usually had plenty of weekend volunteers though, and there had been a number of people around doing various jobs. So why had he called her? Was it because she was a donor? Or because he knew who she was? She groaned. That was ridiculous. He wasn't going to betray her secret. He had no reason to. A tiny voice in the back of her head asked what made Jerry different than Ben. She pushed it away. People kept telling her she needed to trust, so why not start with Jerry?

She gave each cat another treat and a light scratch under their chins before pushing to her feet and punching in a number on her phone.

"Hi, Sweetheart. Your father and I were just talking about you."

Rebecca smiled. "Oh? Anything interesting?"

"Just wondering how you were doing and if you'd been out with your young man again. All the usual things parents wonder about when their children grow up, leave the nest, and move across the country."

Her young man? "Mom. I told you there can't be a future with Ben. Or anyone."

"I know you say that. But you don't see how you look at him. I did. There's love there, Becca. Don't be afraid to grab it."

Oh please. Even her mother was jumping on the bandwagon? This wasn't why she'd called. Not that she'd had a certain motive for calling, but a lecture about her life choices and Ben were definitely not what she'd been going for. Time to change the subject. "Did you get the pictures of Mr. Tumnus and Lucy I sent you?"

Eleanor sighed. "I did. They're precious. Though Mr. Tumnus is a mouthful. Are you really sticking with that name as opposed to something like Mr. T for short?"

She snickered before she could stop herself. "I pity da fool who calls my cat Mr. T."

"What?"

Rebecca's snicker turned into a full belly laugh. "Don't you remember those horrible reruns Dad used to put on all the time? Some group of mercenaries in a van and the one burly guy with a Mohawk and too many necklaces?"

"Not really. I was usually reading when your father was in charge of the television. Hang on."

Rebecca listened as her mom asked her dad about the show. Her dad's laughter warmed her heart. It was a good memory. One from before he had book contracts and speaking engagements and a need to offer solutions for all manner of parenting issues. Did he always have to pretend to walk in their shoes instead of just giving advice from an observer's position? Her smile faded. Her heart ached for that time, when she could curl up on the couch with her dad, and his arm around her shoulders made it seem like there was nothing in the world that could hurt her.

"He says the show was the A-Team and that they made a pretty decent, if somewhat silly, movie remake that you might enjoy renting."

"I'll put it on my list." Rebecca sighed. "I miss you guys."

"Why don't you come visit? I know it's not a holiday, but if you can arrange a long weekend, we can get you a ticket."

It was tempting. She had the time. Even having taken a week when they were visiting, another two days wouldn't be too hard to swing. But the open house at the mission and the cats made disappearing more complicated. "I can't right now. But I'll see what I can swing down the road. Soon."

"All right. You know the offer stands for whenever you need it, right?"

"Yeah. I love you, Mom."

"Love you too, Becca. So does your dad."

"I'll call you later this week." Rebecca ended the call and plugged in her phone. If he loved her so much, why didn't he make a move to bridge the gap between them? He'd caused it, shouldn't he be the one to heal it? And was that even possible? She didn't have an answer.

ELIZABETH MADDREY

22

Ben pushed back from his desk and stretched his neck from side to side. The response from the invitation to the open house was promising. He'd received his invitation on Monday, which meant others in the area probably had as well. Three days later, they had close to a hundred people committed to coming. That was faster than any event he'd run. With the open house just three weeks away, he'd worried people would be unable to attend. It's why he'd pushed to do an open house, where people could come and go as they pleased, instead of a sit-down dinner with a program. The format also allowed them to invite more than they normally would have. Of course, it also encouraged people not to respond and still show up. But that was a risk they could account for. Probably. Rebecca would be excited, wouldn't she?

Before he could talk himself out of it, he picked up the phone.

"Hey, Ben."

He smiled. She recognized his number. Maybe even had it programmed in, under his name. That was a step in the right direction. "Hey, yourself. I'm glad I caught you, I was going to leave a voicemail."

"I'm actually almost finished for the day. I had two cancellations this afternoon so I figured I'd head down to the mission, see if they needed an extra hand with anything. It's an open pantry day, so they'll be swamped on that side of the building."

That would be worth seeing. He'd helped on food distribution missions overseas, but hadn't seen how something local worked. Did they require paperwork of some sort to prove that the food was going to people who needed it? Or did they just assume that if you went to the trouble of figuring out where and how to get it, you were needy enough? Did they worry about people taking advantage of the system? "Think I could tag along? I'd love to get a feel for that end of the operation."

Rebecca cleared her throat. "I guess. I'm not sure where they'll need help...it might just be hanging out with the tutoring kids again."

"That's fine. I like tutoring too. It'd be a kick to tell Zach I helped someone with homework for his class. Can I pick you up, take you to dinner after?"

"I have my car..."

"Sure, but you could leave it there, right? I'd drop you back after we eat."

"Yeah, okay."

"Give me half an hour?"

"'K."

Ben ended the call and grinned. That had gone better than he'd hoped. He'd fully expected her to say no, and keep saying no, when he offered to pick her up. She must not have thought too carefully about what it meant in terms of his driving. It wasn't as if his office was very close to the PT clinic. But if she didn't think about it, he wasn't bringing it up.

He packed his laptop and a few files into his bag, threw his blazer over his arm, and hit the light switch on his office wall as he headed out.

Feet aching, Ben opened the car door for Rebecca then rounded the hood and slid behind the wheel. "Wow. That's...quite the operation."

Rebecca nodded. "The emergency food area is always open, I think 24/7. Anyone can come for one of the grocery boxes. They're packed to provide two meals a day for a family of four for one week. That gives people time to apply for S.N.A.P.—food stamps, basically—and free or reduced lunches for the kids when their parents face an emergency, like an unexpected layoff or illness. I know the mission records basic information of people who use the emergency services, to cut down on anyone who tries to abuse the system. But they don't have many problems. Those boxes aren't what most people would choose to live on, no matter that they're free."

Ben nodded. He'd been guilty of that—filling the food drive bags with the cans in the pantry that were accidental purchases. Things that he had no intention of eating. Stood to reason though that if he wasn't excited about canned peas and beets, that wasn't really what the hungry were looking forward to either. He cringed. He'd do better from here on out—actually go shop for the food drive and buy things that made sense. "And the other side? It looked like a grocery store."

"It is, essentially. We get donations as well as low-cost purchases from government programs. Then we sell them at cost, sometimes below cost, to folks who participate in the food stamp program but who need a little extra to round out their rainy day supplies. S.N.A.P. covers weekly meals, basically, but it doesn't allow for building up any kind of surplus or even some of the extras that we take for granted. The program allows folks to do that and take home more than if they spent the same amount at an actual grocery store." Rebecca dropped her head back against the headrest. "You saw how empty the shelves were at closing time. It'll build back up, slowly, over the next month. Just in time for our next open pantry day."

"It's incredible. And you do hot meals every night, plus sleeping accomodations, too?"

She nodded. "And lunches for kids during the summer, when the schools are out and they aren't getting a meal there. Some of the families only eat the two meals a day we offer them. But if you were to ask my neighbors how many Americans faced hunger, they'd have no idea it was one in six."

One in six. It still surprised him, even though he'd looked it up when he first proposed the joint effort with a local agency to his boss. "There are more people trying to make that information available now. A lot of celebrity chefs play for national food charities when they're in competitions. That's how it first came to my attention."

Rebecca laughed. "You watch food shows?"

"Guilty pleasure. Mostly late at night when there's nothing on and I don't feel like going into the living room to fire up the game console. You've seen their knives, right? You've gotta be hardcore to wield those things. They're manly."

"Fair enough. Where are we eating?"

"Do you like barbecue? Paige told us about this place, a friend of her dad's runs it. It sounded amazing and I've been looking for a reason to get over to try it. She says the brisket's better than anything you'll find in Texas."

Rebecca's eyebrows arched. "That's quite a recommendation. I'm game. I haven't had good brisket since the last time I went back to see my parents."

"That's right, your mom said they live in Texas. But you didn't grow up there?"

"Nope. We moved right before I went to college. So it's never really felt like home. But you can't beat the barbecue."

"We'll have to see. Paige is pretty good at the food thing, so I'm willing to take her word for it. And hey, if it's as good as she says it is, then you'll have a place to take your folks next time they visit." Ben glanced over and caught her quickly suppressed grimace. "Or not."

"It's not that. I just...my dad always picks Thai food. I guess Texas is full of good barbecue but severely lacking in the finer points of Asian cuisine. At least in his mind that's the case. I like Thai as well as the next person, but there's only so much you can eat, you know?"

He pursed his lips. "Depends. I could probably do the mango sticky rice every day without any issues."

Rebecca laughed. "I'm not positive that counts."

"Thai iced tea?"

She shook her head.

"Ah, well. I tried." He signaled and turned into the parking lot. "Here we are. Let's go see if it's all Paige says it's cracked up to be."

Ben reached for her hand as they walked into the restaurant. She jolted but didn't pull away when he twined his fingers through hers. Progress. When they were seated and had placed their drink orders, Ben set his menu aside and held her gaze. "So what sent you into physical therapy? At camp, you were planning to be a missionary, weren't you?"

Rebecca pulled her lip between her teeth and fiddled with the silverware. She looked down at her hands as she spoke. "I applied to a semester long mission trip. It was basically a chance to see if you were suited to the life and get a serious feel for what was involved. When you finished, you're pretty much guaranteed that the agency would take you on once you graduated. I didn't get accepted."

"Oh. Why not?" Ben frowned. She probably hadn't changed her name legally yet, which would mean that the agency believed the stories about Becky MacDonald and didn't want to take the risk. On the one hand, he could see their point—if what Dr. MacDonald had said was true, Rebecca would've been a huge liability. But to not even bother finding out how true it was...how could they?

Rebecca shrugged and cast a grateful look at the server who deposited their drinks on the table. They placed their orders for brisket.

Ben watched her sip her sweet tea. Should he push?

"It was probably the essays. I've never been particularly good at them. They don't exactly give you a long list of reasons with your rejection letter. They invited me to apply again the following year, but there didn't seem to be much point. It just felt like God had firmly closed that door. So I did a lot of soul searching, praying, and talking with my mom...and physical therapy jumped out as a way to still do something useful that helped people."

"You're good at it. And you definitely help. My knee's almost back to one hundred percent, and I know for a fact I wouldn't have pushed myself without your encouragement."

Pink blossomed on her cheeks, making her even lovelier. Did she have any idea how pretty she was? Probably not. The women who did rarely captured beauty in their soul. But Rebecca? She was beautiful inside and out.

"Well, I can't take all the credit. Sara's been seeing you lately."

He nodded, acknowledging the point. "I'm sorry about that."

Her movement jerky and tentative, she reached across the table and laid her hand on his. "Don't be. It's my fault. I'm sorry. I know I haven't been completely fair to you. Ten years ago or now. I...it's..."

He shook his head. "Please don't say it's complicated again."

She laughed. "All right. But it is. I will say I'm trying to untangle the complexities and figure out what I'm doing. I...for the first time in ten years, I'm considering the possibilities I thought were beyond my reach. Be patient with me?"

His heart sped as a weight lifted off his chest. Maybe there was hope after all. If she told him the whole story, that would clear everything up. Wouldn't it? "I can do that."

The server returned with their food and Rebecca snatched back her hand. Rich, tangy spices wafted through the air and Ben's mouth watered. If it tasted anything like it smelled, they were in for a treat. "Can we pray?"

Rebecca nodded.

Ben reached for her hand and bowed his head. So many thoughts raced through his mind and he took a deep breath to settle them. "Heavenly Father, thank you for this food. Thank you for Rebecca and the mission. For the work they do to provide for those who are hungry. Guide and bless our steps as we work to be salt and light in the world. Amen."

"Amen." Rebecca tugged her hand away and leaned over her plate, breathing in. "Smells good."

Ben sliced into the tender beef and took a bite. Flavor exploded on his tongue. "Mm. I haven't been to Texas in a long while. But I'm not sure I need to now that I know this is here."

They ate mostly in silence. Ben focused on his food, but his eyes kept straying to Rebecca. She was neat, not a drop of sauce dripped from her fork. He'd already had to wipe at three different places on his shirt, and he was pretty sure there was at least one on his pants that he'd missed. Zach was the only one of the three of them with any laundry know-how, so he was going to have to beg for help to get the sauce out. He made a mental note to wear a t-shirt next time he came here. Preferably a black one.

"Ugh. I'm stuffed." Rebecca leaned back and dabbed at her lips.

Ben chuckled. "They have carrot cake."

She grimaced and shook her head. "Nope. I'm not giving in."

"It's your favorite. Or it used to be."

"Still is." She closed her eyes. "I can't. I really can't."

The server came to the table and reached for their empty plates. "Can I get you anything else?"

"Can you do dessert to go?"

The girl nodded. Ben looked at Rebecca. "What do you think? Breakfast of champions?"

She sighed. "You're evil, you know that? Fine. Yeah."

"Two slices of carrot cake to go. Separately packaged? And the check."

"I'll be right back." The girl slipped away, balancing their empty plates in her hands.

Ben sucked the last bit of tea from his glass. "Thank you."

"For what?"

"I didn't want to be a pig. But carrot cake...how do you have the willpower to turn it down?"

"I don't run anymore, remember? You have to develop a lot of willpower when you stop that. You really don't exercise?" Her gaze flicked over him.

161

Heat flooded his face and he shook his head. "Not really. Sorry. Just one of those metabolism things, I guess."

"Unfair." Rebecca took one of the bags from the server and tried to reach for the check.

Ben glared and handed the server his credit card. "Nuh-uh. My treat. I asked you to dinner."

She cleared her throat. "So, was this a date?"

Was it? It wasn't what he'd had in mind for their first real date. But then, nothing about having her back in his life had been what he imagined. Maybe in the long run the ups and downs of reality were better than the blissful perfection of imagination. "Yeah. It was."

Rebecca's lips quirked up. "Then thank you. I had a good time."

When the bill was settled, they went out to the car. The trip to the PT office where Rebecca's car waited was short and quiet. Ben started to ask a question several times but stopped himself. The quiet was companionable. It didn't need to be broken for the sake of noise. He parked next to her car in the deserted lot.

"Here we are. Do you want me to follow you home, make sure you get back safely?"

She shook her head. "I'll be fine. I do drive at night, you know."

Ben chuckled. "Sorry. It's weird not dropping you off at your door. My mom would be appalled."

"Well, I can tell her you offered. It doesn't make any sense for you to drive to Springfield when you live a few miles from here."

"Okay. Will you at least text me when you get home? Or call?"

"Sure." She unhooked her seatbelt and pushed open the door. "I had a good time. I didn't think I would, but I did. Thanks for tagging along."

Ben pulled the keys out of the ignition and stepped out of the car, circling around to where she was unlocking her own car. "It was my pleasure. I enjoyed seeing more of what the mission does. And having a chance to eat dinner with you was the icing on the cake."

"Oh. My cake." Rebecca's gaze darted back to Ben's car. "I think I left it..."

He held up a bag and smiled.

"Ha. Thanks." She grabbed the bag.

Ben stepped forward and slid his palm up her arm. He curved his hand around the back of her neck, his fingertips buried in her hair, and lowered his mouth so his lips hovered just above hers. "I've been thinking about this for ten years."

Rebecca's eyes fluttered closed, her lips parting slightly as she leaned forward.

He pressed his lips to hers. Her hands balled into fists at his waist. Electricity sizzled through his body and a hunger that had nothing to do with his stomach seized him. He needed to stop. To step back. But, oh...he didn't want the beautiful torture to end. With his breath locked in his chest, he forced himself to raise his head a fraction of an inch, breaking the kiss. He held her glassy-eyed gaze and eased back a half-step.

"I...I should get home." Rebecca fumbled behind her for the handle to the car door and wrenched it open.

"Okay. Right." Ben's tongue darted between his lips. "Good night, Rebecca."

She nodded, swallowing, and slid behind her steering wheel. "I'll let you know when I'm home."

"'K. Drive safe." Ben closed her door and stepped back from the car. He lifted a hand as she backed out of her space and drove away. He got back into his own car and started the engine, every nerve ending tingling. Her kisses had been potent ten years ago. Compared to now, they'd been child's play.

23

Lucy jumped up on the couch and curled up next to Rebecca, not quite touching her leg. Rebecca reached over and gently stroked her silky fur. During dinner, she'd been exhausted, ready to go home and head straight to bed. Then that kiss. All the emotions she'd crammed into a box and locked away had burst out. Now they wouldn't go away. A husband. Family. Grandchildren. Kisses...and more. She swallowed and blinked back tears. *Oh, God...why did You let him kiss me? Why didn't I pull away?*

For ten years, she'd successfully avoided any kind of relationship that had the slim chance of turning into more than an occasional, casual date. She'd justified it with memories of Ben. How could anything compare to that summer? For the first time in her life, she'd poured out her soul to someone and he'd soaked it up. There'd been no rejection. No questioning of her sincerity. He'd shared his heart, his deepest thoughts and fears and desires. Love had been easy under the summer sun and on clear, moonlit nights walking in the woods or on a gravel path between cabins full of sleeping campers. How could anything in the real world compete with such effortless idyll?

She hadn't written back. When she'd gotten back home, she'd had to endure the full force of Dad's latest talk, complete with a daughter who snuck boys into her room and the loving-yet-disappointed father who cried as he pleaded with God to show him where he'd gone wrong. That icy dose of reality had ruined her sun-soaked summer. Ben's letter arrived the same day as the thanks-but-no-thanks rejection letter for the missionary internship. She'd tucked his letter away, changed her name, and made new plans.

Somewhere along the way, she'd gotten back on speaking terms with God. It had been touch and go for awhile. After all, what good was a heavenly Father who didn't protect you from the Earthly one? And maybe, as Dad continued to protest, he hadn't come right out and said it was his daughter in the illustrations, but he hadn't said it wasn't her, either. And people were quick to draw conclusions. The one time he'd tried to set the record straight it had been too little, too late. Rebecca sighed. At least he'd tried. Sort of. That put a tiny mark in the credit column, but it didn't make things right. And still, the strain in her relationship with Dad clogged up her prayers. Not as much as before, when it was as if every word bounced off the ceiling and landed back in her lap with a thud. But the days of believing God was approachable and concerned were long gone.

With a final rub to Lucy's head, Rebecca pushed off the couch and strode to the kitchen for a glass of water. What was she supposed to do now? Ben wasn't going away. She'd pushed, though she lacked the heart to be cruel like she'd been to guys in the past. This was Ben. The one person who knew her inside and out. Maybe a few things had changed over the years, but not enough to make that statement false. She closed her eyes and leaned against the sink. The truth was, she didn't want him to go away.

And that limited her options.

"Do you have plans for tonight?"

Rebecca chewed the inside of her cheek even as her heart leapt at the sound of Ben's voice. She didn't. Yet. That was mostly because Sara had been slammed with patients all morning, so they hadn't had a conversation about it nor had Rebecca had time to text Jen. "Not really."

Ben's voice brightened. "Would you like some?"

Her thoughts drifted to last night's kiss and sent tingles through her body. "What do you have in mind?"

"Dinner? Then something fun, I don't know, bowling?"

She laughed. When was the last time she'd been bowling? It had to be college. "You any good?"

"Ha. Not really. I'm not sure where that idea came from, to be honest. But it sounded good in my head. We could see if Jackson and Zach want to tag along, maybe Sara and Jen, too? If you want."

Did he sound hesitant? Rebecca signaled to her patient that she'd be right there and cleared her throat. "Why don't I check with the girls, you can talk to the guys and then text me where to meet you? I've gotta run. Bye."

She dropped her phone in the pocket of her scrubs and hurried across the room. "Hi, Mr. Jenkins. How are you feeling today?"

The man wasn't even in his fifties, but he prattled on about aches and pains like an eighty-year-old. How did his wife put up with it? Maybe she just didn't ask how he felt. Rebecca pasted on a smile and helped him through his exercises, ignoring his complaints. Did Ben want everyone to tag along? Or was he hoping she'd press to keep things just the two of them? What did she want, besides another bone-melting kiss?

Once she'd passed Mr. Jenkins off for his massage, she ducked into the staff room and grabbed Sara's arm.

"Hey. How'd you get Mr. Jenkins?"

Rebecca rolled her eyes. "I traded with Jack. He had to run out for an eye appointment. Everyone else asked who Jack was scheduled with before they'd agree to swap. Mr. Jenkins isn't too bad, I just tune him out."

Sara grinned. "That explains why he was getting peevish and loud. He can tell when you're not listening, you know."

Rebecca shrugged. The man needed to get a grip. He had a weak ankle, not a life-threatening illness. "Look, Ben called and asked if I had plans."

"Ooh. So Jen and I are on our own and you'll call us with details tomorrow, right?" Sara flipped open the folder on top of her stack and made a note.

"That's the thing. He said dinner, then was like maybe you two want to come and he'd ask his roommates. How am I supposed to respond to that?"

Sara moved to the next folder in the pile. "Did you blow him off when he first asked about dinner?"

Had she? "I don't know. He asked if I had plans. I said no. He asked if I wanted some and I asked what he had in mind. Is that blowing him off?"

"It's sure not jumping up and down, fluttering your eyelashes and saying, 'Oh Ben, of course I want to go out with you tonight.'" Sara shook her head. "Honestly. Have you not dated before? Guys have egos and you have to stroke them. Otherwise they get insecure and you end up on endless group dates."

Rebecca hunched her shoulders. "I like group dates."

"Sure. 'Cause you're always looking for reasons not to get too close to anyone. But this is Ben, not some random guy from church who thinks he might have a shot with you. You know, Ben, the love of your life, who you've been mooning over for ten years?"

"Mooning? I object to that term. Vigorously." Rebecca crossed her arms.

"Whatever. When you find reasons to push every guy away after two dates, maximum, because they're not Ben, you're mooning." Sarah sighed and closed the file, folding her hands on top of the stack. "Call him back. Tell him Jen and I are busy but that you'd still like to go out with him. And say go out, not hang out."

"What's the difference?"

"If you say hang out, his roommates can still tag along. Go out implies a date. Date implies two. Two makes it more likely that there'll be interesting details to share with us tomorrow." Heat burned Rebecca's cheeks. Sara narrowed her eyes. "Unless there are already details that you've somehow managed not to mention?"

Rebecca's mouth was a desert. She licked her lips and tried for a casual shrug. "He might have kissed me last night."

"Seriously? Why didn't you call us immediately? That's a rule. Maybe even a law. I'd have to look it up. Come on, scale of one to ten."

"Eighteen?"

Sara fanned herself. "I don't understand you. Go call him back and make a date. And if Jen and I don't get details, we're showing up at your house and sitting on you until you spill."

Rebecca laughed.

"Not joking." Sara stabbed a finger at Rebecca's chest. "Go call."

Rebecca rubbed sweaty palms on her jeans. It was just a date. Though something in the back of her mind capitalized the 'D', regardless of her stern mental reminders. Was it because Ben was picking her up at home? That was silly. It just made more sense to drive one car. Plus, she hadn't brought a change of clothes to work, and wearing scrubs out to dinner wasn't particularly delightful, no matter how comfortable they were.

"I'm being ridiculous, Mr. Tumnus."

The cat sat back on his haunches and studied her. Did she measure up? Or did he find her as ridiculous as she felt? Needing to do something, she dumped out their water bowl and refilled it at the sink.

"There you are. Fresh, cool water for his highness. Where's Lucy?"

Mr. Tumnus gave the feline equivalent of a shrug and jumped onto the counter.

"Get down. You know better." Rebecca scooped him up, rubbed his head, and set him back down on the floor. Chances were, he'd be right back up as soon as she left, but she could maintain the illusion that she was training them to stay off counters. The doorbell rang. "There he is. You be good while I'm gone. Okay?"

Rebecca checked her hair in the mirror by the door before pulling it open. Her heart exploded into a gallop when her eyes landed on Ben. He was dressed casually in jeans and a burnt-orange Henley, and he held a bunch of bright yellow sunflowers.

"These are for you."

"They're beautiful. So sunny and fun. Um. I should put them in water. You want to come in for a minute?"

"Sure." He stepped in and pushed the door shut. Mr. Tumnus and Lucy darted through the room, skidding to a stop and tumbling over one another. Ben laughed and squatted down, wiggling his fingers at the cats.

Rebecca shook her head as they danced over to him, arching their backs under his caresses. She knew how they felt. Where had that thought come from? Sheesh. She grabbed the mason jar she used as a vase on the rare occasions she bought flowers and filled it at the sink, one eye on Ben and the cats. They liked him. Maybe they were the kind of cats who liked everyone, but it still warmed her heart that they got along. If they did end up together, Tumnus and Lucy would...she nipped off the thought. Good grief. He brought her flowers and she was planning a wedding.

"There we go."

Ben stood and raised his eyebrows. "I'll get you a vase next time, too."

"I like my mason jar."

"It suits you. But a pretty vase is nice, too. Ready?"

Rebecca grabbed her purse from the counter and nodded.

"You two stay out of your mom's flowers. Got it?" Ben pointed at the cats who meowed and batted at his shoelaces. He offered his elbow as he opened the door.

Rebecca slid her hand through his arm. Why did such a simple thing feel so right?

24

"You look nice." Ben glanced over as he wound his way out of her neighborhood toward the highway. Nice didn't really begin to describe it, but it was probably the better choice of words. No need to come on too strong and scare her. It had taken so long to get her to agree to a date. He wasn't going to mess this up if he could help it.

"Thanks. Where are we going?"

Ben smiled. "How do you feel about surprises?"

"Um. Okay, I guess."

"Then it's a surprise."

She laughed and looked out her window. "Getting on the highway doesn't actually help me guess, does it?"

"Not around here. Hmm, we can play twenty questions if you want." Ben watched as she drummed her fingers on her leg. What was she thinking? Was that too silly? He wanted lighthearted, but maybe he should just tell her. It's not as if it was anything earth shattering. "I thought..."

"Hey. I haven't asked my first question yet." Rebecca's eyes sparkled. "All right, is it in Virginia?"

He nodded. "Yes."

She frowned. "That didn't narrow it down as much as I'd thought. It's been a while since I played this game."

Ben chuckled. "Me too. I wasn't actually serious."

"No, no, no. This was your idea. We're playing. Um...is it inside?"

"Ah. Good question. No." Ben steered onto the highway, manuevering into the lanes that would let him continue on I-395.

"Okay. See, now we're getting somewhere. Though I don't know of any outdoor bowling alleys."

"I didn't say we were bowling. That was just a suggestion, before all our friends bailed on us." Bailed wasn't really the right word. He'd pretty much told them they weren't invited anymore after she called him back. He hadn't misread her intentions, had he? No. He pushed that thought away. She would've said something about Sara and Jen if she'd wanted a group outing. Right? Last night...that kiss...it had to have meant as much to her as it had to him.

She inclined her head. "All right. So, outside in Virginia. Is it a restaurant patio?"

"No."

"Hmm. But we're eating, right?"

"Is that one of your questions?" He flipped on his turn signal and jammed down the gas pedal. He scooted in front of a car in the left lane and zipped around the practically broken-down car hobbling up the right lane not much faster than he could walk.

Rebecca clutched the door handle and nodded. "Yeah."

"Not sure it qualifies, but since I did ask you to dinner, I'll go ahead and answer: yes. That's four, by the way."

She rubbed her hands together. "Sixteen left. This should be easy."

He grinned. "Next question?"

"Is it a park?"

He sucked air through his teeth. "Difficult to answer. I'm going with yes."

"How do you not know if something's a park or not?"

"That's not a yes or no question."

She groaned. "Fine. Is there a playground?"

"Nope." Ben watched as she looked out the window. Would she figure it out by virtue of their location?

"Oh! I've got it. That place by the airport on the river? Are we going there?"

He snickered. "Can you be more specific?"

"Good grief, I don't know its name. That park. It's right at the end of the Reagan airport and the planes come down super low and it's like they're going to land on you. I love it there, though I don't go very often. I used to ride my bike up that bike path from Mount Vernon though and stop there to rest before heading back."

Ben nodded. "It's called Gravelly Point."

She clapped her hands. "What a great idea. Are we getting takeout?"

"I packed a picnic, it's in the back." His stomach clenched. Should he have gotten something fancier from a restaurant? His cooking skills weren't stellar, but they were decent. Especially when it came to picnic food. And he'd snagged the tub of artichoke dip Paige left in the fridge on Sunday. If Jackson hadn't eaten it by now, it was his own fault. That stuff was killer.

"Even better." Rebecca reached over and patted his leg. "Thank you. This is special."

He grabbed her hand and threaded his fingers through hers. "You're special."

He turned into the parking lot and found a space in one of the crowded rows. The grassy area was deserted, why so many cars?

"I guess people like to park here and go for a bike ride?" Rebecca pushed open her car door and stood, her gaze roving over the parking lot.

"Guess so. At least there aren't a ton of people eating. Come on, I like it over near the water." Ben grabbed a cooler out of the trunk before taking her hand. Did she feel the electricity? Chemistry wasn't everything, but it sure didn't hurt. In this case, it rounded out the friendship and general admiration he had for her as a person. Even if he wasn't entirely sure that the woman he knew was the real Rebecca, he was sure enough that he wanted to stick around and find out. She just didn't seem like someone who could pull off a deception of that level. Change her name? Sure. Hide the aspersions her father cast on her character? He could believe that, too. But present such a convincing personality that remained consistent with a ten year gap? No. He wouldn't believe it.

"This looks like a nice spot." Rebecca stood looking out over the Potomac River. "It's beautiful."

Ben set the cooler down and slipped his arms around her waist, leaning his cheek against hers. "So are you."

She turned in his arms and tilted her chin up to meet his gaze. "I want—need—you to know, I never forgot you."

He lowered his mouth to hers, a gentle, undemanding kiss that filled him with yearning. *I love you.* It was too soon to say the words again. He needed the truth, whatever it was, before he could say them aloud. But they were there, on the tip of his tongue. Instead, he stepped back and reached for the cooler. "Hungry?"

"I take it you had a good evening?" Zach hit pause on his game and grinned when Ben came in whistling.

"Yeah. Why aren't you out?" Ben sat and frowned at the game. "This new?"

Zach tossed the case for the game to Ben. "Picked it up after dinner. Jackson stayed to hang with Paige. I didn't feel like being a third wheel and my phone battery was dying, so I couldn't even just sit and play some mindless game. So I swung by the game store."

"Any good?"

"Eh, it's all right. Want to join in?"

Ben cocked his head to the side and studied his friend. "You okay, man?"

"I don't know. I'm restless, I guess. We seem to have a replay of Jackson and Paige with you and Rebecca. And I'm interested in Amy but the signals she puts out are so mixed they'd make a blender look boring. What's going to happen in the spring when the Garcias come back to the States and want their house back? You'll be married and living in Springfield, Jackson and Paige can live in her condo, and I'll be trying to bum a room of some random strangers at church."

"If you're lucky, you can find the perfect place where you can grow old and die alone." Ben shook his head as Zach snorted out a laugh.

"Fine. I'm having a pity party. So what?"

"Nothing. Long as you realize it. Why don't you ask Amy out? Put it on the line?" Ben tossed the game case on the coffee table and reached for the second controller.

Zach rubbed his neck. "I dunno. What happens when she says no? Then what?"

"When? What if she says yes? Isn't that even a remote possibility?"

"Yeah, I guess. I don't want to mess anything up. We work together. She's trying to get me to be involved in more stuff after school. I just..."

"You're scared." Ben clicked through the player options and selected a muscle-bound two-headed creature dressed in camouflage that strained at the seams.

"I'm..." Zach sighed. "Yeah I guess I am."

Ben punched Zach in the shoulder. "That's the price of romance, man. I've been in a state of nearly perpetual terror the past six weeks. But you know what? It's worth it. So far."

"And if it all falls apart, what then?"

Ben shrugged. It wasn't the scenario he wanted to explore, but the thought crossed his mind more often than it probably should. "Then I pick up the pieces. But at least I know I gave it my best shot and didn't pull any punches. Are we playing, or what?"

ELIZABETH MADDREY

25

Rebecca paced in front of Jerry's office door. He'd sent someone to get her five minutes ago, but he was still on the phone. It was unusual for him to have any calls this late in the evening. Frankly, it was unusual for him not to be on his way out, with Melissa taking over for the night. What was keeping him, and what could it possibly have to do with her?

D'Andre was struggling with his math. It probably had more to do with figuring out how to process his grief over losing Kira than the actual math problems, but still, Rebecca should be out there with him, not waiting in the hall like someone called into the principal's office.

Jerry pulled open his door and motioned for her to enter, closing the door behind him. "Have a seat, Rebecca."

She sat, her brows drawing together as she took in his frown and the deep furrows in his forehead. "What's going on?"

"I've been fielding calls all afternoon wanting me to verify that Becky MacDonald was a resident here."

She closed her eyes, her head shaking. "So I'm living homeless in D.C. now? At least when I was in rehab I got to be in Switzerland."

Jerry didn't smile. "Several board members received calls first. They referred the questions to me. I've tried to dodge, but I'm afraid the party line might have come across as an admission."

"The party line?"

"You know, we don't disclose the names of any of the people who utilize our facilities for any purpose." Jerry sighed. "And as much as they seemed satisfied with the answer, I know it's going to be reported. Someone got a photo of your mom, when she came to help."

ELIZABETH MADDREY

"And she was obviously coming to visit me, plead with me to return to the fold." Rebecca let out a breath that was half-groan. "I'm sorry, Jerry."

"I'm the one who's sorry. I think I made things worse for you by trying to protect your privacy. I just don't understand why this is such a big deal for people. It's been years since Becky MacDonald was any kind of news, why don't they let it go?"

Rebecca shrugged. Why wasn't this bothering her? Normally news like this would have her blood boiling and she'd be formulating a new exit strategy. But not today. "Don't worry about it."

He cleared his throat. "Here's the thing. The Board—and it's all the Board, not me—is worried that this is going to be negative publicity for the mission right before the open house. They want me to ask you to take a break from coming down here. Just in case people are watching, trying to get a shot of you coming or going."

Her heart sank. "But the kids..."

"I know. D'Andre in particular will take it hard. It's a double whammy for him, losing Kira, now you." Jerry stopped and cleared his throat again as he wiped his eyes. "I tried to fight it."

"It's okay. Thanks. Can I at least finish up tonight? Maybe if I explain...wait. How did the Board know I *was* here?"

Jerry winced. "I had to explain why your mom was here. Which led to explaining about you."

"And the donations?"

Jerry nodded.

Great. Just great. The one time she managed to do something that was anywhere close to her lifelong dream of helping people, someone has to try and twist it into ugliness. Maybe that was an overreaction. But honestly. Why did they need to know? She ran a hand through her hair. "All right. Well. I'm going to go finish helping D'Andre with his math and anyone else who needs it. Then I'll head home and...I guess you can let me know when it's okay to come back. What about the open house?"

"For now, if you can coordinate with Ben on your own, I'd appreciate it. The Board wants me to take it over, but I just don't have the time. Do you mind? I'll understand if you do. But..."

Jerry's face was hopeful. And nearly gaunt from grief and his usual workload. "No, that's fine. I'll keep you posted via email. I'm sorry, Jerry. Really sorry."

He shook his head and stood, rounding the desk. "Like I said, I'm the one who's sorry. You're an amazing asset to the mission, physically and financially, and I'm furious that the Board is more concerned with potential fallout based on decades old innuendo. But I couldn't get them to change their minds."

"I appreciate that you tried." Rebecca offered a wan smile as she turned and left the office.

Jen tucked her feet under her on Rebecca's couch and pulled Lucy onto her lap. "Wow. That's quite the capper to a Monday. What are you going to do?"

Rebecca dropped into a chair, running her hand down Mr. Tumnus' back when he jumped up. "Nothing. Stay away 'til Jerry gives me the all clear. What's there to do? If the Board thinks it's better for the mission, I don't want to go against that. Nor do I want to do anything that would hurt them. They do good, necessary work downtown. And none of that is about me or my involvement."

"Did he say what reporter? Don't take this the wrong way, but you're not really news these days."

Rebecca snickered. "I had the same thought. All I can figure is that the open house at the mission is news. Particularly since it's combined with Bread of Heaven. They're doing some write ups in the bigger papers to attract more attendees and, hopefully, donors. If they saw Mom and put things together, that would make an interesting side-piece. Maybe try to explain why B of H is involved? Famous pastor slash speaker enlists the aid of major non-profit to save daughter?"

"People have too much time on their hands." Jen frowned.

"Yeah, well. Can't change that either. All I can do is hope it blows over." Rebecca shook the cat hair off her hands as Tumnus hopped down and wandered off. "In the mean-time, I have more opportunity for hanging out on weeknights. That's a good thing, right?"

"Sure. Though are you sure it's only your girlfriends who are going to benefit from that time?" Jen opened her eyes wide and fluttered her eyelashes.

Heat seared Rebecca's face and neck. She cleared her throat and tried for nonchalant. "I don't know what you mean."

"Uh-huh. You promised us details. All you managed to say was that you went on a picnic and that he kissed you." Jen pointed a finger at Rebecca. "The red on your face suggests that those kisses were more than a chaste peck."

"Don't you and Sara talk behind my back? I already told her they were incredible." Rebecca stood and headed for the kitchen. "You need a soda or some water or something?"

Jen laughed. "Don't change the subject. I needed to hear it for myself. So..."

"So, nothing. I sat with him at church, which you know because you were there, too. We had lunch after church. Again, you were there. And I didn't talk to him yesterday, or today. He's texted a few times, but we were both busy." Rebecca shrugged and walked into the kitchen to fill a glass with water. She called over her shoulder, "But I'm hoping he'll call."

"Are you going to tell him everything?"

She was going to have to, wasn't she? She sauntered back into the room and plopped down on the chair. "I don't really feel like there's a choice anymore. And I'd pretty much decided I needed to do that already. This just escalates the time-table some. I wish I knew when the articles were going to print. And where."

"Better to tell him *before* that happens then have him figure it out and feel betrayed."

Rebecca swallowed. Betrayed. It was a harsh word. Accurate, but harsh. She nodded.

"So tell him tonight. I can go, you give him a call and lay it all out." Jen lifted her hands in the air, palms up. "Easy peasy."

Rebecca snorted. "Right. So simple. Besides…I think this is an in-person conversation. Don't you?"

"Yeah, I guess." Jen glanced at her watch. "I should run. I've got an early meeting tomorrow. Thanks for dinner and a chance to meet your cats. They're adorable."

"Thanks for coming." Rebecca pulled her friend into a tight hug. "I needed this."

"You know I'm always up for hanging out, right?"

Rebecca nodded.

Jen gathered her things and opened the door. "Go call Ben. At least get the ball rolling. Then call and tell me how it went. Or text. Or something."

"Go home, Jen." Rebecca chuckled and stood in the doorway while Jen walked to her car. She waved, watching until Jen's taillights disappeared around the corner.

With a sigh, she closed the door and flipped the locks. Her cell rang. Her heart raced off and she pictured Ben on the other end of the line.

"Hello?"

"Hi, Sweetie. It's Mom."

Rebecca deflated. "Oh. Hi."

Her mother laughed. "Well, that's one of the least enthusiastic greetings I've gotten in a while. What's wrong?"

"I'm sorry. I was hoping it was Ben." Rebecca turned off the lights on the main floor and started up the stairs. "I haven't talked to him since Sunday. I miss his voice."

"I'm so happy you two are dating."

Rebecca smiled. "I don't know that we can call it dating yet, Mom. We've gone out a few times. That's all."

"Mm-hmm. I'm sticking with dating. And I'm hoping the two of you move fast. You lost enough ground over the past ten years. When something's right, the way the two of you are right, you don't want to waste time dithering."

"How do you know we're right, Mom? You met him once. I don't even know he's right. Not really." Rebecca turned the water on in the bathroom to let it warm up so she could wash her face and get ready for bed.

"Oh, Becca. Yes you do. Stop over-thinking."

Rebecca sighed. Was her mom right? Maybe. Probably. "I'll try. Can I ask a random question?"

Eleanor chuckled. "Always. You just did, in fact."

"Ha. Ha. Have any reporters been asking Dad about me with all the press he's doing for the new book?" There was a long stretch of silence. "Mom? You there?"

Her mom sighed. "We weren't going to say anything. There've been a couple of calls this week from papers up near you, asking if we'll confirm your residence at a homeless shelter in the District. Oh, Honey, I'm sorry. Mostly your father has just been hanging up on them."

That was a pretty standard response. And not necessarily a bad one. If you didn't talk to reporters, they couldn't misquote you. But like with Jerry, in this case the response probably fed the beast rather than defusing it. She blinked back tears and plopped onto the closed toilet. "It's okay. This is all my own fault."

"It isn't, Becca. Don't worry about it. Roland's working on a statement. The publicist from the publisher wants him to give them a statement on Friday to use in a press release. He's going to admit that the stories he used in your teen years weren't about you, specifically, but were constructed to pose common parenting problems and his suggested solutions. If people go back and look, they'll see he never really said it was you. But he allowed it to be assumed. As did I. Though I can't see his publisher going through with the book if he does it."

"Mom. You can't let him do that. What about everything you've said these last years about how many people he's helped? The greater good, all that?" Hollowness spread out from her heart as the implications of her father's admission became clear. Even though it was what she'd always wanted...to have her dad lose everything, for *him* to end up in all the magazines with speculation running rampant...she couldn't do that to him. She couldn't let him do that to himself.

"I don't know, Bec, he's pretty adamant. He says they've gone after his daughter one too many times."

She shook her head. What a nightmare. "Friday. You said Friday, right?"

"Yeah. Friday morning at nine."

Rebecca squeezed the bridge of her nose. It was Tuesday night. She'd need to go to work tomorrow, rearrange her schedule, and get time off. "I'll be there Thursday. Don't let him talk to anyone about this until I get there. Please?"

"Becca, I don't understand. Isn't this what you always wanted?"

She let out a short laugh. "I thought so. Just...don't let him make any decisions 'til I'm home. Okay?"

"I'll do my best. Call me when you have your flight information."

ELIZABETH MADDREY

26

Ben sighed as Rebecca's voicemail picked up. Again. She got busy. It happened. But he really needed to talk to her.

"Hey, Rebecca, it's Ben. I've got a meeting tomorrow—that's Friday in case you don't get this right away—with my manager and, possibly, the head of Bread of Heaven about the open house. I don't know what's going on, but apparently, something's come up. They need you there too. Please call me back so I can get you details, maybe arrange to pick you up? After, could we get dinner? I...dang it, there's another call. Look, call me. Okay?"

He switched over to the incoming line. "Ben Taylor."

"Oh thank goodness. I've been trying to call you all day, but every time I think I have a minute, I get pulled away. Um, this is Rebecca."

He laughed. "Apparently we've been playing phone tag without realizing it. I just left you a message."

"Okay. I'll listen to it when we're done. Look, something's come up with my folks and I'm taking off tonight and heading to Texas. I'll probably be back on Saturday or Sunday. I don't actually have a return ticket yet, but I'm hoping for something this weekend."

His stomach dropped. "Are they okay? Is there something I can do?"

"No, no, they're okay physically. It's all...part of that big, complicated story. I need to run, but I didn't want to disappear without letting you know."

What about the meeting tomorrow? "Look, when you listen to the voicemail, just ignore it. The folks here want to have a meeting about the open house Friday. I'll give Jerry a call and see if he can come instead."

"That's...probably a good idea. Sorry."

He frowned. What was that in her voice? What was going on? "Are you okay?"

"I don't know yet. You could pray for me. For us."

"I'll do that. Will you let me know when you get there? Text me at least?"

"Yeah. And if you need to email or whatever about the open house, go ahead and do that. It's just Texas, not the end of the world." Her chuckle was strained. "I'm going to run. Take care, Ben."

"I'll see you when you're back."

"Mmm. Goodbye."

Ben ended the call, his chest tight, her goodbye echoing in his mind.

"Thanks for coming down, Jerry. I haven't been able to pry any information out of them about this, but with Rebecca out of town, I really thought someone needed to be here to represent the mission." Ben raked a hand through his hair. Other than a brief text last night after she landed, he hadn't heard from Rebecca. Of course, they were two hours behind in Texas, so it was just barely eight a.m. Maybe she was sleeping in and having a quiet breakfast with her parents. His stomach churned. There was something in the air and it had him on edge.

"I'm glad you thought to call me." Jerry glanced around Ben's office. "Are we meeting in here?"

Ben shook his head. "They told me they'd send someone to get us when they were ready."

"Are meetings always like that around here?"

"No." Ben tucked his hands in his pockets and focused on keeping his fingers from balling into fists. "It's very unusual."

Jerry nodded and mimicked Ben's pose. Minutes ticked by before the director's administrative assistant knocked on the door. "They're ready for you."

Why did it feel like he was marching to his doom? Ben gestured for Jerry to follow her and brought up the rear. Had he done something wrong? He hadn't been able to find anything that suggested two non-profits couldn't work together for a common goal. The accountants hadn't seen a problem, nor had legal. He walked into the conference room and his eyebrows lifted. The director sat at the head of the conference room. His manager, the head of PR, and the VP of Fundraising were already seated at the long, oval table.

"Ben. Thanks for joining us. This is...?"

Ben cleared his throat and introduced Jerry.

The director watched them as they sat then folded his hands on the table. "I appreciate you coming, Jerry. We received this message on Wednesday and feel like it's in everyone's best interest to clear it up before proceeding further with any association between Bread of Heaven and the mission."

The head of PR pushed a button and the screen on the far wall lit, displaying an email that had the draft of an article suggesting that Becky MacDonald was using the mission as a location for meeting up with underage lovers. After giving people a minute to read, she opened the attachment, which was a photo of the back of Rebecca, her arms around D'Andre, his tear-stained face barely visible above her shoulder.

"That's ridiculous." Ben shook his head. "I was there when that was taken. That boy is grieving the death of one of their volunteers."

"But is that Becky MacDonald? She has quite the reputation...if she's a resident there..."

Ben sighed. "That's Rebecca Fischer, a volunteer at the mission who I've been working with on the open house plans."

Heads swiveled to Jerry. "Is that true?"

"It looks like Rebecca, yes. And she is one of the volunteers who tutors the kids after school. D'Andre had been working with my god-daughter, Kira, before she passed away. He's taken it hard. I imagine, if this photographer wanted, they could have taken a picture of just about every volunteer, and at least half of the residents, comforting D'Andre over the last two weeks."

"Hmm. So Becky MacDonald isn't a resident at the mission?" The director drummed his fingers on the conference table.

"That's correct." Jerry clasped his hands together. Ben noted his knuckles turning white. Hopefully that went unnoticed by everyone else at the table. Still, it meant Jerry knew the truth and was protecting Rebecca as well.

"All right. That's all we needed to know. We get enough correspondence from whack-a-doodles, we'll file this along with it and let legal know. Thanks." The director nodded a dismissal.

Ben ushered Jerry back to his office and shut the door. "You know."

Jerry nodded. "I'm surprised you do. She told you?"

Ben let out a mirthless laugh. "No. I did some digging. I guess it stands to reason that if I could piece it together, so could anyone. Though it wasn't until the church magazine spotlighted her mom that I got curious."

"Her mom visited the mission, too. I wonder if that's what started this. Our Board made it clear that Rebecca isn't to volunteer anymore until this blows over. If it does."

Ben paced the length of his office. "I don't understand why this is coming up. I mean really, who cares? It's not as if she's a Hollywood starlet. And to be honest, her dad's not even an A-list speaker in church circles anymore."

"I don't know. Did she say anything about why she went to Texas?"

"No. But she doesn't know I know."

Jerry's jaw dropped. "Oh. That...complicates things."

Ben sighed and perched on the edge of his desk. "I wanted— want—her to tell me."

"I can see that." Jerry crossed to Ben's window and looked out. "I should get back downtown. I'm going to call Rebecca and tell her about the meeting. She knows I know...and I think it's important she realize that this has spread beyond the mission."

Ben nodded. When Jerry had left, he sat back down at his desk and stared at his monitor. After a few minutes, he browsed through the contacts on his phone and opened up an email.

ELIZABETH MADDREY

27

Rebecca sat in her parent's living room and studied her father. He looked older. Even older than he'd looked when he was in D.C. Her heart ached. Had she done this to him somehow? "Dad? Are you okay?"

"I'll be fine, Sweetheart. I'm sorry you flew all the way out here, though it's always good to have you come visit. But I'm afraid you're not going to change my mind. This is what I should've done years ago. The first time someone assumed I was talking about you in my examples. I didn't set the record straight. And then it went on from there, like it had developed a life of its own. I know I've apologized before, but I need to say it again. I'm sorry. And I hope you'll be able, someday, to forgive me."

The wall she'd built around her heart cracked. "I do, Dad. I can't say we're back on the same ground that we were before. But I forgive you."

He smiled. "Then that's all I need. The rest will come."

"Here's the thing, Dad. I can't let you throw your career away."

"No, Becca just..."

"Just let me talk, okay? Look. I ran for years, changed who I was—at least on the outside—and it hasn't done anything except keep me looking over my shoulder. People still think horrible things about me. They still write articles wondering what kind of mischief I'm getting into these days. If you go out and say it was all made up, that's not going to stop."

"Sure it will."

"No, Dad. It won't. They'll think it's some last-ditch effort by a father to save his daughter. They found me. In D.C. at the mission. They think I'm living there homeless, but when Mom came to help, they put two and two together. So you making a statement now, when this is all about to break? It's not going to do anything but make you look stupid."

Her father's shoulders sank. "So, what...we do nothing?"

Eleanor strode into the room, trailed by a man in a business suit. "Honey. Steve's here."

"Steve." Roland nodded and gestured to Rebecca. "This is my daughter, Rebecca. Rebecca, this is Steve, the publicist from my publisher."

"You're here." Steve scratched his chin and looked at Roland. "I thought she was in rehab overseas."

Rebecca laughed. "You need to stop reading tabloids, Steve. I've actually never been overseas. Not once, in my whole life. But it's on my to-do list."

Steve ducked his head, pink tingeing his cheeks. "Sorry."

"Don't be. I came because Dad was saying you all wanted him to prepare a statement and I think, really, the better idea is for me to give you one."

"Becca."

"Daddy." Rebecca shook her head as her heart leapt. She hadn't thought of him as daddy in over a decade. For it to just slip out...maybe true forgiveness would be possible after all. "So here it is; you should probably take notes."

Steve took out his phone set it on the table. "Okay if I record it? That'll make transcription easier."

"Sure." Rebecca took a deep breath. She was doing this. It wasn't as if there was anything people didn't already think. "When I left for college, with the permission and understanding of my parents, I legally changed my name so that I could get a fresh start and work to live a life that was free from the stigma of the past. A new life that would be honoring to God. I have never used drugs or been in rehab, despite speculation in the press. If anyone had bothered to ask my parents, they would have received confirmation that those reports were untrue. I completed a Master's degree and am now working as a physical therapist. I also volunteer at a homeless shelter, working primarily with disadvantaged youth as a tutor, though I also help, as necessary, with food distribution from their food bank. I have also set up a foundation that uses the annual distributions of the trust fund my parents created for me to help support this ministry. At no time have I ever personally benefitted financially from this trust, though it would be within my rights to do so. At this time, I would ask that people allow me to live my life without the constant reminders of the past or wrongful speculation."

"That's it?" Steve reached for his phone.

"It's enough, isn't it?" Rebecca shrugged and turned to look at her father. Tears ran down his face and he held out his arms. She walked into them, her heart filling with the warmth of his embrace.

"Should be. I'll go get this put into a press release. Hopefully it'll squelch whatever has started the latest round of interest in you and let you get back to what was your anonymous life." Steve smiled and headed for the door. "I can show myself out."

"Becca, dear, you didn't explain." Eleanor's arms wrapped around her from the other side, making her the middle of a parent sandwich. She smiled. They'd hugged like this all the time when she was younger. The sense of belonging was almost tangible.

"Why should I? They drew their conclusions a long time ago. I also didn't admit to anything. If they want to read that as confirmation of my malfeasance, then so be it." Rebecca sighed. "I want a future with Ben—or at least the possibility of one. I can't have that if I can't be honest with him. About everything. He's more important than my pride."

Rebecca shuffled down the jetway, shoulders slumped. She dragged her small rolling bag behind her. Home. She just wanted to get home, pet her cats, and sleep for...oh, a week should be long enough. Why did air travel suck the life out of you? It was one of those mysteries. Of course, Sara and Jen both said it invigorated them, so maybe it was just her. Either way, if she didn't have to get on an airplane again for another year or two, she wasn't going to complain. Thanksgiving. Christmas. Ugh. Maybe she could talk her parents into coming East? Or she could drive. Though twenty-whatever hours in the car wasn't any better.

"Welcome home, Rebecca."

She stopped and looked up, blinking. Her ruminations had taken her out of the gate area, past security. Her heart thundered in her chest. "Ben?"

He grinned and held out the bouquet of deep red roses that were in his arms. "How was your flight?"

"How did...who...what are you doing here?" She reached for the flowers and buried her nose in them. These were real flowers, no hot-house beauties, but blossoms with a sweet scent. Where had he found them in the fall?

"I asked Sara. It wasn't hard to convince her to share the details. Was she not supposed to?"

Rebecca shook her head. "No, it's fine. I just...I have my car."

"I took the Metro. I'm kind of hoping I can catch a ride home, maybe take you to dinner as payment?" Ben closed the distance between them and looped his arms around her waist. He lowered his head so their foreheads touched. "I missed you. I realize it's ridiculous, you were only gone two days. But you'd been so busy all week..."

She angled her head, pressing her lips briefly to his. Even with the brief contact, shivers raced through her. "You're the most amazing man."

"Is that a yes?"

She laughed, nodding as she stepped back. "Yes. I might even let you drive. And I don't let anyone drive my car."

He flashed a grin and reached for the handle of her rolling bag. "Is this it, or do you have something checked?"

"That's it. I've never been one of those women who has to travel with seventeen extra outfits just in case." She wove her fingers though his. "The car's in the garage."

They strode through the mostly empty check-in area and up the ramp to the garage elevators, chatting about inconsequential things. Rebecca's heart settled back into its normal rhythm, though the electricity from their joined hands was a constant current running up her arm.

"Are you hungry?" Ben lifted the suitcase into the trunk of her car.

Rebecca shook her head and tossed him the keys. "Not really. Sorry. But I'll still let you drive."

He chuckled, nipping the keys out of the air. "I'll get you home then. I'm glad you're back."

She settled into the passenger seat then paused with the seatbelt stretched half-way. "How will you get home?"

"You're not far from the Springfield Metro. I'll walk over, hop on, and have one of my roommates come get me at Dunn Loring. Easy." He reached over and rubbed her knee. "Don't worry about it."

Rebecca snapped her mouth shut. She should object—drive him home, drop him off, and then head the rest of the way to her house but...weight settled on her shoulders. Too much effort. If he didn't mind, she wasn't going to. "You're sure?"

"Absolutely." Ben glanced over at her before starting the car. "Did you talk to Jerry at all?"

She took a deep breath. The car wasn't where she'd pictured having this conversation. She hadn't actually gotten as far as picturing a location for the conversation—she'd only envisioned it would have to take place soon. Whenever soon translated to. "Not since before I left...why? Something happen at the meeting on Friday?"

"There's some odd stuff going on. Basically, my boss wanted to know if anyone had been in contact with the mission directly with weird accusations that could lead to bad publicity for all of us. I think Jerry got it all cleared up. He seemed to think he had, at least. And the responses to the open house invites keep rolling in. It really looks like we're going to have a massive turn out. Hopefully they won't all show up at one time."

Now she was going to have to call Jerry and find out what was going on. She'd hoped to give him, and the mission, some time. Had no one picked up the press release? Steve had sounded so sure that once the publisher put it out there, new outlets would snap it up and the situation would disappear. Of course, in some ways it was good that no one was reporting it, since she hadn't talked to Ben about it. She really needed to do that before he read it somewhere else. "That's great. On both fronts. Are you busy tomorrow after church?"

Ben shook his head and eased over a lane to avoid all the merging traffic.

"I'm probably going to sleep in. But do you want to come for lunch? I picked up some chilies while I was in Texas. I thought I might make enchiladas."

"You can make them?"

She laughed. "I can. And frequently do. But with the chilies, I can even make the sauce from scratch instead of using canned."

"What time?" He flipped on the turn signal and took the cloverleaf for the exit much faster than she usually did.

"Say noon? Maybe you could bring something for dessert?"

"Deal. My mouth's going to be watering all night."

"Well, just try not to drown in your sleep, okay?"

He snickered and slowed for the turn into her neighborhood. Everything looked the same as it had when she left. And yet, it was as if she was seeing it for the first time, as some kind of amalgam of Becky and Rebecca. Had she locked a part of herself away when she changed her name? Or was it simply the freedom that came from having forgiven her father?

Ben pulled into her parking spot and cut the engine. "I'm really glad you're home."

"Me too." Rebecca unbuckled her seatbelt and pushed open the door.

Ben got out and gathered her suitcase, clicking the lock on her key fob as he carried it up the two steps to her townhouse. He handed her the keys and set down the bag before taking her face in his hands and pressing a long, bone-melting kiss to her lips.

When he eased back, he tucked his hands in his pockets, one side of his mouth quirking up. "Go inside and get some sleep. I'll see you tomorrow for lunch."

"Okay. Ben night. Erm, 'night, Ben." Heat crept across her cheeks. Had he kissed her so completely senseless that she was mixing up her words? She fumbled the keys in the lock before finally managing it. Ben reached around her to put her suitcase inside the door then stepped back. Rebecca hovered in the door for a minute, just looking at him. "See you tomorrow."

Rebecca closed the door and flipped the locks, then hurried to the front window to watch him leave. Ben stood for a minute on her stoop before he turned and sauntered down the sidewalk toward the Metro. She sighed and let the curtain fall over the blinds. Home. And Ben. Maybe all the pieces of her life were finally coming together.

28

Ben clutched the bottle of sparkling cider and hesitated on Rebecca's doorstep. Should he have brought flowers instead? Wine? He wrinkled his nose. Not wine. Not only did he not know her feelings about drinking, it wasn't something he particularly enjoyed. And showing up with a bottle seemed...pretentious. Maybe chocolate? He frowned. Should he stash the cider in his car and take it home? Without a doubt, Jackson and Zach would drink it.

The door jerked open. Muttering to herself, Rebecca stepped out and crashed into him. "Oh. Hi. You're here."

Heat swamped him. "Yeah. Just. Everything okay?"

"I realized all I have in the house to drink is water and the enchilada sauce turned out a tad spicier than is probably going to fly with you so I was going to run out and..."

He held up the bottle of apple cider. "This work?"

"You're a life saver." Rebecca chuckled and pushed the door open. "Come on in."

"Smells amazing. And, for the record, I still like spicy." Ben set the bottle down on the kitchen counter. "Can I do anything to help?"

Rebecca pressed her lips together and studied him before she nodded. "Do you mind setting the table?"

"Nope. Just point me in the right direction."

Rebecca opened a drawer and the cabinet directly above it, revealing silverware, plates, and glasses. "Napkins are already on the table. I thought we could eat at the actual dining room table. I hardly ever get the chance. Most of the time it's the coffee table. Or, if Sara and Jen are over...still the coffee table."

He chuckled and collected two place settings, bumping the drawer closed with his hip. What would it be like to be able to cook a meal that smelled this good? He could get around in the kitchen well enough not to hurt himself or poison someone. But enchiladas? Not happening unless it was throwing a pan of frozen ones into the oven. Which wasn't necessarily a bad way to go. There were some tasty options available in the frozen dinner aisle.

Rebecca came in as he finished arranging the second set of silverware. She set a bubbling dish of enchiladas, smothered in dark red sauce, on the trivet between their plates. "I have a little salad, too. Let me grab it and we'll be set. Go ahead and sit."

Should he sit at the head of the table or the side? He'd set the two places next to each other because it seemed cozier. Should he have put them across from one another? Shaking his head, he pulled out the side chair. It was ridiculous to be in a lather over where he sat. Or the apple cider. But she'd said she wanted to talk to him and it was either a good thing or ominous. He was focusing on the positive.

Rebecca set the salad down and sat before she took his hand. "Will you bless the food?"

Ben squeezed her fingers and said a quick, but heartfelt, prayer. "This looks amazing."

"Dig in." Rebecca reached for the salad bowl.

Ben scooped two enchiladas dripping with sauce and cheese onto his plate then held out his hand for hers. "Switch?"

When they both had food, Rebecca put her napkin in her lap, folded her hands, and cleared her throat. "So. Here's the thing."

The mouthful of savory spices in his mouth turned to dust. He swallowed, the previously amazing enchilada. It hit his stomach with a thud. "Okay?"

"It's not bad. Or, not all bad?" She blew out a breath and offered a weak smile. "You know how I went by Marie when we were at camp?"

He nodded, tense muscles relaxing. She was finally going to tell him the truth. All of it, hopefully. He stabbed another bite, savoring the flavors as they cascaded over his tongue.

"So, that is my middle name. Rebecca Marie...MacDonald." She winced as she watched him.

He took a sip of the apple cider. "Okay?"

Rebecca drew her eyebrows together. "Don't you...Becky MacDonald? The girl every Christian mother of our generation held up as an example of what not to do?"

"Yeah, I guess I remember a few stories. But that's not you now, right? It wasn't you at camp, either." He shrugged.

She cocked her head to the side and pursed her lips. "You already knew."

Ben set down his fork. It wasn't a question. In fact, it sounded a lot more like an accusation. In these situations, particularly with women, less was usually more. "Yeah."

"How? Did Jerry tell you?" Sparks shot from her eyes.

Ben shook his head and held up a hand. "No. No one told me. I figured it out on my own. Your mom is a very lovely, very distinctive looking woman. That article..."

Rebecca hissed out a breath. "That article. I could kill someone."

"That's a bit extreme, isn't it? Anyway, it got me wondering, so I did a little digging and put two and two together." No need to mention Colin's very brief involvement. If the set of her jaw was any indication, it wouldn't go over well.

"Why didn't you say something?" She crossed her arms and pinned him with a glare.

So many different reasons. Did he have to explain them all? Better to stick with the most important one. "I wanted you to tell me."

Rebecca blinked, her eyes shimmering with unshed tears. "I guess that makes sense. But if I'd known you knew, it would've made these last few weeks easier."

One corner of his mouth quirked up. "Love isn't always easy. It isn't supposed to be."

Her laugh bordered on hysterics.

"What?" Ben frowned. "I love you, Rebecca. I have since camp. I've wanted to say it to you for weeks now, but I also knew I couldn't do that until you told me the truth. On your own."

She shook her head. "I never suspected you knew. What else are you hiding?"

What was he hiding? His stomach churned and he scooted his chair back from the table. This wasn't exactly what he'd been expecting after his declaration of love. Or what he'd hoped for. "What are you saying?"

"Let's see, you invade my privacy then keep secrets from me, I think it's pretty clear what I'm saying. You said you needed to hear me tell you the truth, well you got it. I'd like the same from you."

Ben's blood pounded in his veins. He dabbed his mouth with his napkin before setting it on the table and standing. "You know what? I've never hidden anything from you. I didn't ask about your name change because it was your story to tell, even though I knew there could never be anything between us until we had honesty. Maybe I shouldn't have looked into it, but what was I supposed to do when you pushed me aside with all your 'it's complicated' nonsense? But I'm sorry. I'm sorry I cared enough to try and figure out a way that we could be together. And I'm sorry it bothers you that I don't care about your supposed past which, for the record, I don't believe. Anyone who paid attention could see that your Dad never actually mentioned you by name. Thanks for lunch. I'll see you around."

"Ben..."

He shook his head and strode out the door. How had this become about him? On what planet had he done anything wrong?

"Let me get this straight. She told you her not-so-secret secret, you told her you loved her and she got mad that you already knew." Zach dipped his hand into a bag of corn chips.

"That about sums it up, yeah." Ben sighed and reached for the bag. "And on top of all that, those enchiladas were killer and I only got like six bites."

Zach snickered. "Yeah, I'm sure that's what you're upset about."

"It's easier than focusing on the fact that I bared my soul and she didn't even blink."

"I can see that. So what are you going to do?" Zach spun the bag back to grab another handful of chips.

"I don't know. Pray about it. I'm not sure I can just jump back in for a third—fourth?—time? I mean, really, at some point don't you move on? Don't you have to?" Ben dropped his head on the table. "Whether you want to or not?"

29

"You did what?" Sara thumped down on Rebecca's couch and stared at her friend, mouth agape.

Rebecca sat in the chair opposite and wrapped her arms around her knees. Sara was supposed to have understood. Why didn't she? "Someone leaked all this to the press. That's why I got asked not to come back to the mission, why I had to go and talk to my dad, make that statement. If that hadn't happened..."

"You'd still be trussed up in your lie, letting the best thing that ever happened to you slip through your fingers. Honestly, Rebecca. The man tells you he loves you and you accuse him of keeping secrets?"

Put that way...she hunched her shoulders. "But he knew, Sara. The whole time. So who's to say it wasn't him that tipped off a reporter?"

"If you believe that, even for a second, you're an idiot."

Jen burst through the door. "Sorry it took so long, traffic is nuts. I don't know where everyone thinks they're going on a Sunday afternoon, but it's making it hard for those of us who actually do have places to be. What'd I miss?"

"Ben came for lunch. Rebecca told him the truth. Being an enterprising sort and not a moron, he'd already pieced it together. Since he didn't get upset and storm off, Rebecca then accused him of hiding secrets until he did finally storm off. After telling her he loved her, mind you. Now she's accusing him of being the leak that got her name back in the sidebars of obscure magazines." Sara patted the seat next to her on the couch.

Jen sat and blew out a breath. "Please tell me that was exaggerated."

Rebecca shook her head. "Why don't you guys get it?"

"You can't honestly think it's Ben. It could just as easily have been me or Sara. Or Jerry. Didn't you say he knew?" Jen kicked off her shoes and crossed her legs.

Jerry. He was a possibility she hadn't considered. But she knew him well enough...and he'd been open about the fact that he'd put it together. No. It couldn't be Jerry. Rebecca shook her head. "I've known Jerry long enough to trust him. Same with you two. It has to be Ben."

Jen sighed. "Gee thanks. Didn't Jerry tell you at the mission? Couldn't someone completely unrelated have overheard? Or the Board? Did he tell them?"

"He said he didn't." Rebecca chewed on her lower lip as other possibilities presented themselves. The walls at the mission weren't particularly sound proof. He'd closed the door...but if someone had been in the hall, they could've easily overheard. "Say someone did overhear, what possible benefit could there be to telling someone?"

"Money? Jealousy? Anger?" Sara ticked off the options on her fingers as she said them.

Other than money, none of them made sense. Rebecca got along well with the people at the mission. Sure, there were little things now and then when she didn't like how things were organized. And yeah, Jerry took her suggestions seriously more often than not. Was that because of her donations? She didn't want her ideas put into place simply because of her money. She'd have to ask Jerry about that. "I guess money's a possibility. But I just don't think it's likely."

"Even if it's not likely, it's possible. And, in my mind, more probable than it being Ben." Jen looked at Sara. "Isn't there something about innocent until proven guilty?"

"Oh, ha, ha." Rebecca frowned. "Like either of you would have done any differently in the same situation."

"Uh, yeah we would've. Have you *looked* at him? Plus he's a Christian. He's kind."

"Gentlemanly." Jen piped up, nudging Sara with her elbow. "And did she tell you about the kisses? Being a good kisser can make up for all kinds of other failings."

"Mmm. It's true." Sara angled her head to the side. "What are you going to do?"

Other than find new best friends? "I don't know. I'm still not convinced that I'm wrong."

"Then that's where I'd start."

Rebecca looked at Jen. "What do you mean?"

"If you want to be sure it's Ben, then you need to rule out the other options."

It wasn't a terrible idea. Not a great one, either. But not terrible. "And how, exactly, do you propose I do that?"

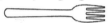

"Thanks for meeting me, Jerry." Rebecca cradled her cup of coffee between her hands.

"Of course. What can I do for you?" Jerry sat across from her at the tiny table in the jammed coffee shop a few blocks away from the mission, just on the edge of the business area in the city.

She rubbed the back of her neck. Where was she supposed to start? "I was wondering if you'd mentioned to anyone what you found out about me."

"No...I didn't see any reason for people to know. And I figured if you went to such lengths to hide it, then you probably didn't want just anyone to hear about it. Why?"

Rebecca sipped her drink. It was what she'd expected him to say. Was that because she believed him or because he obviously wouldn't admit to having spread the word after she'd asked him not tell? The lines were blurred. Who was she supposed to trust? She'd known Ben for a summer ten years ago and a few months now. And yet...she wanted to trust him. Still, look at her dad, she'd trusted him...and wasn't going back down that road. She'd forgiven him, she wasn't going to hold on to the hurt. She wasn't. So. Jerry or Ben? Or both? "Do you think there's any way someone could have overheard you talking to me about it?"

"Yeah, I guess. What's this about?"

"I'm trying to figure out how I got tracked down to the mission. I just don't understand the sudden interest."

"Ah. Ben told you about the meeting at Bread of Heaven, I take it? I'll tell you what, you've got a champion in him. He nipped any negative aspersions right in the bud and made it very clear they weren't going to fly. I think if he hadn't been so thorough they would have tried to back out of the open house. At this point, there aren't any objections from them about your involvement. And I'm using that to try and convince the Board that you're a needed part of the ministry. The kids miss you."

Ben had stood up for her? Before she'd told him the truth? In fact, he hadn't asked any questions yesterday. She'd been prepared to argue, to have to convince him that the stories weren't true. Why did he just accept her word? Did she dare do the same? "I miss them, too. I appreciate you talking to the Board, Jerry. But if they don't want me, maybe it's better if I stay away."

The color drained from Jerry's face. "No. Rebecca, you're..."

"Don't worry, I'll still give. You don't have to worry about the funding."

"That's not what I meant." He looked down at the table. "Not entirely, at least."

She gave a wry chuckle. "I know how tight the budget is, Jerry. I'm not going to take the support away. But maybe it's time for me to find another way to use my free time."

Jerry's eyes searched her face. "I still consider you a valuable member of the team."

"Thanks. That means a lot. Maybe down the road I can figure a way to come back. But for now, I think it's better if I make a clean break."

"What about the open house? I really don't have time to be in charge of it on top of everything else. Ben's already been flooding me with email this morning."

Her chest constricted. Had he just assumed she wouldn't keep working with him? "Are you sure the Board won't mind?"

"They said to get the work done. Since I can't handle it, it's up to me to delegate. They don't need to know. Plus, you've put in so much effort already, you should get to see it through to the end. Please?"

She sighed. "I'll talk to Ben. If he's still willing to work with me, then fine."

"Why wouldn't he be? If that boy's not in love with you, he will be soon. And having spent a little more time with him on Friday, for what it's worth, I think the two of you would be great together."

His words were like a knife twisting in her heart. He wasn't the first to say it—hadn't her mom, Sara, and Jen all made the same comment? So why did it suddenly matter? She flicked the corner of the paper heat shield on her coffee cup. Why did trusting someone take so much effort? She managed a slight smile. "Thanks. Things are complicated."

Jerry scoffed. "That's life. And love is maybe more complicated than anything else. At least if it's worth your time it is. I never pegged you as someone who was looking for the easy way out, not when you work so hard with the kids at the mission to help them succeed and give them a chance to rise above the scant opportunities they have. Don't wuss out and think that if it's not something you can control one hundred percent that it's not worth your time. Why not step back and give the complicated part to God, see what He does with it?"

"I'm not..." Rebecca stopped and pressed her lips together as reality crystallized. Letting go had never been her strong suit. "All right. I'll see what I can do."

"Atta girl." Jerry patted her hand as he stood. "Now, I need to get back to the mission. Let me know what last minute things you need from me for the open house, but otherwise, I'm going to be counting on you to handle it."

She watched him leave, the coffee in her stomach turning to acid. Handle it. Which meant Ben. Which meant...humble pie. Rebecca blew out a breath. Better to get it over with than have it hang over her head.

"Knock knock. Got a minute?" Rebecca held her breath as Ben looked up from his computer monitor. His eyebrows lifted as a mix of expressions flitted across his face before finally settling into a mask of polite welcome.

"I guess. Come on in. Did we have an appointment?"

Her heart sank. He was so stiff and formal. Clearly irritated, not without a good reason, but it didn't make apologizing any easier. Rebecca trudged in and perched on the edge of one of the chairs facing his desk. "You know we didn't. I...came to apologize."

"Ah. Maybe it'd be better to save that conversation for a time when I'm not at work." Ben shifted his attention back to his monitor.

He might have meant it as a dismissal, but Rebecca wasn't buying. She bristled then took a deep breath and reminded herself to stay calm. It wasn't going to help anyone if she let him push her buttons. "Maybe. But I'm here now, and I'd just as soon go ahead and say it. I'm sorry, Ben, for not trusting you from the beginning. I don't imagine you'll believe me, but I almost told you my real name a thousand times when we were at camp. And then, when you came for physical therapy, it was like a dream. Or a nightmare. I should have told you right away. I'm sorry I didn't. And more, I'm sorry for yesterday. All of it."

"Don't be sorry for the enchiladas, they were fantastic." Did she see the barest hint of a gleam in his eye? At least his tone had thawed. A little.

The tightness in her chest loosened. She swallowed. "Can you—will you—forgive me? Please?"

He held her gaze for several long heartbeats before nodding. "Yeah. I spent most of last night and this morning trying to convince myself to move on. I didn't make much headway. All I really managed was to spend a lot of time thinking about and praying for you. I was going to wait and call on Wednesday. Maybe Thursday."

She laughed, the tension in her muscles easing. "I'm glad I came by today...I would've been a wreck by then. I love you, Ben Taylor."

A slow smile spread over his face, morphing into a goofy grin as he stood and walked around his desk. He pushed his office door shut before tugging her into his arms. It was like being wrapped in a toasty blanket, snug, comfy. Home. He touched his forehead to hers. "You have no idea how good it is to hear you say that. I love you, Rebecca."

She rose to her tiptoes and pressed her lips to his in a chaste kiss that still had her nerve endings on fire before she eased back. He kept his arms looped loosely around her waist. "So."

He laughed. "So?"

"Since I'm here, is there anything I need to know about the fundraiser?"

Ben searched her face. "You talked to Jerry."

She nodded.

"He told you about Friday."

She nodded again.

"I wanted to tell you, but..."

"I hadn't told you who I was yet. I'm not mad. I was. But I'm not anymore. He told me you stood up for me. Thank you. I can't remember the last time someone did that."

Ben shook his head and released her, moving back around his desk to sit. "You need to read your father's interview more carefully."

She frowned. "What do you mean? I read them."

"Take some time tonight and give them another look. I think you'll find he's your biggest champion."

Dad? Clearly Ben was seeing something she didn't. Never hurt to look, though she didn't believe she'd find anything she wasn't expecting. Still, maybe it would give her another lead to chase to figure out who told the press she was at the mission. "All right."

"I think the open house is under control." Ben paused and cleared his throat. "Since we're working on openness and honesty here, I emailed a friend of Jackson's who has some fairly impressive computer skills to ask if he could dig around, see if he might find any ideas where the press got info about you being in D.C."

Rebecca raised her eyebrows. "Why?"

"I figured if I could help you find the real culprit, then maybe you'd forgive me."

She snickered. "Culprit seems a bit harsh, but the idea is nice. Has he gotten back to you?"

"He's chasing a few leads, but apparently thinks he might be on to something. Does the name...hang on..." Ben grabbed his phone and swiped the screen several times. "Carl Perkins mean anything to you?"

"Maybe. There was a guy at my high school named Carl. I don't really know his last name. He was a jock. Star quarterback. Played basketball and lacrosse, too. Dated anyone who'd go out with him. And I use the term 'dated' loosely. I think his reputation might even have been worse than mine. And his was real."

"Hmm. Can you find out his last name?"

"I've got my yearbooks at home. But what possible reason could he have?"

"I don't know. It's just a trail Colin's following. I'll keep you posted."

She smiled and leaned across the desk to kiss him. "Do that."

30

Ben tucked his hands in his pockets and bounced up and down on the balls of his feet. What was taking Zach and Jackson so long? It wasn't that he couldn't do this on his own but...he needed advice. Maybe this was stupid. Too fast. Too...something. He pulled out his phone. He'd call them and tell them just to forget it.

"Hey. Traffic is insane. What's so important that we had to do this right now?" Jackson's gaze drifted to the sign above the store they stood in front of and paused. "Uh...Ben?"

Zach let out a low whistle. "Look at those. Hey, isn't this the same place you got Paige her ring?"

"Yeah. Which begs the question...why are we here?"

Ben pushed his shoulders back, stretching the suddenly too-tight muscles. "I was thinking I might be purchasing something for Rebecca, and I wanted outside opinions."

"Dude." Zach shook his head. "After yesterday's lunch? I thought you were figuring out a way to move on?"

"I was. But she came to my office and apologized. She said she loves me. I can't turn away from that—from her. She's the one. It feels right, here." Ben thumped his chest, then his head. "And here. With as much prayer as I've put into this relationship over the past ten years, let alone these last two months, if this isn't what God wants, then He's either going to need to thwack me upside the head so I hear Him or I have no idea how to hear His still, small voice."

"Works for me." Jackson shrugged. "Let's go in and have a look. And you can tell us about Rebecca's visit to your office."

Ben tugged open the door. "There's not a lot to tell, though she's also trying to figure out who would've spilled the beans. I told her I'd emailed Colin and he's got a possible lead he's researching. She's going to look through her yearbooks to see if she can figure out why this particular guy would care about her. So it's not a long-time boyfriend or anything. I was kind of hoping it would be that easy. You know?"

"What can I help you gentlemen with?" The shopkeeper's eyes landed on Jackson and he grinned. "Here to pick out a wedding band?"

Jackson chuckled. "I haven't asked her yet, actually. No, this is my friend Ben who was, apparently, so impressed by my taste in jewelry that he's here on his own accord."

"Well then, let's see what we can find. Tell me about your young woman."

Ben took a deep breath. Where should he start? "She's got a heart the size of the ocean, though she thinks she hides it. She's smart and dedicated and a fighter."

"Hmmm." The man tapped his lower lip. "I have an idea. Just one moment, it's in the back."

Zack looked up from his study of a case of watches. "How much do you think the reporter paid the guy for the tip?"

"Why would that matter?" Ben slid his fingers over the glass cases, the glare from some of the rings causing him to blink. Rebecca was understated...should he have mentioned that? One of these huge rocks wasn't going to work for her. Or did she want that? Should he have brought her along or did that spoil the surprise? Was a surprise even a good thing in this situation?

"Seems to me it'd help narrow down your suspect list. If it's just a little money, then that wasn't the motivation, but if it was enough to get high, that might change things." Zach shrugged. "Just a thought."

"Get high?" Ben turned to face his friend. "Something we should know?"

"Ha ha. I work in one of the worst parts of D.C. A good number of my students, even the good ones, come to class buzzed on something on any given day of the week. Shockingly, the 'Drug Free School Zone' signs at either end of the parking lot don't keep the school clean and sober. Many of those kids, and their parents, use the mission for meals, food for the kitchen, and sometimes even a place to sleep. So yeah, drugs are a potential motivation."

Ben nodded. "All right. I'll mention it to her."

"Here we are, gentlemen." The storekeeper came back with a small velvet box. "Let's see if this will do the trick."

"Hey. Got a minute?"

Ben clamped the phone between his ear and shoulder, snapped the ring box closed, set it on his nightstand, and hit mute on his TV. "For you, Rebecca, always. What's up?"

"Carl Perkins. That *is* the name of the football player from my high school. He signed my yearbook. And then a friend signed under it and made a nasty comment about why I'd let a player-slash-party-boy sign my yearbook. I don't remember him that way, but like I said, I don't really remember him at all. He did, apparently, ask me out. But I didn't really date in high school. The few times I did, people expected me to be the person Dad talked about in his speeches. So when I didn't put out, they got...put out."

A laugh escaped. He couldn't help it. "You have a way with words."

"Yeah, well, I'm starting to see a tiny bit of humor in the situation. I ran, for so many years, from this specter I thought my father had created and yet, the people who matter never believed it. So...why was I running? Anyway. Can you pass that on to your friend and see if it helps?"

"Will do." Ben scratched his jaw. "The party-boy think is interesting. Zach said something along those lines. I was going to talk to you about it later this week. I didn't want to bother you again today."

"You're never a bother. Especially not now that I can tell you I love you."

His heart sped. Would hearing that ever get old? He didn't see how. "I love you, too. It's late."

She sighed. "And I have an early day tomorrow. 'Night."

"'Night."

Ben ended the call and flipped open the ring box again. He was fairly sure she'd say yes. The key now was finding the right time to ask.

31

"I'm still not sure this was a good idea." Rebecca reached up to straighten her father's bow tie. He'd always looked handsome in a tuxedo. The passing years hadn't changed that.

"Why not? Since your statement two weeks ago, there hasn't been even a whiff about you anywhere. And I know this because I made sure Steve was looking for it. So if having your mom and me here can help bring new donors to the mission, or to Bread of Heaven, or both, then we're happy to do it. Plus, it's more time with you. Now that you're speaking to me again, I'd like to soak up your presence and make up for lost time."

Rebecca linked her arm through his and smiled up at him. "That's why I'm glad you're staying with me this time. Though, to be honest, I'm not doing a perfect job at this whole forgiveness thing. I have to keep reminding myself to let it go. I've prayed for that so many times...why can't I just be past it?"

Her father's smile was warm with a tinge of sadness. "Aw, baby, I wish it worked like that. But it doesn't usually. The way we think about things is a habit just as much as anything we do. And when we couple it with sin, like bitterness or unforgiveness, it can be even more entrenched. What matters is that you're asking the Holy Spirit to help you continue to let go. You're committed to a new way of thinking. Over time, it'll get easier."

"I'm sorry, Dad."

"Don't be. Neither of us is perfect. What matters is that we're practicing forgiveness and mending the rift." He kissed her forehead and gave her a bright smile. "Now, show me around this open house. And I'd also like to meet this man of yours. Your mother has a leg up on me there and I need to catch up. Though if he got her stamp of approval, he's already got mine. She's much harder to please than me."

Her cheeks grew warm. Where was Ben? He'd obviously been here earlier in the day since all the stations were set up around the room. But he was supposed to be here now, too. Of course, so was Paige with all the food. So maybe he was helping her? If he hadn't appeared by the time she was finished showing her dad around, she'd text him. "I should be able to arrange both of those things."

Rebecca led her father to the nearest display. "Our theme is 'Faces of Hunger,' so each area highlights a different aspect of hunger nationally and internationally. This one is urban hunger. We have facts and figures for the statistically minded, but we also networked with various charities in the major cities around the U.S. to get photos of their clientele. We wanted to showcase the fact that gender, ethnicity, age, and education aren't necessarily predictors for hunger or food insecurity."

Roland stood for a minute, his eyes moving back and forth between the large print statistics and the photos. "This is incredible. Why don't more people know?"

Rebecca shrugged. "That's the question, isn't it? We're trying to do our part to open a few eyes. And while we'd love that to turn into volunteers and donors, we also think it's important that people are simply aware. That way, if they see their church organizing a food drive or they get a plastic bag delivered to their doorstep, they can help in little ways and know that, in reality, it makes a huge difference."

"I'm so proud of you."

Rebecca looked up at her dad. The expression on his face brought tears to her eyes. She ducked her head. "Thanks. Come on, there's still suburban, rural, and international hunger to get to. Plus the display on ways you can help and the silent auction table."

Roland shook his head and slipped an arm around his daughter's shoulders. "Lead on."

D'Andre let out a whistle that was awfully close to a catcall. "Lookin' *good*, Miss Rebecca."

Rebecca laughed. "Flatterer. What are you doing here? I know the mission's still open for regular operations, but most of the folks who don't sleep here were planning on grabbing dinner in the cafeteria and then heading home."

The boy gave a shrug of studied disinterest. Rebecca fought a smile. He tried so hard to be cool. Did the other kids see through it as easily as she did? "Figured I could see what everyone's talkin' about. Maybe I can work it into an essay or somethin', save myself some research. Libraries are the worst."

"Ah, well then make sure you grab one of the booklets down on the far wall. They have all the important facts from the displays, plus some practical suggestions on how to help. Just make sure you do your report in your own words and don't copy mine. I sent one of those to all the schools in the area, so they'll know."

He frowned. "I'm not a cheater."

"I know that, D'Andre, but you could spread the word. Help keep other kids from getting caught."

He snorted. "If they're too stupid to do their own work, they deserve to get caught."

"Now that's a sentiment I like to hear." Zach strolled up to Rebecca, followed closely by Ben and Jackson. "Hey there, D'Andre. We'll be doing some fun math with those stats next week. Study up."

The boy shook his head. "Fun math. Only you Mr. Wilson. Catch ya."

Rebecca watched D'Andre melt into the growing crowd before turning. What a sight the three men made in their suits and ties. "Mmm. We should have the three of you stand outside and flag down cars. I'll bet our attendance would skyrocket."

Jackson snickered and raised his hand. "Spoken for. Speaking of which...where's Paige?"

"Try the kitchen. Out that door, turn left, follow your nose." Rebecca looked at Ben. "Everything looks amazing. I'd planned to help you set up but when I got here, it was all done."

"Yeah, I had something come up that I needed to take care of, so I asked Jerry if it'd be okay to come early. He didn't mind. And Zach was just grading exams, so any excuse to get away from that suited him just fine."

"The life of a teacher. Work all week, grade all weekend." Zach grinned. "I'm going to go look around. I do actually have some ideas on ways we can play with the stats in class. Maybe having it be practical will help some of the kids pay passing attention."

Rebecca hooked her arm through Ben's and studied the crowd. "Even if this is all the turnout we get, I'm going to consider it a success. Some of the conversations I've overheard have been encouraging."

"Rebecca?"

She tilted her head up to meet Ben's gaze. Something was off in his tone. Nerves? "Yeah?"

He cleared his throat. "You remember I mentioned Jackson's friend Colin? How he was looking into that guy..."

"Sure. Carl. Did you find out more?"

Ben nodded and pulled his phone out of his pocket. He freed his arm from hers and swiped the screen a few times before offering her the device. "You need to see this."

Rebecca frowned and took the phone. The webpage was titled "The Life and Times of Bad-Girl Becky." She winced and scrolled. Photos of her doing various things around the mission were accompanied by vitriolic rants about her pretending to be a do-gooder. Her stomach churned. At least there were no pictures of her home, or work. But still. "I don't understand."

"This is all done by Carl. Colin was able to track the IP of the posting computer to the public library down the block. Thankfully, they have security cameras everywhere. I'm not sure what strings

Colin pulled, but he sent me this photo." Ben swiped the phone again before turning the screen toward her.

She drew in a quick breath. "I've seen him around here...not recently. Jerry had to ask him to leave. He got caught trying to sell drugs to the kids. We know not everyone who comes here is clean, but generally they understand that they're not to do, or sell, drugs on the premises. But if you get caught, or someone reports you, the first strike is you get asked to leave. You can ask to come back, but if you do and it happens again, then Jerry turns you over to the police. He makes that very clear. But what does this have to do with Carl?"

Ben tapped the phone. "This *is* Carl."

Rebecca frowned. The photo didn't look anything like the boy she'd seen in the yearbook photos, or the one she had vague memories of from school. The Carl from school had been well-built—that was part of what kept the girls flocking to him—and he'd had a thousand-watt smile full of gleaming, perfectly straight teeth. This man was gaunt and his visible skin was covered in scars and scabs. She couldn't see his teeth, but the smile was missing, replaced by a curled lip and an expression that would keep all but the bravest from even bothering to say hello. "I...how can you be sure?"

"Library card. And I confirmed it with Jerry. That's the name he gave when he came here looking for a place to bed down for the winter." Ben gently pried her fingers off his phone and slipped it back into his pocket. "Do you remember who told Jerry he was selling?"

"A couple of the kids mentioned he'd approached them, so I mentioned it to Jerry. He said he'd look into it. I didn't think anything more of it...accusations like that aren't as rare as I'd like them to be. Jerry, and the rest of the staff, check them out thoroughly to make sure they're true, not motivated by something else." Rebecca rubbed the back of her neck. "I just do what we're trained to do as far as reporting and leave the rest to the paid staff."

Ben kissed the top of her head. "Sorry. I should have waited and told you another time. But I wanted you to be aware, so if you see him around...you should let someone know. I don't think he'd hurt you, but from what we can tell, he's been selling the pictures and little snippets about you for a couple hundred bucks. Probably to feed his drug habit."

Tears pricked her eyes. Rebecca blinked rapidly. She wasn't going to worry about this now. With a firm mental shake, she nodded and forced a smile. "All right. Now we know. I guess I should just be glad it wasn't someone I trusted or called a friend in the past. Maybe I'll feel better about it after I get some sleep. But until then...we have an open house going on, and I'm desperate to try some of the food Paige's staff keeps refilling. Plus...my dad wants to meet you."

Just after eleven p.m., Jerry escorted the last guest to the door. Rebecca kicked off her shoes and let out a gusty sigh before she grinned. "That is what I would call an unmitigated success."

Ben shrugged out of his suit jacket and loosened his tie. "I agree, one hundred percent. Our goal was to educate and garner interest, and I'd say we did both. The silent auction was a good addition...though I was surprised to see your novelty salt and pepper shakers made up some of it."

Rebecca smiled. "It occurred to me last night when I was putting the box of yearbooks away, that I have so many of them and hardly ever use them, let alone display them. I keep out my favorites and that's enough of a reminder. So why not let others get a fun little reminder that they're to be salt and light out there in the world, too?"

"And if it benefits the open house, then even better?"

"Something like that. They all sold for well over their minimum."

"I liked the reminder cards you put with each one, that just a pinch of salt promised great rewards for the kingdom." Ben took her hand. "You're an amazing woman, Rebecca."

Warmth spread through her. "Thanks."

"I suspect the mission and Bread of Heaven will both be seeing an influx of donations and volunteers in the coming months. I know I'm going to recommend we do this annually and start a program to coordinate efforts in other cities nationally."

Rebecca wound her arms around Ben's waist and laid her head against his shoulder. "I don't think I've ever met someone who has such open hands when it comes to God's blessings."

"What do you mean?"

"There are so many different ways you could have used this for your own gain, but instead, you're focused on how it can help everyone and how to spread the success to others, even if ultimately it means Bread of Heaven has a slight downturn."

Ben shook his head. "It's all God's Kingdom."

"Like I said, I don't think I've met someone with that attitude before."

Ben hugged her tightly before easing back so their eyes met. "Yes you have."

Rebecca furrowed her brow. "Who?"

"Your father."

Her father? No. Dad was a good man, and their relationship was on the mend, but he was always focused on his own gain, even as he went about doing God's work. The money he earned from his books and public speaking wasn't something he invested further in the Kingdom...was it? Examples of Dad doing just that flickered through her mind. Maybe...she sighed. How had she allowed her hurt to color her understanding of him so badly?

"You okay?"

She nodded. "Just thinking about what you said. I hadn't ever seen him in that light...but it fits. Thank you."

"I enjoyed meeting him. He's so proud of you it practically beams off him in neon letters. And it doesn't come across like that's a new development for him either. It's nice that we have that in common."

Warm tingles spread through her. "I'm just starting to see him that way. I can't help but be sorry for the years I wasted."

"There've been a lot of those." Ben lowered his mouth to hers for a long, tender kiss. "I plan to make up for lost time whenever possible."

"I love you." Rebecca clasped her hands behind his head and gently tugged. A throat clearing made her stop and she tried to jerk away as her cheeks lit on fire. Ben loosened his grip, but didn't let her go as they turned.

Jerry offered a sheepish smile. "Sorry. We're all locked up on this side of the building..."

"Got it." Ben chuckled and let go of Rebecca. "Grab your shoes. We'll load up the last display and be on our way."

"I didn't see your car, Rebecca. Do you have a way home?"

"My mom and dad borrowed my car. Letting other people use it is starting to be a bad habit. Regardless, Ben's going to drop me off." Rebecca hastily jammed her screeching feet back into her heels. They were coming right back off as soon as she was in the car. She snagged the poster while Ben collected the rest of the display pieces. "Night, Jerry."

32

"Hey, Ben. You're going to want to see this." Zach voice was muffled by Ben's bedroom door.

Ben rolled over, holding the pillow over his head. The only thing he wanted to see right now was the back of his eyelids. He was going to the late service today and had left his roommates a note to that effect. With the open house the night before, cleaning up, taking Rebecca home, it'd been after two by the time he crawled into bed. And even then, he hadn't fallen asleep immediately. That was completely his own fault, though. There wasn't enough fall night air, no matter how chilly, to undo the effects of kissing Rebecca. Ben needed to propose soon. And she'd better not want a long engagement. He might not live through it.

"Come on, Ben. Rise and shine." Zach pounded on the door.

"Go away."

Zach just laughed and pounded on the door. "There's coffee."

Muttering under his breath, Ben threw aside his covers and grabbed a t-shirt off the floor, pulling it on. He yanked open the door and stumbled down the hall. "This better be good."

"Good morning, sunshine." Jackson grinned at him from the table and pushed a section of the newspaper toward him. "Zach, go get the man some coffee before he bites your head off."

"Too late. But I can still grab the joe."

"It's a newspaper. Please tell me you didn't wake me up at, what time is it?"

Jackson glanced at his watch. "Just after ten."

His blood cooled slightly. After ten wasn't unreasonable. Not really. "Why aren't you at church?"

"Thought we'd hit the late service with you. My sister's picking my mom up at the airport this afternoon, so no huge family lunch. Instead, we're having an impromptu barbecue here for dinner. Wanna invite Rebecca and her parents?" Jackson lifted his mug.

Ben reached across for the coffee Zach offered. Did Rebecca already have plans? Her parents were staying another day or two, but what were they going to do? He should've asked, though it gave him a reason to call her. "I'll see if they're free."

"Do that. But read the paper, first." Zach nudged the section closer to Ben before straddling a chair.

Ben rolled his eyes and, sipping his coffee, scanned the headlines. The fog of sleep lifted when he saw a photo of Rebecca and her dad at the mission. His brain was still fuzzy. They'd invited the press, hadn't they? Probably. Publicity for things like this was usually standard. After all, the mission did good work locally, it made sense for locals to come and find out more. He skimmed the article and shook his head. "Well. They say no press is bad press, right?"

Zach's jaw dropped. "You're not serious."

Ben blew out a breath. "Not really. I mean, we invited some reporters. That's not the kind of article we were hoping for, but I guess I'm not as surprised as I should be. I guess with the emails that B of H and the mission got...even figuring out who tipped off the reporter, it figures that they'd try to get some kind of story. From what I understand, they made a pretty decent investment in their source, even if he's just an addict with an axe to grind."

"What do you mean?" Jackson reached for the paper. "I didn't see that in the article."

"You wouldn't. Your friend Colin..." Ben's phone rang. "Hold that thought."

Ben hurried back to his room and grabbed his phone off the charger. "Hello?"

"Is this Ben Taylor?"

Ben sank to the edge of his bed and banged his forehead with a fist. Always check the caller ID. When was he going to remember that? "Yes?"

"Hi, Ben. It's Jerry from the mission. I'm sorry to call on Sunday morning, but I wanted to talk to you before I called Rebecca."

Ben's heartbeat quickened. "Hey, Jerry. What's going on?"

"Carl came back last night. Now that it's October and the night air's getting colder, we fill up faster. Anyway, he agreed to the rules, so we readmitted him, only to find him smoking meth in the men's showers at three in the morning. So we called the police and he had enough on him that they're saying it's intent to distribute. I thought you'd want to know."

"That's great. I mean..." Ben winced. He sounded heartless. The guy clearly needed help for more than just his drug problem, but it was hard to see past the hurt he'd caused Rebecca. Even if, in the end, it had pushed her to forgive her father and let go of her own past. Or start to. Hmm. Maybe he owed this guy a thank you note. Nah. Let's not take it too far.

Jerry chuckled. "I know what you mean. It clears the way for you and Rebecca, though I think that was already pretty clear, given what I saw last night."

Heat crawled up the back of Ben's neck. "Sorry about that."

"Don't be. It's good to see her with someone who appreciates her. She's a good girl. I expect an invitation to the wedding."

"Um." Ben cleared his throat.

"It just happens that the walls around here aren't very soundproofed. So I caught some of your conversation with Rebecca's dad. I won't say anything. But it did get me thinking that Carl was still hanging around when I first mentioned to Rebecca that I'd pieced it together. It's possible he overheard and then put things together. Easier for him to do than someone else, since he'd been around her in high school."

"Yeah, I guess. You see the article in the paper this morning?"

Jerry laughed. "I did. Rebecca will be annoyed, but I imagine it'll put an end to all the speculation and gossip. And if it brings more folks to the mission—on either side of the coin—it'll be a good thing. The Board is talking about expanding our housing area, so it's possible we'll be able to help even more folks if the funding comes through."

Ben nodded. God had an amazing way of working things out. "That's great. If B of H can help, let me know and I'll see if we can put something together."

"Will you let Rebecca know about Carl?"

"Sure. Thanks, Jerry."

Ben set the phone back in its charger and went back down the hall. He recapped the conversation for his roommates as he finished his coffee.

Jackson shook his head. "Seems kind of bizarre that he'd come back and be that stupid."

"No one ever said druggies were smart, man." Zach shrugged. "Besides, I can think of at least ten people who've been praying for a quick and thorough solution to the problem. Why should we doubt it when we get one?"

Ben hunched his shoulders. He'd doubted it, too. It was so easy to ask for a miracle and so much harder to believe it when you got one. After all, that kind of thing was for Bible stories and fiction.

"Anyway, if you think about it, it got down to forty last night. We'll be getting frost soon. If I was homeless, I'd be seriously thinking about checking in to a shelter, too. Even if I'd already used my one strike. Maybe he really planned on keeping his drug use to non-shelter hours. But when you've got an addiction that's as advanced as the photos you showed us of that guy? Intentions don't mean anything. I see it with my students." Zach crossed his arms over the top of the chair and rested his chin on his wrists.

All right, so maybe it wasn't a case of miraculous intervention. Not that Ben didn't fully believe God orchestrated it, but it was more believable when you looked at it from Zach's viewpoint. And why did he feel the need to justify God working in a situation? *Sorry, Lord. What is it the man said? I believe...help my unbelief.*

"If we're going to get to church, the grocery store, and get set up for a barbecue later tonight, we'd best get going." Jackson stood and pointed at his roommates. "You two coming?"

Ben's palms were sweaty. He pushed the vacuum around the living room and ignored the churning in his gut. Rebecca and her parents would be here soon, as would everyone else. Where Jackson had gotten the idea that a party this huge was a smart idea was beyond him, but it'd probably be fun. And if the opportunity presented itself...he wiped his hands on his jeans, brushing over the ring in his pocket. The box made too big a bulge, so he'd pulled it out. Was that a mistake? He'd checked for holes six or seven hundred times. There weren't any. But did you need the box? He hit the switch on the vacuum. Laughter from out back reached his ears. Someone must be here already. He rubbed his hands over his face with a harsh chuckle. *Forget the ring. Your name is not Frodo. Or Gollum.*

He put the vacuum away, double-checked that Zach had cleaned their shared bathroom like he said he would, and went outside. Jackson's sister and her enormous family were there, along with an older woman who had to be Jackson's mother. She was lovely and the family resemblance was strong. He scanned the crowd but didn't see Rebecca or her parents yet.

"Need any help?" Ben sidled up to Jackson as he manned the grill.

"Sure. You want to take over here? I could go spend a few minutes with my mom. Paige just texted, she's on the way, as are her parents. And my friend David is coming, too. Have you seen Zach?"

"Nope. But the bathroom is clean, so he at least did that. Was he inviting anyone?"

Jackson offered Ben the grill tongs. "No idea. But maybe he went to pick up Amy and drag her here. That boy needs to get it in gear. Did you see the way she looked at him last night?"

Ben grinned. "Missed that. I take it she wasn't glowering with distaste?"

Jackson snorted. "Not so much. I'm going to go sit with Mom a bit, you can handle the dogs?"

"Please. I'm a grill master, or did you forget." Ben chuckled as his friend walked away. He peeked under the lid of the grill, his mouth watering as the smoke from grilling burgers and dogs wafted out. Closing the lid, he looked around, where was Rebecca?

"Boo."

Ben whirled, laughing. "I was just wondering when you were going to get here."

Rebecca laced her fingers through his. "Sorry. Mom and Dad decided to head downtown to see the museums instead. So I ran them downtown. They'll take the metro later this evening, though I suspect they're going to stay and find dinner at one of Dad's favorite places. Basically, they told me not to worry about them, took a house key, and...I feel like a bad daughter but it's nice that they're not coming."

He kissed her forehead. "You're not a bad daughter. You spent all day with them for the past two days. I'm guessing they might've been looking for a break themselves. You wanna stay and man the grill with me, or wander off and mingle?"

Rebecca looked out over the crowd that seemed to be growing bigger by the second. "Hmm. I think I see Sara and Jen over there. Did you invite them?"

"I didn't. Maybe Zach did? Doesn't matter. I'm glad they're here. Why don't you go hang with them a bit and I'll come find you when the grilling is over. Or, if you get lonely for my sparkling wit, you know where to find me."

She laughed and skipped down the two steps from the raised portion of the patio. Ben watched her weave through the crowd, stopping now and then to smile and lift a hand in greeting. She fit in well with his group of friends and the various other random people hanging out. Who were all these people? Did they have enough food? He peeked under the cover of the grill and frowned.

"Anything ready yet?" Zach poked his head out the sliding door that led into the living room.

"Not yet. But where are all these people from?"

"I heard Jackson yammering about it at church, so he probably invited people, who invited people. You know how it is."

"Well, I hope we have more burgers and dogs, cause what's here right now isn't going to cut it."

Zach chuckled. "I'll check the fridge and grab some platters. Need anything?"

"Nah. Thanks." Ben opened the lid again and started turning hotdogs and flipping burgers. Hopefully some of the people brought side dishes or they were going to need to run to the store.

When the second round of burgers and dogs had been served, it looked like everyone had gotten at least one serving of something meaty. Ben turned off the grill. They could always fire it back up if they needed, but the sun was starting to set and a chill was creeping into the air. People weren't likely to hang around too much longer. Rebecca had visited briefly with Sara and Jen in tow. He'd spied Zach and Amy eating together. And Jackson and Paige had spent the better part of the afternoon at the picnic table with Jackson's mom and Paige's parents. From what Ben could surmise, everyone had a good time. Ben spotted Rebecca across the yard and started making his way that direction.

"Heya stranger." Rebecca smiled.

Ben dropped a kiss on her lips before sliding an arm over her shoulders. "Hey. You looked like you were having fun."

"I did. Sara and Jen did, too."

"Where'd they go?" Ben scanned the crowd.

"They had to run. But I did see that guy," Rebecca nodded her head toward a cluster of men tossing bean-bags, "give Jen his card. He watched her all afternoon."

"Which one?" All the guys in the group were good guys, but it'd be interesting to know.

"Khakis, green polo."

"Ah. David. Jackson's friend. I don't know him super well, but he's the guy who hooked me up with Colin."

"Colin...he found Carl?"

Ben nodded.

"Hm, so a computer guy?"

"Yeah. Jen's a programmer, right?"

Rebecca smiled. "She is. He might have an uphill battle ahead of him, but it'll be fun to watch. Jen doesn't believe in dating other coders. Says they're intimidated by a woman with brains."

Ben laughed and was about to reply when Jackson climbed up on the bench of the picnic table.

"Can I have everyone's attention, please?"

What was he doing? Ben saw Rebecca's curious look and shrugged.

"As most of you know, Paige and I met this summer when she was chosen to cater a fundraiser for my then-boss, Senator Carson. We've had some ups and downs, but at the end of the day, knowing her has helped me better understand God's call on my life and just, in general, made me a better man. Now that my mom has finally been able to make the trip up here to meet Paige, I don't want to wait any longer." Jackson jumped down from the bench, took Paige's hand, and sank to his knee. "Paige Jackson, will you do me the honor of becoming my wife?"

Paige squealed and threw her arms around Jackson while everyone looking on clapped.

"I guess that's a yes." Ben chuckled, though the ring in his own pocket threatened to burn a hole into his leg.

Rebecca elbowed him in the side as she wiped her eyes. "Of course it's a yes. The two of them are perfect for each other."

Ben took her hand. "Come on, let's go say congratulations."

Ben shuttled the last trash bag out to the curb and wandered out to the back yard. Rebecca was sitting at the picnic table, staring up at the evening sky. Jackson's mother had given her grandchildren some of the roses from the arrangement Jackson's sister brought to the airport, the kids had used them as swords for a while, then dropped them. Ben scooped up two blooms that remained mostly unscathed by the kids' exuberance.

"For you." Ben offered the roses and sat next to Rebecca on the bench, slipping his arm around her shoulder. "You didn't have to stay and help clean up, but I'm awfully glad you did."

Rebecca sniffed the roses and smiled. "I was hoping we'd end up with a chance to be alone. Even for a few minutes. How's your knee holding up? I saw you've been moved to once a week on the schedule."

"It's good. I'm still doing my exercises and sometimes it aches, but the doc says that's to be expected for a while. You know, when I got hurt, I was so mad at Jackson for dragging me into that football game. Now...I feel like I owe him a thank you. To think that you've been here in the same place as me for so long...I'm glad you're back in my life."

Rebecca rested her head on his shoulder. "You say the sweetest things. I'm glad you're in my life, too. And I'm even glad for all the changes I had to make to get to this point. Some of them probably hurt almost as much as your knee injury."

Ben chuckled. "Probably so."

Rebecca set the roses down on the tabletop, covering a couple of silver-toned plastic forks that hadn't made it into the trash, then snuggled closer.

The diamond in his pocket dug into his leg. Was this the right time? Would she prefer something big and splashy like Jackson had done? Or a fancy dinner? Out of all the things they'd discussed, her ideal marriage proposal had never come up. Not too surprising, though marriage had been on his mind even toward the end of summer camp. He offered a quick prayer and gulped. "Can I ask you something?"

Rebecca sat up and turned to look at him, concern etched into her features. "Always."

Ben stuck his hand in his pocket and pulled out the ring, his breath catching in his throat. "I know it might feel fast, but for me it's been so incredibly slow. For all those years, I prayed for you, I prayed that God would bring you back into my life. And now He has and...I don't want to ever let go. I love you, Rebecca Marie Fischer MacDonald...will you marry me?"

Rebecca's mouth popped into a tiny 'O' and her eyes darted between Ben's face and the ring. Tears streamed down her cheeks as she began to nod, slowly then more rapidly. "Oh, yes. Oh...I love you, Ben. Of course I will."

Sliding his thumb across her cheek, Ben wiped away her tears. With a shaking hand, he slid the ring onto her left hand. It was a little big, so it slipped to the side, showing off the tiny inset diamonds that made up the entire band.

She sniffled, beaming, and looked down at her hand. "It's beautiful. Thank you."

She'd said yes. The woman he'd loved for all these years had said yes. Ben pulled her close, their lips almost touching. "I love you."

"You have no idea how glad I am of that. I love you, too." She leaned forward, sealing their future with a kiss.

Author's Note

Thank you for reading *A Pinch of Promise!* I hope that you enjoyed getting to know Ben and Rebecca. I would appreciate it if you'd help others enjoy it too by leaving a review on Amazon and Goodreads and telling your friends about it. Any success my books have is owed to readers like you who take the time to tell others about my stories. Thank you, from the bottom of my heart.

I continue to owe a huge debt of gratitude to my husband and sons for giving me the time to write, my sister for her unflinching support and encouragement, and my critique partner Jan Elder for catching all the time I use the same word six times in two paragraphs.

More than anything, I'm grateful that God continues to give me words and makes it possible for me to write them down.

I'd love to hear from you! You can connect with me on Facebook (www.Facebook.com/ElizabethMaddrey) my webpage (www.ElizabethMaddrey.com) or via email. To stay current with news and occasional giveaways, please subscribe to my newsletter.

About the Author

Elizabeth Maddrey began writing stories as soon as she could form the letters properly and has never looked back. Though her practical nature and love of computers, math, and organization steered her into computer science at Wheaton College, she always had one or more stories in progress to occupy her free time. This continued through a Master's program in Software Engineering, several years in the computer industry, teaching programming at the college level, and a Ph.D. in Computer Technology in Education. When she isn't writing, Elizabeth is a voracious consumer of books and has mastered the art of reading while undertaking just about any other activity.

Elizabeth is the author of more than ten books, both fiction and non-fiction. She lives in the suburbs of Washington, D.C. with her husband and their two incredibly active little boys.

More Books by Elizabeth Maddrey

Contemporary Romance:

"A Splash of Substance" (Taste of Romance Book One) by Elizabeth Maddrey

She doesn't vote. He works for a Senator. Is it a recipe for romance or disaster?

Paige Jackson has always stayed out of politics, leaving it to God to govern the world. She has enough on her plate as the owner of a catering company founded on convictions to buy local, sustainable fare. Jackson Trent works on Capitol Hill for Senator Carson, putting his beliefs in action to help shape national policy.

Hoping to find high-end clients to keep her business afloat, Paige bids on a contract to cater the Senator's next fundraiser. Shake-ups in the Senator's staff leave Jackson grudgingly in charge of the event. After Paige is chosen as caterer, she and Jackson must work together despite opposing beliefs on how God calls Christians to participate in government. As Paige introduces Jackson to sustainable fare, it's not just the food that piques his interest.

When Senator Carson becomes front-page news in Washington, Paige is sucked into the whirlwind of scandal. Can Jackson convince Paige he wasn't complicit and win her back or has politics burned his chance at love?

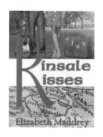

"Kinsale Kisses: An Irish Romance"

She wants stability. He wants spontaneity. What they need is each other.

Colin O'Bryan cashed out of the software company he founded and started a new life in Ireland. Content to wander from town to town as a traveling musician, he had no goals beyond healing from the betrayals that led to his career change, and finding his next gig.

After the death of her parents, Rachel Sullivan hoped her aunt's B&B on the Southern coast of Ireland would be a place for her to settle and start a new life. Though she can't deny the sparks in Colin's touch, his lack of concern for hearth and home leave her torn.

Can this free-spirited minstrel win her heart or will Rachel choose roots and stability over love?

"Wisdom to Know" ('Grant Us Grace' series Book 1)

Is there sin that love can't cover?

Lydia Brown has taken just about every wrong turn she could find. When an abortion leaves her overwhelmed by guilt, she turns to drugs to escape her pain. After a single car accident lands her in the hospital facing DUI charges, Lydia is forced to reevaluate her choices.

Kevin McGregor has been biding his time since high school when he heard God tell him that Lydia Brown was the woman he would marry. In the aftermath of Lydia's accident, Kevin must come to grips with the truth about her secret life.

While Kevin works to convince himself and God that loving Lydia is a mistake, Lydia struggles to accept the feelings she has for Kevin, though she fears her sin may be too much for anyone to forgive.

"Courage to Change" ('Grant Us Grace' series Book 2)

Should you be willing to change for love?

When Phil Reid became a Christian and stopped

drinking, his hard-partying wife, Brandi, divorced him. Reeling and betrayed, he becomes convinced Christians should never remarry, and resolves to guard his heart.

Allison Vasak has everything in her life under control, except for one thing. Her heart is irresistibly drawn to fellow attorney and coworker, Phil. Though she knows his history and believes that women should not initiate relationships, she longs to make her feelings known.

As Phil and Allison work closely together to help a pregnant teen, both must re-evaluate their convictions. But when Brandi discovers Phil's new relationship, she decides that though she doesn't want him, no one else can have him either. Can Phil and Allison's love weather the chaos Brandi brings into their lives?

"Serenity to Accept" ('Grant Us Grace' series Book 3)

Is there an exception to every rule? Karin Reid has never had much use for God. There's been too much pain in her life for her to accept that God is anything other than, at best, disinterested or, at worst, sadistic. Until she meets Jason Garcia. After his own mistakes of the past, Jason is committed to dating only Christians. He decides to bend his rule for Karin, as long as she comes to church with him. As their friendship grows, both will have to decide if they'll accept the path God has for them, even if it means losing each other.

"Joint Venture" – A 'Grant Us Grace' Novella

Laura Willis is busy planning her wedding to Ryan when she catches him cheating. Again. This time with her best friend. She throws her fist, and her ring, in his face and immerses herself in work at Brenda's House of Hair. But the salon is awash in drama too as Brenda cuts corners and goes on a rampage.

Laura's coworker hairstylist, Matt Stephenson, is searching for other employment options and a new place to live. Deciding to take a risk, he determines to open his own salon and invites Laura to partner with him.

Can their friendship survive the undertaking or will this joint venture be more than either of them bargained for?

Women's Fiction:

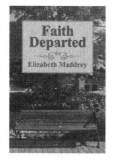

"Faith Departed" ('Remnants' series Book 1)
Starting a family was supposed to be easy.

Twin sisters June and July have never encountered an obstacle they couldn't overcome. Married just after graduating college, the girls and their husbands remained a close-knit group. Now settled and successful, the next logical step is children. But as the couples struggle to conceive, each must reconcile the goodness of God with their present suffering. Will their faith be strong enough to triumph in the midst of trial?

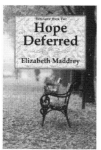

"Hope Deferred" ('Remnants' series Book 2)
Can pursuit of a blessing become a curse?

June and July and their husbands have spent the last year trying to start a family and now they're desperate for answers. As one couple works with specialists to see how medicine can help them conceive, the other must fight to save their marriage. Will their deferred hope leave them heart sick, or start them on the path to the fulfillment of their dreams?

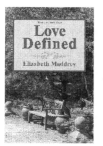

"Love Defined" ('Remnants' series Book 3)
Dreams Change. Plans Fail.

July and Gareth have reached the end of their infertility treatment options. With conflicting feelings on adoption, they struggle to discover common ground in their marriage. Meanwhile, July's twin sister, June, and her husband, Toby, are navigating the uncertainties of adoption and the challenges of new parenthood. How much stretching can their relationships endure before they snap?

Non-Fiction

"A Walk in the Valley: Christian Encouragement for Your Journey Through Infertility" by Julie Arduini, Heidi Glick, Elizabeth Maddrey, Kym McNabney, Paula Mowry, and Donna Winters

Everyone's journey through infertility is different. Even women who have the same physical problems will have different courses of treatment, different responses, and different emotional ups and downs as they walk this path. But we also have so much in common: the hurt, anger, frustration, pain, sorrow, hope and joy that we have experienced along the way.

We are women who have experienced infertility. Some of us have gone on to conceive, others have adopted, and others remain childless. All of us have found peace in the loving arms of our Father God at the end of our journey. We want to share our experiences and thoughts with you. It is our hope and prayer that you'll be encouraged.

This devotional workbook starts with how each woman discovered her infertility, then explores the diagnostic testing pursued, how they processed the official diagnosis, what decisions had to be explored regarding treatment, their experiences during infertility treatment (including pregnancy, miscarriage, and childbirth), and finishes with their experiences in remaining childless, adoption, foster care, child sponsorship, and the emotional healing regardless of the outcome of their infertility journey.

Each devotional has a Scripture focus and questions for thought and discussion.

Made in the USA
San Bernardino, CA
15 June 2015